P9-DNU-525

FINNEY COUNTY PUBLIC LIBRARY
605 E. Walnut
Garden City, KS 67846

SNAKEROOT

A **NIGH†SHADE** *Novel*

Also by the same author:

RIFT

RISE

NIGHTSHADE

WOLFSBANE

BLOODROSE

INVISIBILITY (with David Levithan)

ANDREA CREMER

SNAKEROOT

A NIGH†SHADE *Novel*

PHILOMEL BOOKS
AN IMPRINT OF PENGUIN GROUP (USA) INC.

PHILOMEL BOOKS
An imprint of Penguin Young Readers Group
Published by The Penguin Group
Penguin Group (USA) Inc., 375 Hudson Street,
New York, NY 10014, USA

⊕

USA I Canada I UK I Ireland I Australia I New Zealand I India I South Africa I China

Penguin Books Ltd, Registered Offices: 80 Strand, London WC2R oRL, England
For more information about the Penguin Group, visit penguin.com

Copyright © 2013 by Seven Crows, Inc.
All rights reserved. No part of this book may be reproduced, scanned or
distributed in any printed or electronic form without permission in writing from
the publisher. Philomel Books, Reg. U.S. Pat. & Tm. Off. Please do not participate
in or encourage piracy of copyrighted materials in violation of the author's
rights. Purchase only authorized editions.

Library of Congress Cataloging-in-Publication Data
Cremer, Andrea R. Snakeroot / Andrea Cremer. pages cm.—(Nightshade ; 4)
Summary: Bosque Mar haunts Adne and Logan's dreams, trying to turn Adne to the
dark side as he attempts to escape the Nether, where Calla, Shay and the other
Guardians trapped him in the final battle of the War of All Against All.
[1. Werewolves—Fiction. 2. Love—Fiction. 3. Supernatural—Fiction. 4.
Shapeshifting—Fiction.] I. Title. PZ7.C86385Sn 2013 [Fic]—dc23 2013011331
Published simultaneously in Canada. Printed in the United States of America.

ISBN 978-0-399-16422-4
1 3 5 7 9 10 8 6 4 2

Edited by Jill Santopolo. Design by Amy Wu. Text set in 10.25-point Apolline.

The publisher does not have any control over and does not assume
any responsibility for author or third-party websites or their content.

ALWAYS LEARNING   PEARSON

For Sharon and Garth, with all my love

Forbid us something, and that thing we desire.

Geoffrey Chaucer, *The Canterbury Tales*

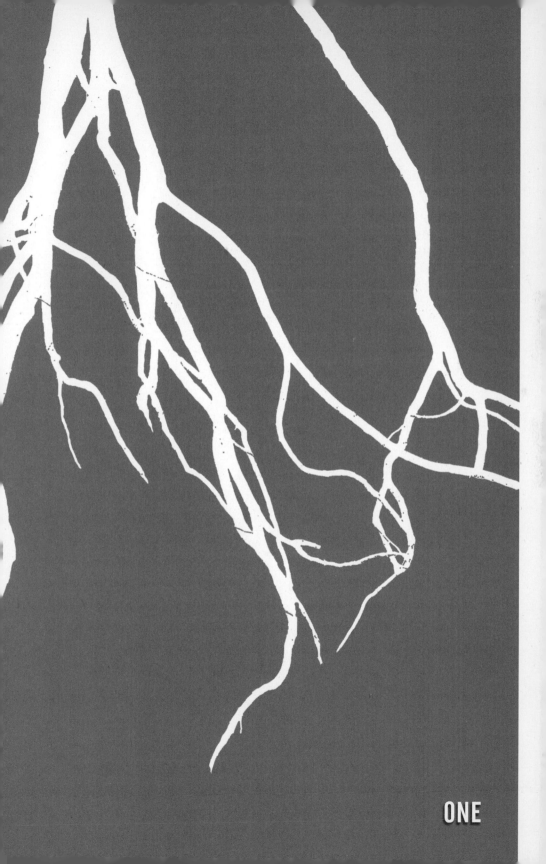

ONE

ADNE HAD LEARNED to live with nightmares years ago. Since the day her mother suffered and died, tangled in the shadow grip of Bosque Mar's evil wraith, Adne often woke trembling, covered in sweat, with a throat raw from screams. Wanting to show a brave face, she hadn't told anyone—not her father, not even Connor—how frequently the night terrors shook her from sleep, sudden and violent. But life had changed and she couldn't continue to keep that secret, because now she rarely spent a night alone.

When Adne jerked up with a cry that night, Connor was awake immediately. He cradled her trembling body in his arms.

"It was a dream," he whispered before she said anything. "Easy now."

He stroked her hair, his fingers pausing briefly when they found the sweat on the back of her neck.

"Your mother?" Connor asked quietly when Adne's limbs had stopped shaking.

Adne shook her head. She wasn't ready to talk yet.

Connor stiffened beside her, and Adne knew why. The nightmares she'd told Connor about had been those of her mother and the wraith. But since the war had ended one month ago, something had changed. The shadows that visited her now were different, and yet unsettlingly familiar.

"Do you want to tell me about it?" Connor asked.

Shaking her head again, Adne turned her face to press her lips against Connor's cheek. He took her chin in his hand, turning her farther until her mouth met his. Adne waited for the warmth of Connor's skin and the gentle strength of his touch to chase the nightmare away, as she knew it would. Though guilt caused a slight twinge in her chest, she hurried to lose herself in the sensation. In the joy and ceaseless thrill of having this man—whom she'd desired since she first knew what it was to want a man that way—in her arms each night, holding her, kissing her. When they were twined together in the dark, Connor made it clear how long he'd wanted her too.

After the nightmare, Adne's desire for intimacy wasn't only about loving Connor, it was about using him to chase away her fears. And she didn't want to use him. But Adne couldn't think of anything else to do. She was frightened by her dreams, but she was more afraid of what Connor would think if she shared the visions with him.

Telling Connor the truth was out of the question. Telling anyone was out of the question.

Connor's lips were on Adne's neck and she closed her eyes. The cold sweat that covered her body gave way to heat spreading over her skin. Adne twisted her fingers through Connor's silky hair before wrapping her arms around his neck. She clung to him, willing the shadows still creeping into the edges of her consciousness away, her body electric with tremors of fear and desire. Connor had always been light to her. Pure light and hope in the face of sorrow and despair. Whatever darkness threatened her now, Connor would keep it at bay.

He had to.

The library at Rowan Estate looked like a tornado had torn through it. As Sabine turned in a slow circle, observing the damage, she thought it looked like it had a few weeks ago, right after Shay had closed the Rift that separated the human world from the Nether realm. Considering all the cleanup work and restoration she'd helped with to get the place back in shape since then, Sabine was not amused by this new development.

"Over here!" Adne called.

Sabine picked her way through the rubble until she reached Adne's side.

Adne crouched among what had been dozens of bookshelves, riffling through splintered wood and torn pages. "Things have been taken."

Sabine leaned over her. "How can you possibly know that?"

"You're not the only one who spent hours getting this place organized," Adne said. "I gave up days of my life cataloging this section, and I swear it's not all here. There are books—important books—that are missing."

"Are you sure this isn't what's happened to them?" Sabine asked, picking up a pile of debris that looked like it had gone through a shredder.

Adne laughed, but Sabine recognized the determined set of her jaw. "No. I'm sure that's what whoever did this wanted us to think," Adne said. She swept her arm toward the rest of the library . . . or what was left of it. "They wanted us to think it was an attack, when it was actually a theft."

"So case closed?" Connor kicked aside pieces of a shattered marble bust. "Good work, Adne. Can we go home now?"

"Hardly." Adne was bent over the remnants of books at her feet.

"I didn't sign on to play detective," Sabine said. "Can I go beat up the thieves for information instead?"

"Sounds like fun." Connor laughed. "But it's *thief,* not thieves. The second one managed to get away."

"How'd that happen?" Sabine asked. The Searchers weren't sloppy and the thieves were human; catching them should have been easy.

"He displayed his immensely noble character by tripping his associate, so we were busy catching that guy while the first one made it to the getaway car," Connor said. "He drove into a populated area where we couldn't pursue him without drawing unwanted attention."

"The tripped associate's a no go," Ethan said as he walked up, apparently having overheard the last bit of their conversation.

"Why's that?" Sabine asked.

"He's been hexed." Ethan sat down next to Sabine. "He can't answer questions about who employed him or why."

Sabine's gaze swept over the ransacked shelves. "What do you mean, hexed?"

"Hexed, cursed," Adne said. "Whatever you want to call it."

"Black magic?" Sabine's frown deepened. "How is that possible?"

"Why wouldn't it be possible?" Connor twirled a lock of Adne's hair in his fingers. She batted his hand away, but not without throwing a teasing smile at him.

"Because the Rift is closed and the Harbinger is gone," Sabine said. "I thought that meant the Keepers' magic was cut off. No more wraiths. No more hexes. Nothing."

"The magic from the Harbinger, yeah," Connor said. "So you're right about no wraiths, but magic—basic magic—is still around. That won't ever go away."

"Don't sweat it." Ethan put his arm around Sabine's shoulders. "Black magic keeps us employed. We have to make sure it doesn't get out of hand."

"So you think Logan is behind this hex?" Sabine asked, pulling Ethan's arm farther around her so she could nestle against him. "And the theft?"

"He's our number one suspect," Ethan said. "Wait—replace *number one* with *only*. Only suspect."

Adne smiled, but her eyes remained worried. "Why did he want those books?"

"What were they about?" Connor asked. He'd picked up the

pieces of a broken vase and was entertaining himself by trying to fit them back together.

"That's what worries me," Adne said. "They were about the Keepers' heritage. Family lines. Legacies."

"You're worried because Logan's checking out his family tree?" Sabine asked. "Maybe he's just lonely. After all, he's the only Keeper left, right?"

"No, he's not." Ethan frowned. "There are a few younger Keepers still scattered around the world. They've gone into hiding, trying to prevent us from tracking them down. Though it's sort of a moot point. I think they're more paranoid about us finding them than we're interested in hunting them. They're harmless now. Just humans dabbling in the dark arts."

"Exactly," Adne said.

Connor dropped the vase fragments. They broke into even smaller pieces when they hit the floor. "I think you skipped a few steps. I didn't get a resolution from that conversation."

Adne smiled. "Sorry. I mean that the Keepers who didn't end up as withered husks—because they were living on borrowed time—are still out there. But they don't have power—at least, not power like they used to."

"You think Logan wants to get it back." Sabine ground her teeth.

"Maybe . . . probably," Adne said. "The books that are missing aren't only family trees. They recount the origins of the Keepers."

"Hmmmm," Connor said. "Oh . . . uh-oh."

"Uh-oh is an understatement." Ethan fingered the hilt of the dagger belted at his waist.

Sabine asked, "Can he do it? Find a way to restore their power?"

Adne rubbed her temples, suddenly looking weary. "I don't know and I'm not sure how we find out. Logan took the books that hold the clues we need."

"But we do have this." Connor produced a small wooden box from inside his long leather duster. "Check it out."

"What's that?" Sabine asked. She took the box from him, since Adne's head was still bowed. The box was intricately carved of ebony wood, and it was locked.

"We took this off the thief we did manage to catch," Connor said. "It was the only thing he was carrying. The other guy had the books."

Sabine ran her fingers over the patterns and deep grooves of the wood. "I wonder what's inside."

"Let's find out," Connor said. He snatched the box out of Sabine's hands and picked the lock. He opened it, peered inside, and frowned.

"Give it here." Adne reached up and Connor handed it to her.

Adne gave a little gasp. "Oh!"

"What is it?" Sabine peered over her shoulder.

Within the box lay a torn sheet of paper, a small, oddly shaped white stone, a pair of gold rings, and a pendant.

Sabine reached inside and picked up the rings. "They're engraved on the inside of the bands." She peered at the tiny markings. "A. Hart, E. Morrow. *Amor et fidelitas.*"

"'Love and loyalty,'" Adne murmured. "Wedding rings?"

"That'd be my guess," Sabine said.

"Women." Ethan reached over Sabine and grabbed the piece of paper. "Going for the jewelry before the evidence!"

Sabine elbowed him. "The jewelry *is* evidence."

"Right." Ethan winked at her before reading the faded ink. "Alistair Hart Nightshade, 1388–1666, Great Fire of London."

"That's weird." Adne took the paper from Ethan, turning it over in her hands.

"You mean that he died at age 278?" Connor asked. "I'd say that's par for the course in our line of work."

"No," Adne said. "I mean that the stuff in the box is way older than this note. This is paper, not the parchment they would have used in the Middle Ages." She held the paper up to the light. "I think it's signed on the back, but the ink is really hard to make out. Wait . . . yeah . . . here's the name. 'C. Nightshade, 1859.' Oh great."

"What?" Sabine asked.

"That has to be Cameron Nightshade," Adne said. "He built this place. Rowan Estate is named after his wife. He came over from England in the eighteenth century, she showed up a little later—they were the first Keepers in North America."

"Are you jockeying for Silas's old job?" Connor asked. "What's up with the history lesson?"

Adne stuck her tongue out at him. "I just happened to spend some time reading the books I was cataloging and not trying to get out of my responsibilities . . . like some people I know."

Connor shrugged. "I'd rather be out in the field than in a musty old room."

"It wasn't musty until all the shelves were obliterated," Adne said.

"So Cameron left a note in Alistair's box?" Sabine asked.

Adne nodded. "If I'm remembering right, Cameron was Alistair's son."

"But why would Logan care about this stuff?" Ethan reached into the box, picking up the small white stone. "And what the hell is this white rock doing in here?"

Sabine took a closer look at the object and began to laugh.

Ethan threw her a sidelong glance. "What?"

"That's not a rock," she said. "It's a knuckle bone."

"Gah!" Ethan dropped the bone. Fortunately, Adne shoved the box out in time to catch it.

"Why would anyone keep a bone in there?" Ethan said, rubbing his hands on his coat.

"It was a thing," Adne said. "Usually it was only for saints and other famous types, but the bones of the dead were thought to have great power . . . that's more bad news for us."

"You think Logan wanted this stuff to work some nasty mojo?" Connor asked.

"I'd say that's a safe bet." Adne picked up the pendant. "This is a lot prettier than the bone."

Sabine leaned close. The pendant was an oval about the size of her palm, hanging from a thin gold chain. The bloodred ruby was rimmed with gold, and a ghostly image—a rose centered between two crossed swords—hovered in the gemstone's depths.

"That's beautiful," she whispered.

Adne nodded. "I've never seen anything like it."

"That's an *intaglio*," Connor said. "It's kind of a cameo in reverse. They inscribed the image into the gem's surface—that's what gives it so much depth. They were sentimental gifts, and the words carved into the setting usually had mystical significance or power—like a talisman."

They all stared at him.

Finally, Ethan said, "How the hell do you know that?"

Connor coughed, looking at Adne and then away. "I . . . uh . . . may have been doing some reading about jewelry recently . . . uh . . . yeah."

Adne blushed, lowering her gaze back to the contents of the box. A small smile played on the corners of her mouth.

"Anyway," Connor said. "That's what the necklace is."

Sabine reached out, taking the pendant from Adne. She turned it over.

"This is inscribed too," she said. *"Sanguine et igne nascimur."*

"'In blood and fire we are born.'" Adne shivered. "Anything else?"

"Another name," Sabine said, her voice growing quiet. "Eira."

A numb silence fell over the group.

"The first Keeper," Adne said. She snatched the pendant from Sabine. She shoved it into the box and slammed the lid, mimicking Pandora's futile effort to stop horrors from spilling out into the world. When she looked up at them, she was trembling. "Logan's going back. Back to the very beginning."

Adne felt the others' eyes on her as she grabbed the box and fled the library. She had no idea where she was going, but soon she was outside, breathing fresh Colorado air. The day was bright, and though the air still carried a chill, Adne could taste the promise of spring. Her swift walk picked up to a run, her feet seeming to have a will of their own, while her mind was muddled.

When she finally stopped, she was breathing hard. Her breath rose in small puffs. Adne looked around, trying to get her bearings as well as understand why putting together the pieces of Logan's break-in had sent her into a panic. When she saw where she was, her knees buckled and she dropped to the ground.

The garden. Bosque Mar's garden. She couldn't be here. Not here.

Why is this happening?

Adne had never fainted before, but now, even on her knees, she couldn't keep her balance. Black fog poured into her mind, blotting out the real world and forcing her into a waking nightmare.

She knew the scene immediately, but somehow being in the garden amplified her awareness that this dream was something more than a product of her own imagination. She was too aware of the earth beneath her, how alive it was. With her hands on the ground, Adne could feel everything—the channels and pathways of roots and rivers, minerals and magma. And the earth knew her. Beneath her palms, it shuddered.

"Very good."

Adne squeezed her eyes shut. She knew the voice but refused to acknowledge it. *This is not happening. He is not here.*

She wished she could close her ears along with her eyes so she wouldn't hear the footfalls that brought him next to her. His presence was overwhelming. Powerful, and inexplicably alluring.

"I love this place," Bosque Mar said, his voice cool as silk. "The garden was what brought you to me. This is our place."

Still huddled with her eyes closed, Adne whispered, "No."

Bosque laughed. "Such a fighter. You remind me of her."

"Stop." Adne felt tears rising in her throat.

He was close. Too close. She could sense his body as he crouched beside her. "It's time for you to come with me."

Adne screamed, rolling away from him. "No!"

She lashed out with one arm, finally opening her eyes. She struck at nothing but the air.

Bosque wasn't in the garden. Adne was alone. Choking on her breath, she began to sob.

It would have been easier for Adne to face the idea that between grief and exhaustion she was having some sort of psychotic episode. But Adne knew magic. And she felt its presence all around her, along with the overwhelming sense that something was coming for her.

Adne always thought she would welcome the absence of nightmares about her mother's death. But those dreams had fled only when the new visions had arrived. Though she could hardly believe it, the new dreams were worse. These weren't grief-ridden images of the past. Adne sensed they were portents of the future.

The nightmares had begun when the sun set on the day of the Searchers' greatest victory. The Rift had been closed. The war was over. With her limbs tangled in Connor's, Adne had fallen asleep. She'd expected a peaceful night. Though her heart still ached from losing her father and her brother, Adne believed that their sacrifices had helped set the world right again.

She wasn't ready for the tide of horror that visited her while she slept.

In her dream she'd been walking through the Rowan Estate gardens. Dead wolves lay on the frozen ground all around her. Adne passed them without hesitation. The wolves weren't her concern. She was needed elsewhere.

Adne stopped when she reached the withered hedge.

"I knew you'd come." Bosque Mar materialized before her. "We have so much to discuss, Ariadne."

Bosque reached out to her. Without hesitating, she took his hand. He smiled at her. His smile contorted, mouth stretching wide into a grotesque grin until the skin split open. The handsome face of the man dropped off in clumps of flesh until his true visage was revealed.

Adne screamed until her cries roused her from sleep.

The details of the nightmare weren't always the same. Sometimes it took place in the Rowan Estate library. Sometimes in the bowels of the Pyralis volcano while the fire wolves, the Lyulf, stalked around her. But no matter where Adne found herself in the dream, Bosque was always waiting for her. And she always went to him when he beckoned.

The first night she'd woken trembling after the dream, Adne thought she could pinpoint its source. Her first and last encounter with Bosque Mar was branded on her mind, vivid and disturbing.

"What a lovely young thing." Bosque watched Adne move, running his tongue over his lips as if tasting the air. "And with such power. You've been playing with my garden, dear. Without permission."

He twisted his fingers and Adne stumbled. "Please stay awhile. I think you could be quite useful to me."

She rolled over, clawing at the rug beneath her feet, which had begun to unravel. Its loose threads wound together into thick ropes that wrapped around her ankles and continued to snake their way up her body.

Amid the chaos of that final battle, Bosque had singled Adne out. When he'd spoken to her, she'd felt his gaze as acutely as if he'd been touching her. Even as she'd struggled against the bonds he'd invoked to hold her captive, Adne had shivered, unable to fight the awareness that with one look, Bosque understood who she was and the power she could wield more than anyone else ever had.

She didn't know what that meant.

Adne had pushed aside the unpleasant dream as she would any other, assuming the nightmare was simply the aftermath of the war.

But the next night she'd dreamed of Bosque Mar. And the next. And the next.

Adne had told herself repeatedly that the nightmares meant nothing, that they were the last shreds of fear left from years of fighting the Keepers. Bosque Mar had been banished from her world and he had no way of returning.

And yet, every night the Harbinger visited her while she slept.

Today the dream had intruded upon her waking mind. She couldn't bear it.

Crumpled on the ground, Adne held the wooden box tight against her chest. Logan needed something from Rowan Estate, but he didn't have it—at least not everything. They'd kept this box from him. That meant Adne could stop him before he managed to pull off whatever scheme he was concocting. By outmaneuvering Logan, she would keep the nightmares from coming true. Whatever Logan was searching for, Adne had to find it first.

The crunch of boots sounded on the garden's gravel path. Adne looked up to find Connor bearing down on her. He crouched beside her.

"What's up, buttercup?" Connor's tone was casual, but the skin around his eyes was tight with concern.

Adne knew her face was streaked with tears. Trying to pretend they weren't there was pointless.

"I shouldn't have run out of there," she said. "I freaked."

"Uh-huh." Cupping her face in his palm, Connor rubbed the tear tracks on her cheek with his thumb. "I got that much. But it's not like you, Adne. Why'd you spook?"

Adne grimaced, wishing Connor had picked a word other than *spook*. It was too close to the truth. She felt haunted.

Choosing her next words carefully, Adne told him, "Knowing Logan was here. Seeing all that history of the Keepers. I thought it was over. The war. The loss."

"It is over," Connor said with a dry laugh. "Logan Bane might have the coin to hire half-competent thieves, but can you imagine him pulling off anything more?"

"I don't know." Adne lowered her gaze.

Logan had been a spoiled child and an arrogant S.O.B., but Adne suspected that much of Logan's behavior had been posturing. None of them had seen beneath the surface of the Keeper heir's façade. The break-in made Adne realize she was afraid to find out.

"So." Connor cleared his throat. "I don't mean to be insensitive, but Sabine and Ethan would like to get back to the Academy. Me too."

Adne nodded, letting Connor pull her to her feet. She tucked the box under her arm. Connor looked at it and frowned.

"You keeping that?"

"Yeah," she answered. "I want to put it somewhere Logan won't be able to get at it. Just in case."

Connor shrugged, but then he looked into Adne's eyes. "Are you sure there's nothing else you want to talk about?"

"I'm okay," Adne insisted. "Just an overreaction."

"You know we're not going to let Logan mess with the glorious future that awaits us." He grinned and Adne laughed.

"Yeah, I know."

When Connor put his arm around her shoulders, Adne's mood lightened. His presence made the waking dream fizzle to insignificance. For a moment, Adne would have called herself happy. But something flickered on the edge of her vision. She turned and her heart stuttered. A wolf watched them from the edge of the forest that bordered the garden.

"Connor." Adne clutched his arm.

"What is it?" He was instantly tense. She didn't have to look to know he'd already drawn a weapon.

Adne was about to point, but she blinked and the wolf was gone.

"Adne?" Connor scanned the space around them, searching for the cause of her alarm.

"It's nothing," Adne said, her throat still tight. "I thought I saw . . . but it was nothing."

"You sure?" Connor asked, still waiting for any signs of imminent danger.

"Yes." Adne leaned into him, trying to convey an ease she didn't feel. "I'm just on edge. Please get me out of here."

"With pleasure, little lady." Connor gave a whoop and scooped Adne off the ground. Adne shrieked as Connor carried her back to the manor, making her laugh by kissing her noisily and teasing her about his plans for the night until a blush scorched her cheeks. But when she stopped laughing and laid her face against Connor's neck so she could smell his skin and the leather of his duster, Adne wondered if she wasn't losing her mind after all. A wolf had been watching them. She knew she'd seen it.

But seeing the wolf wasn't the problem. The wolf wasn't a stranger. Adne could never have mistaken that charcoal fur, which she'd wept into after the wolf warrior had been slain. Nor would she ever forget those silver-flecked eyes—eyes that had been gazing at her just moments ago in mutual recognition.

It didn't matter if her brother was a wolf or a boy. Adne would always know Ren Laroche.

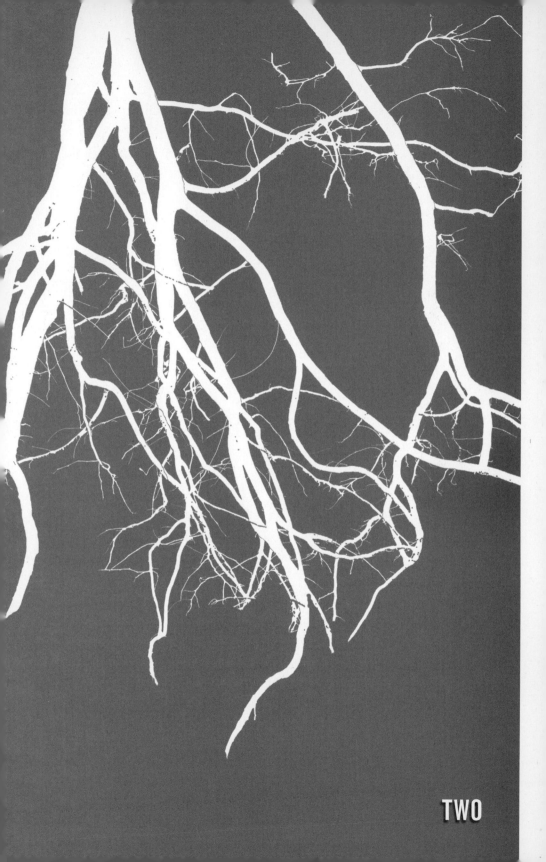

TWO

MAGIC PROVED TO be much more work than Logan Bane had ever imagined—at least magic you had to do yourself. It turned out that most spells required an array of ingredients, many of which were very unpleasant to handle and even worse to smell. Other spells required bodily fluids—*his* bodily fluids. Magic was rank sweat, putrid odors, congealed blood, and gag-inducing dissections with no guarantee that the spell would even come off right.

But as unappealing as all of that might be, the greatest obstacle to Logan's goal was what he needed most, the key to successfully casting the most powerful spells: multiple casters.

Realizing how much he'd taken for granted all of his life was another hard lesson, as if the whole dreadful business with the Scion and his Searchers hadn't been bad enough. Day after day, the same question dogged Logan's steps. Had he made the right choice?

At the time, Logan had convinced himself that giving aid to the Searchers was the only choice. A matter of survival. He'd seen the writing on the wall the moment his pack of Guardians divided, half of them going over to the Searchers. Rebellions were like plagues: catching, devastating.

If his father, Efron, hadn't blamed him for Calla's betrayal, things might have gone differently. But Logan's father made it clear that he teetered on the verge of disowning his only son and heir. More concerned with keeping the taint of rebellion off himself than protecting Logan, Efron had effectively demoted his son. With no pack to rule, Logan would have been denied his father's legacy. And while the wealth and privileges of a Keeper's life remained his to enjoy, Logan knew well that his reign as lordling among his peers would soon end.

With his inheritance stolen, Logan went to the Searchers, offering his services to their misguided yet indefatigable cause. He freely admitted to himself that he'd gone out of spite and in haste, not thinking through the full ramifications of his actions. He'd thought he'd made allowances for all possible outcomes.

Should the Searchers lose, Logan still had the pretext of being their prisoner. Efron Bane's arrogance ensured that he would much more readily accept the possibility of his son's failure than his treachery.

But they didn't lose. And Logan had no idea how ill prepared he was for that scenario, despite his laying bets on the Searchers' chances. His self-assurance began to crumble when Sabine tore out his father's throat. Rebellion from a distance was an interesting concept. Up close, made of spilled blood and rent flesh, it was nothing other than a ghastly reality.

Logan would have run at that point, if not for the knowledge that his throat would be the next one torn to shreds by a Guardian. Forced to remain beside his father's corpse while the Nightshade and Bane alpha males battled, Logan couldn't fight off the creeping knowledge that all of this was horribly, horribly wrong. He was not meant to be here. Had no business being a part of this folly. This was not his legacy.

Logan's mind had fogged with doubt. He was surrounded by a haze of blood and violence, and then Calla had been at his side, forcing him to say the words. To invoke the source of the Keepers' power: Bosque Mar. Logan renewed his blood oath, calling Bosque from beyond the Rift. When Bosque appeared, condemning Logan for his treachery, Logan had been surprised by the sting of Bosque's words. As Bosque spoke to him, Logan's blood felt like barbwire, twisting and tearing within him.

Cowering from fear and shame, Logan had watched as the Scion—he couldn't think of that force of wild magic as the boy who'd been called Shay—drove his master into oblivion, sealing the Rift forever. As Rowan Estate shook and Logan literally saw his world crumbling, he'd summoned the strength to crawl along the quaking library floor. When the ground beneath ceased its violent shifting, Logan scrambled to his feet. And he ran.

He didn't stop running until he reached the private airstrip where his father's Dassault Falcon 7X was waiting for him. Logan had called the airstrip as he ran, knowing the pilot and crew were on call 24/7 to accommodate spur-of-the-moment trips. Wheezing, Logan boarded the plane and ordered the pilot to take off immediately. Once they were airborne, the flight attendant offered him a cocktail, which Logan refused. As much as he felt like he needed one, Logan knew he needed a clear head more. The glossy-lipped stewardess then took off his shoes for the usual foot massage she provided, and gasped. Logan's feet were bleeding. He wasn't surprised. Without a word, the flight attendant washed and bandaged his feet. His father's staff knew better than to ask questions. No matter what they witnessed.

Logan practically lived aboard the private jet for the first month after he fled Colorado. He didn't feel safe staying in one place for more than a few days. It was only a matter of time before the Searchers came after him. Once the fallout from the last battle at Rowan Estate had settled, those wretched, duty-bound warriors were sure to begin hunting down all the Keepers. At least the ones who survived the war.

As it happened, there weren't that many.

The Keepers had always been selfish with their powers. That

hoarding, territorial quality paired with preternaturally long lives meant very few Keepers had children. Offspring were considered necessary for the future, to carry forward the blood oath and maintain the link between Bosque Mar and the earth. But nurtured and coveted Keeper children were not. Logan had always sensed that his father regarded him as a nuisance. Logan had never known his mother, and his father rarely spoke of her. Lumine Nightshade had more kind words about Marise to offer than Efron did. Despite the absence of affection between them, Logan and his father reached a common accord: they were both waiting for Logan to grow up.

And grow he had. Logan was eighteen. He'd come of age. And his life had shattered into a thousand jagged pieces. He didn't know what to do with himself—with the exception of avoiding the Searchers. Logan definitely knew to do that. But he decided it was time to stop running. He ordered the pilot to fly to Montauk, where he knew he would find someone—or two someones—willing to take him in.

"I don't know what you're complaining about," Audrey said, offering Logan a clove cigarette, the day after he'd arrived. "It could be much worse."

Logan took the slim black cigarette with a nod of gratitude.

"She's right, you know," added Chase. "Take Mother and Father, for instance."

Audrey smirked, settling on the divan next to her brother. Chase and Audrey Roth were twins and thus the rare exception to Keepers having no more than one child. They were unexceptional as Keepers, however, in their lack of regard for their deceased parents. That they could speak with such nonchalance of their parents' devolving suddenly from living beings to rotting flesh and, finally, to bones and dust, leaving Chase and Audrey orphans, was a testament to that.

The Roth family had steered clear of Keeper politics, focusing on the economic strings their kind liked to pull. Montauk's distance from any of the sacred sites also kept the Roths out of the bloodier side of Keeper affairs. Logan hoped that meant this place and its inhabitants weren't on the Searchers' radar. He felt safe enough to stay in Montauk. For now.

The waterfront estate was too modern for Logan's taste. He preferred residences that recalled the grandeur of Europe, and a time when the notion that all people are created equal was known to be hogwash. He couldn't deny, however, that the mansion and guesthouses offered every comfort and were architecturally stunning, with their clean lines and airy rooms.

Though they'd elected to receive their education via private tutors rather than enroll at the Mountain School—the Roth twins subscribed to the popular East Coast idea that the world ended west of the Mississippi—Chase and Audrey had long been friends with Logan. Their father, Weston Roth, had partnered in investments with Efron Bane for over a century. And Logan and Efron had visited the Roths' Montauk home often.

The two men had a natural affinity that Logan supposed was due to their shared origin story. Both originally human, Efron and Weston had been elevated by their wives to join the ranks of the Keepers. Though his father was too powerful for any of his peers to publicly disparage him, Logan knew that an elevated Keeper was considered somehow lesser than those who could claim the birthright.

Logan half agreed with that sentiment. Though he was happy to be his father's heir, Logan's pride derived from his mother's ancestry. Her bloodline could be traced back to Eira: the first Keeper.

Not that it mattered. Now that the Rift was closed, there was no such thing as a Keeper. Logan looked at his smooth, unlined hand and slender fingers holding his cigarette. He sighed, wondering how soon he'd show signs of age.

"Still melancholy?" Chase offered a lazy smile. "How can I cheer you up?"

Logan looked away from Chase, ignoring the flirtatious curve of his lips. With silky black hair and olive eyes, Chase would have been a welcome distraction. But Logan couldn't afford distraction right now. Logan's gaze flicked back to Chase.

"I'll think of something," he answered. Logan didn't want to fan flames, but neither did he want to smother any spark Chase might be kindling.

Logan supposed that might be the one good thing about having the elder generation of Keepers gone: no more antiquated rules about sexuality. No more lying about who he was. And from the sly gleam in Chase's eyes, it was clear he counted that fact as a silver lining too.

Pushing her lip into a pout at being ignored by the boys, Audrey said, "I miss Joel."

Chase groaned, throwing his arm over his eyes. "Not again."

"Who's Joel?" Logan asked.

"Her wolf pet," Chase answered. "Efron sent him to Father to be our bodyguard, remember?"

"Ah, that's right." Logan recalled that Joel had been a brawny wolf of the Bane pack. One of the youngest, but still a decade older than the wolves Logan had been set to inherit.

Audrey threw a silk pillow at him. "He was not my pet. Joel adored me."

"He had to adore you," Chase replied. "You just chose to believe his sentiments were genuine."

"How do you know they weren't?" She flipped her glossy raven ringlets as if to prove a point.

"Because he was a Guardian," Chase said. He lifted his arm to look at Logan. "Am I right?"

Logan shuddered, remembered the gurgles coming from his father's throat after Sabine tore it to shreds. He hadn't revealed the truth of Efron's demise. It was too horrible to repeat. If there were still Guardians around, representing a similar threat, Logan might have felt compelled to warn his peers. But just as there were no more Keepers, there were no more Guardians.

"Even if you're right," Audrey said, sulking, "it was still awful that we had to shoot him."

"There was a wolf running wild through the house," Chase countered. "It's not like we could have released him into the Hamptons."

"Don't mock me." Audrey glared at her brother. "I liked Joel. He was lovely."

"We could have made him into a rug." Chase grinned wickedly. "Or stuffed him. You could still have cuddled him in bed every night."

Audrey jumped up. "That's vile. I was sleeping with the boy, not the wolf."

"I certainly hope so. Though if you're that kinky, I'm kind of impressed." Chase laughed, nonplussed by Audrey's sudden pummeling of his chest. Logan began to laugh too. Audrey was neither kinky nor did she know how to throw a punch.

Finally shoving Audrey back onto the divan, Chase asked Logan, "What's really bothering you?" He paused, drawing a breath. "Money trouble?"

Audrey gasped, narrowing her eyes in warning at Chase.

"No, no," Logan said quickly, and was rewarded by the tension going out of the room. "Money is never an issue."

He wasn't deceiving them. Logan had problems, but none of them were financial. The Keepers were bereft of their magic, but worldly assets they still held in spades. And in terms of net worth, Logan remained among the wealthiest of Keepers. Efron Bane had been shrewd in his investments and solicitous of all the right relationships: finance, politics, entertainment—there wasn't a place Efron was without connections. Now those strings had been placed in Logan's hand to pull as he wanted.

"When you called, we thought"—Audrey threw Logan an apologetic glance—"you might need help."

Logan took a long pull from his cigarette. "I do need help. Just not that kind."

He didn't know if Chase and Audrey would understand, even if they were sympathetic to him. It would be easier if his aim was vengeance or sheer hatred. But neither of those motivations matched the stirring in his blood. The sense of loss that followed him no matter where he went.

"Two things," Logan said. "I need access to your father's library."

"You shouldn't have trouble finding it," Chase remarked. "It takes up half of the east wing."

"His private library," Logan said, tapping ash from the cigarette's glowing tip.

Chase and Audrey exchanged a glance.

"Yes, I know about it." Logan looked at each of them steadily. "I assume you know where the key is."

"What's the second thing?" Chase asked.

Logan smiled at him, noting that he hadn't answered the question.

"Some spells require three supplicants to succeed," Logan said, pointing at Chase, Audrey, and himself. "One. Two. Three."

The twins stared at him for several minutes. Logan found himself enjoying how disconcerted they seemed.

Chase leaned forward. "This is a joke."

"Not at all." Logan stabbed out the cigarette and stood up. "I need to cast a few spells. Learn magics from the books your father has secreted away in his library. Then I'll want to cast more spells."

"Why on earth would you go meddling with magics?" Audrey asked, exasperated. "Didn't you tell us when you arrived that you feel like you have a target on your back?"

Logan pursed his lips but didn't answer.

"Casting spells is like planting a homing beacon on yourself," Audrey continued. "Do you want the Searchers to find you?"

He didn't. "I don't have any choice."

"Of course you do," Chase replied. He waved at their surroundings. "What more do you need than this? Can spells bring you happiness?"

"I'm not after happiness," Logan told him. He couldn't pinpoint what it was that had driven him to an obsession with the Keepers' history. Why he hired thieves to ransack Rowan Estate and bring him as much of Bosque Mar's collection as they could manage. One of the fools had been caught. Damn him. But what Logan had managed to get his hands on proved useful enough. It at least pointed him in the right direction.

Logan couldn't expect the twins to understand something he didn't fully comprehend himself, but he needed their help.

Giving Audrey a direct look, he said, "How do you expect you'll look in ten years?"

She lifted her chin in pride.

But when Logan said, "Twenty?" her face fell.

If there was anything Keepers had in common, it was vanity.

"Bosque Mar kept us from aging," Chase interjected. "And he's gone."

Logan's fists clenched at Bosque's name. "I know."

"So what are you after?"

Logan sighed. He'd talked himself into trusting Chase and Audrey, but that didn't make confiding in them easy. "I just want to know—I need to know—if there's a way to bring him back."

"Bring him back?" Audrey snorted. "Have you forgotten your history, Logan? The Rift was opened by a great knight. You may be Efron Bane's son, but a knight you are not."

"I won't argue with that," Logan said with a shrug, "but I think I could be a warlock if I tried."

"A warlock?" Chase tilted his head, regarding Logan with curiosity. That was a good sign.

"Yes." Logan leaned back against the couch cushions, trying to appear at ease, though his pulse was frantic.

"Interesting." Chase kept his eyes on Logan while Audrey clucked her tongue in disapproval.

"It's a waste of time," she said.

"Then you don't have to help," Logan told her. His gaze moved slowly over her face. "If you find humanity so satisfying, of course you wouldn't want to bother with this."

Audrey blanched, clutching at the edge of the divan. Chase looked at his sister and then returned his attention to Logan.

"All right," he said. "We'll help you."

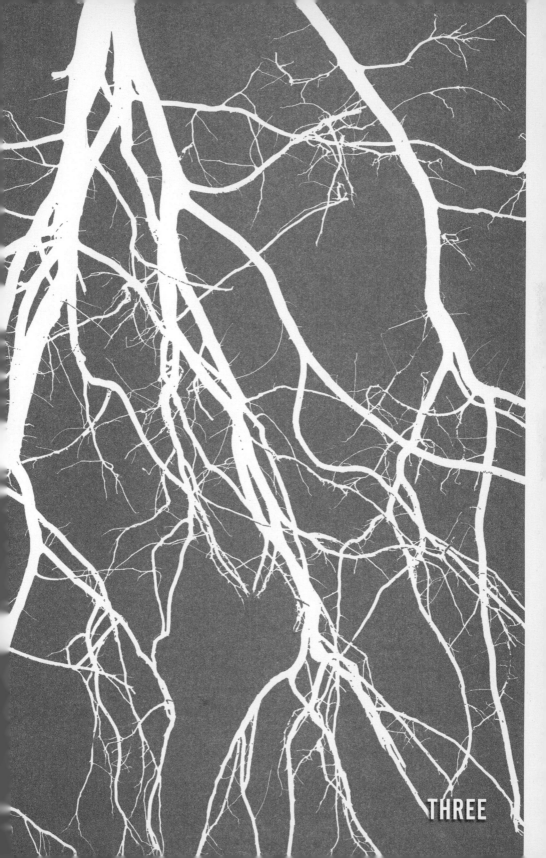

THREE

THOUGH SABINE KNEW the wolf no longer lived within her, she still felt the sway of its feral instincts. She wondered if the lingering sense of the wolf would fade with time, or if it would remain a part of her—like a phantom limb, reminding her of a past now gone forever.

But there were moments when Sabine could feel her hackles rise, warning her of imminent danger. And that bristling along her spine had become a frequent occurrence, taking hold of her at least once a day. Sometimes more.

Shrugging it off as habit, or something as simple as muscle memory, would have been easier if not for the timing of her heightened tension. The gnawing sense of something amiss, something lurking in a shadowed corner, a waiting horror that couldn't be seen but was nonetheless there: all of it began with the ransacking of Rowan Estate's library.

Sabine couldn't bring herself to call it a coincidence. Something was wrong. Very wrong. But what that was, she hadn't a clue. All Sabine could do was watch and wait until the problem revealed itself.

And that was why Sabine, warrior wolf of the Bane pack and sometime sexy beast—as Ethan liked to call her when he wanted to rile her up—had perfected the skill of pasting on a bright smile and simultaneously walking backward and describing the architecture and history of Rowan Estate. All while wearing a name tag.

In Sabine's days as a Guardian, if someone had suggested she would spend her future days wearing a name tag and performing a job with the title "docent," she would have bitten his fingers off. When Sabine had informed Ethan of her intention to take up the post as director of tours at Rowan Estate, he'd laughed. When he realized she was dead serious, he'd first balked, then protested.

"You're a fighter," Ethan had argued. "One of the best I've seen. You belong in the field."

"I belong here," Sabine had countered. And after those words, and a pointed look, there had been no further discussion.

Having just concluded that afternoon's tour, Sabine returned to her watchpost at the top of the stairs, bidding the visitors to return to the foyer and make their way to the exit. The final minutes of the tour were those that most closely touched Sabine's own life, as she discussed people the tourists assumed were long dead but whom Sabine had known, served, and despised. Speaking their names in a matter-of-fact tone always proved a challenge: Efron Bane, Lumine Nightshade. That Sabine was no longer a wolf didn't seem to change the way the memory of the pack masters made her want to snarl.

As the director of Rowan Estate's burgeoning new tourism business, Sabine wasn't expected to guide the tours herself. But she found winding her way through the mansion's halls, recounting its past, and rendering its rooms legible to strangers to be rather cathartic. As the doorways and passages of the estate became familiar, its specters faded along with Sabine's lingering fear. She'd done literal battle in this place, had soaked its priceless carpets with the blood of her former master, given up a part of herself to become someone new. Though she couldn't deny it had been the site of countless horrors, to Sabine, Rowan Estate had come to represent a powerful shift in her life: a moment of choice, of liberation.

As the last tourist disappeared from the mansion's foyer, Sabine anticipated quiet and solace for the remainder of the day. A sudden, overwhelming sense of danger, followed by a loud crash from behind her, chased away those peaceful notions.

Sabine whirled around, her gaze fixed on the closed double doors that led to Rowan Estate's library. The library was one of the sites off limits to tours—not only was that part of the building still under repair, but the Searchers were still discovering secret cabinets and hidden bookcases that contained volumes and paraphernalia deemed valuable and potentially dangerous.

That was where Sabine had killed him. Where she'd felt exhilaration and the release of so many years of pain as her jaws had crushed Efron Bane's windpipe and his wicked blood had gushed over her tongue and painted her muzzle crimson.

More loud sounds erupted from behind the heavy doors. Large objects were either falling down or being thrown around the room.

What the hell?

For a brief moment, Sabine wondered if Logan's thieves had returned for a second shot at their lost bounty.

No way. Sabine chided herself from the brash thought.

Ever since the first break-in, security at Rowan Estate had been tightened to the point of overkill. No one got into the library without clearance. Which meant . . .

Sabine flung the doors open and strode into the massive chamber. These days the two-story space looked more like a theater set in the midst of construction than a functional library. Most of the shelves had been emptied as the Tordis Scribes devoted their time to cataloging and studying the volumes from Bosque's collection. Though the exterior wall that had been obliterated when Shay Doran had closed the Rift was now intact, the fireplace and stained glass windows adorning said wall were still works in progress. Scaffolding and protective tarps now decorated the room instead.

Sabine's gaze tracked through the room, seeking the source of the disruption.

A woman stood in front of a shelf that still held books on the library's second level. Unaware that she was no longer alone, the woman remained focused on her task—which as far as Sabine could tell seemed to be pulling books off the shelf, flipping through the first pages, and then, with noises of frustration, casting the books aside.

Climbing the wrought iron spiral stairs to the second floor, Sabine crept toward the woman, trying to determine who this intruder was.

"It has to be here!" the woman muttered, throwing another the book to the floor.

Whoever she is, she obviously was never a librarian, Sabine thought as she observed the mangled tomes on the floor. The Tordis Scribes would pitch a fit if they saw this—*Well, not a fit, they're too tight-laced for fits.* But there would be weeping and lamentations for sure.

Since the woman was alone, Sabine didn't see her as a threat. With a polite clearing of her throat, Sabine said in her best tour-guide voice:

"Excuse me. Can I help you?"

The woman pivoted to face Sabine, startled by the interruption.

Now that Sabine had a clear view of the woman's face, she gasped. "Oh. What are you doing here?"

A rude question, Sabine knew, but she couldn't think of anything else to say. Sabine had few occasions to interact with Sarah Doran. Shay's mother was obviously much older than Sabine, and since her sudden return to the Searchers, Sarah and her husband, Tristan, had mostly kept to themselves, which made it that much stranger to find Sarah tearing through books in Rowan Estate's library.

"That's none of your business," Sarah answered Sabine sharply. "Just leave me be."

Sabine bristled at the dismissal. "I can't do that. You don't belong in the library and you're damaging the books." She swept her hand toward the discarded volumes. "These are all meant to be sorted and cataloged by the Scribes. You're interfering with the Arrow's directive."

With a derisive snort, Sarah said, "I asked the Tordis bookworms for their help and they ignored me. As for Anika . . . she understands. She wouldn't mind that I'm here."

"I'm afraid I can't just let you keep doing this." Sabine frowned. She wasn't exactly in charge of the library, but Sabine still had a sense of responsibility toward the mansion as a whole.

"Who do you think you are to tell me what to do?" Sarah's lip curled in a snarl that was strangely wolf-like. "Do you have any idea who you're talking to?"

"You're Sarah Doran. Shay's mother." With a smile and a shrug, she added, "I'm Sabine."

Sarah's face fell when Sabine spoke her name. "Sabine? You're . . . you were one of them."

"One of them?" Sabine was taken aback by Sarah's abrupt shift in demeanor. She seemed almost afraid of Sabine whereas a moment ago she'd been haughty.

"A Guardian," Sarah answered. "But you're the one who stayed."

Sabine nodded. Sarah's eyes darkened with a sorrow so fierce, Sabine had to look away.

"I'm sorry," Sarah murmured. "I've been terribly rude to you. It's just . . . no one will help me."

"Maybe I can," Sabine said. "What are you looking for?"

"Anything." Sarah glanced at the half-emptied shelves. "Anything about him."

"About Shay?" Sabine asked. "I'm pretty sure his room is still intact. We don't use it on the tour . . ." Sabine let her words trail off, not knowing whether they would be helpful.

Sarah shook her head. "No. I've been in his room. It's not his things I'm trying to find. It's information about him. About what they did to him. There must be records here. The Scribes say they haven't found anything, but I'm sure there's some account of his life here."

Sabine's chest tightened at the implication of what Sarah had said. "You think the Keepers did something to Shay."

"They must have," Sarah said. "Otherwise how could he have . . . why would he . . ." Sarah's gaze became piercing. "You must understand what I'm talking about. You're the one who stayed."

Sabine's mouth formed a small *o* as the meaning of Sarah's words settled in.

"I'm right, aren't I?" Sarah continued, seizing on Sabine's silence as confirmation. "He wouldn't have become one of them without some dark magic altering his being. Why would he leave us?"

"I think it's more complicated than that," Sabine answered hesitantly. For all she knew about Shay, the Keepers could have done something to him, but she didn't think so. It hadn't been Keeper magic that closed the Rift and returned the world to its natural order. Somehow in that transformation, Shay had become a wolf—a pack leader. Sabine had seen him in the forests around Haldis Cavern; Shay and all of Sabine's former packmates. They seemed happy, and nothing about their existence smacked of nefarious forces at work.

But how could Sabine say that to Shay's mother? Sarah had regained her son only to lose him again in the space of an hour.

"I could take you to see him," Sabine offered. "I visit the wolves. Well, I mean I don't actually visit them. Wolves are skittish around people. You have to watch from a distance, but . . ."

Sarah bowed her head, and though she made no sound, Sabine could tell she was crying.

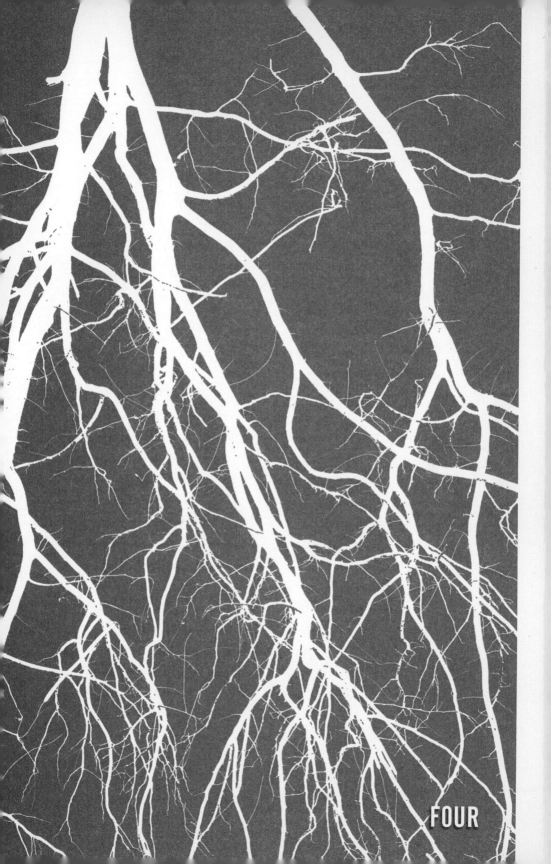

FOUR

REN HADN'T forgotten who he was.

Renier Laroche, alpha wolf, who would rule the newly formed Haldis pack with his mate, Calla Tor.

His path had always been clear. His was the arrow shot straight at destiny's bull's-eye.

But someone had moved the target and Ren had gotten terribly lost.

And it wasn't just because he was dead, which Ren understood that he was. He'd lost his way long before the man who had raised him, Emile Laroche—who Ren believed for so long was his father— had snapped Ren's neck in the library at Rowan Estate.

In the days and weeks since he'd been taken from the world of the living, Ren had tried to pinpoint the moment where it had all gone wrong. It wasn't as though he had a dearth of possibilities to choose from.

It might have been the night he left the house that had been built for him and Calla to live in. The moment he'd turned his back on the Keepers, forsaking the life he was supposed to have for one he never could have imagined. A new life that ended up being much too short.

Or it could have been when Ren watched Emile Laroche kill the man who it turned out was Ren's biological father. Ren never had the chance to know Monroe, but at least he'd met Adne. It was no small thing to have a sister. But in the end, she'd been taken from Ren too.

Another contender had to be the night of his eighteenth birthday. Samhain was a day sacred enough to bear witness to the union of an alpha male and female and the formation of a new Guardian pack. But the ritual had never taken place. Instead, Ren had chased through the dense Colorado forest after Calla, his runaway bride. That she'd left him at the altar was bad enough, but the reason she gave was worse: that everything they'd known about who they were and the history of the war in which they'd fought had been lies. That Ren's own mother had died at the hands of the Keepers.

And of course, there was the day that a new student arrived at the Mountain School. Seamus Doran had seemed as inconsequential as any human, but Ren's first impression of Shay couldn't have been more wrong. As it turned out, Shay had another name—the Scion—and while the Guardians had been fighting on the wrong side of the Witches' War, Shay's destiny was to be the champion of the right side. The Searchers had come for Shay and they'd taken Calla too. Calla and the life Ren wanted, because somewhere between blood and lies and choices, Calla had fallen in love with Shay Doran.

Ren didn't like Shay. He would never like Shay. But Ren knew enough to see that his life had been thrown off course by forces greater and much more complicated than his sometime romantic rival's appearance in Vail.

Maybe that had been Ren's downfall—making the battle one between himself and Shay, rather than seeing how much more was at stake.

He saw all of it too well now, caught as he was between worlds. His state of unrest came with an acute awareness of the unseen forces that hovered around the living at all times, jostling each other as they searched high and low for cracks in the earth's spiritual armor, hoping to slip in even though they'd been banished.

Ren was careful not to get too close to the shades he saw passing to and fro. Along with his sense of them, he also knew somehow that he wasn't one of them.

He was different. Exceptional. And while that sounded like it should be a good thing, Ren knew it wasn't. He didn't belong. He'd been caught betwixt and between, unable to return to the world but equally unable to move past it.

This wasn't how things were supposed to be. Wolves hated to be caged.

Maybe being a ghost wolf wouldn't have been so tedious if there were also ghost deer or ghost rabbits, but besides the shades of creatures from other realms, Ren only encountered living beings. Having no substance, Ren couldn't hunt the woodland fauna that populated the mountain slopes outside Vail. Occasionally he had the pleasure of spooking an animal that sensed his presence, even if it couldn't see or smell him, but he was denied the joy of the chase and the kill.

It wasn't all bad. Though he knew he was a ghost, Ren felt much as he always had. He could shift from his wolf to human form at will, but he never grew tired or hungry. His heightened Guardian senses remained intact, plus he'd gained surprising extrasensory perceptions. In addition to his new connection to realms beyond the earth, Ren found that he could locate people from his past simply by reaching out with his mind.

He'd discovered that he could travel anywhere he wanted at will, instantly. Well, not quite anywhere. His teleporting ability seemed to be tethered to his life. He could only go places he'd been before he died, which made him doubly glad he'd gone over to the Searchers at the end of the war. When Vail became too painful, Ren slipped off to the Mexican jungle or the coast of New Zealand.

Of course, each place wasn't entirely without bad memories. It all reminded him of what was lost.

But none of it compared to how Ren had felt when he'd encountered the pack outside Haldis Cavern.

He hadn't been looking for them. At least Ren told himself he hadn't been. He'd simply been following the patterns of his old life, roaming the mountain slopes in his wolf form.

When Ren realized how close he'd ranged to the cave, he couldn't resist taking a look. He'd even wondered if the carcass of Logan's giant spider pet was still rotting in the cavern depths.

Ren never had the chance to find out. He came to a startled halt a few yards shy of the cave's opening. A place of the dead Haldis was not. Ren had reached the mountain heights just before sunset and the pack was gathering for a hunt.

With yips and playful barks, the wolves dashed in and out of the trees. Nev, Mason, and Ansel tussled, jumping over each other and battling for lead of the group. Bryn stood a short distance apart, wagging her tail as she watched them roughhouse.

Instinctively, Ren rushed forward, barking to announce his arrival. But the wolves continued their play as though he'd made no sound at all. Ren halted and barked again. Then he noticed the movement of the pine trees and realized he was upwind of the pack. They should have caught his scent.

I am a ghost, Ren reminded himself, though accepting that made him feel like he'd died all over again.

That was when they emerged from the cave. A white wolf with golden eyes and a brown wolf with green eyes. Calla and Shay.

The pack rushed to greet their alphas, showing deference by staying low to the ground, licking at their muzzles. It was a scene of pure joy.

And Ren knew he would never be a part of it again. Lifting his muzzle, Ren let out a howl of rage. A howl that no one heard.

What had he done to deserve this kind of punishment? Trapped between worlds, he was alone. It made him furious.

Ren had avoided Haldis after that day. At first he'd stalked through the forests under the moonlight, trying to menace game and restore some sense of his former self. But like his packmates, the beasts of the forests paid Ren no attention.

So instead, he'd turned to shadowing his sister. Ren had thought seeing Adne, even if he couldn't truly be in her life, would give him something of a chance to know her. He'd expected to find her happy. After all, she'd finally captured the game she'd been chasing for years: Connor—the Striker with a roguish manner and an inappropriate sense of humor. That last quality somehow made Connor both endearing and irritating; the former quality inspired Ren to track the Searcher's movements along with Adne's. Maybe animals couldn't sense ghosts, but all the lore about spirits suggested that humans certainly could. The idea of haunting Connor appealed to Ren—it was certainly one way to keep his sister's paramour in line.

But the solace Ren had sought vicariously in observing Adne's new life proved elusive. Adne didn't appear to be happy at all, and despite Ren's best efforts, Connor didn't notice he was being haunted by a wolf. Connor's obliviousness didn't trouble Ren, but Adne's disconsolate mood did. A lot. Ren wasn't sure what hindered his sister's bliss, but she seemed . . . troubled. Deeply troubled.

Thereafter, the purpose of Ren's watch over Adne shifted from the hope of knowing her better to the need to protect her. Something about Adne's sorrow frightened Ren. In his disembodied state, Ren could see the emotion follow her, swarming about her like a plague of locusts. It wasn't natural, and while Ren didn't know what he could do to keep Adne from harm, he was determined to try.

And the pattern of Ren's days and nights had formed. He followed Adne when she was at Rowan Estate and occasionally to the Roving Academy, though since she'd made a habit of passing her nights in Connor's room, Ren decided against keeping an eye on her while she slept . . . or didn't.

Ren supposed there were worse ways to spend one's afterlife, but he couldn't shake the feeling that something more should have happened. He wasn't the only Guardian to die in the last battle, but he seemed to be the only one still around.

There had to be a reason for that. There had to be.

Ghost or not, he was a Guardian alpha. No one could take that from him. Ren knew he'd lost his way between life and death, but that didn't mean he couldn't find his way back. It didn't mean he wouldn't keep fighting.

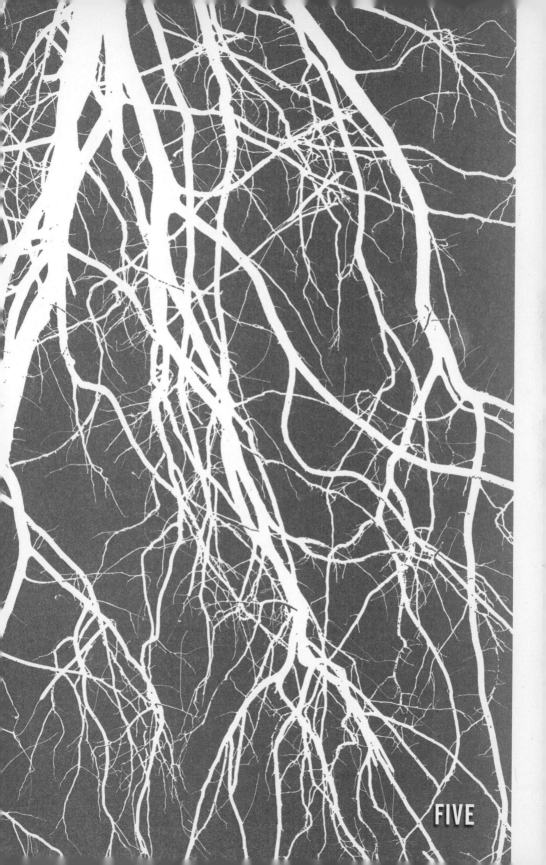

FIVE

MINUSCULE CLOUDS of white mist appeared as Logan's breath mingled with the cold winter air.

"Can't we do this closer to the house?" Audrey complained, twigs snapping under her boots as they trudged through the woods. "It's freezing out here, and the farther we walk, the longer it's going to take to get back."

"We're going to try to open a channel between our world and an alternate dimension," Chase scoffed at his sister. "Do you really want to see our house get sucked into an evil vortex?"

Audrey's eyes widened, then she glared at Logan. "You never said that could happen."

Chase laughed and Logan shot Audrey a derisive glance. "It can't. Chase is just winding you up."

Logan squared his shoulders and pressed on through the tangle of brush and leafless trees. Truthfully, he didn't know what unintended, possibly disastrous consequences could result if the spell the trio planned to cast proved successful. The young Keepers could claim no experience with the type of magic they were about to delve into.

Chase, Audrey, and Logan each had some familiarity with Nether magic, but the spells they'd used in their lives had been easy. They'd been taught at a young age to summon lesser Nether minions: imps, gargoyles, pixies, and as the Keepers grew older, incubi and succubi. The summoning and command of wraiths came later, only after one could demonstrate enough willpower to keep a wraith in check. Chase and Audrey confessed that they'd made games out of pitting various smaller creatures against one another in combat. Logan was relieved they'd had enough sense never to try such a foolish thing with wraiths.

There were other spells. Silly things that amounted to little more than parlor tricks: glamours and memory charms. Audrey, of course, had full command of this superficial magic. Logan wished she'd cared more about harnessing the power of the Nether than guaranteeing her hair maintained a diamond-like sheen.

But Logan knew all of their power, great and slight, derived from a single source: the Nether itself. The small damage they could do as petty warlocks was nothing without unlocking the gate to that ultimate darkness. And access to the Nether had been offered to the Keepers in exchange for their oath of fealty to Bosque Mar. When that fool Shay Doran had banished Bosque and sealed the Rift at Rowan Estate, the well of magic Logan and his peers had always taken for granted was suddenly dry.

Magic itself, however, remained in the world and what Logan deemed the best course required old-school spellwork. Once he'd gotten Chase and Audrey on board, his research time had doubled. It should have tripled but for the fact that Audrey spent half her "research" time complaining or offering disgusted commentary on the spells' ingredients.

Logan didn't disagree with Audrey's reticence when it came to the grit and grime of real spellwork, but his impatience made him quickly irritable toward her. He was fairly certain she'd come around with time, just as Logan himself had.

Chase, for his part, was making much more of an effort toward bringing his skills in line with Logan's. The two boys had taken to staying awake into the early morning hours, poring over books of shadow and the "traditional" occult codices that warlocks and witches relied upon to draw the dark before Eira had made the first blood pact with Bosque Mar.

And with each spell cast, their power grew and their knowledge increased. Even without the abilities they'd once taken for granted, Logan and Chase were on the verge of working magic that could do serious harm. But that was small comfort in the face of what lay ahead.

Since the closing of the Rift, Logan had spent many hours retracing his steps, reexamining his choice, and had come to the conclusion that he'd been a bloody fool. He'd viewed his life, the war, the Searchers, and especially Bosque through a narrow lens of the present when he should have taken a long view.

Wealth and influence, which the surviving Keepers still had, were well and good, but Logan knew that, having been cut off from the Nether, those aspects of his life had been placed in jeopardy as well. Without Bosque, the Keepers were no more than socialites with ties to old money . . . very old money. They were no better than the politicians and financiers they'd become accustomed to commanding.

It was only a matter of time until someone challenged the Keepers' stranglehold on one thing or another. A new player would inevitably appear, someone who didn't believe the rumors of the strange and explicable demises met by those who'd thwarted Keeper wishes in the past. And when that fresh challenge came, the Keepers' bluff would be called. No wraith could be summoned to torment the impudent. No Guardian could be ordered to maim for the sake of making an example.

And it would all be over.

That realization made Logan willing to head into the Long Island woods in the middle of a moonless winter night.

"Here." Logan stopped, surveying the small break in the trees. He looked up at the ink-dark sky, speckled with only a few stars. "This should work."

"Finally." Audrey dropped her pack onto the ground, shivering.

Annoyed, Logan told her, "Unpack the supplies."

Audrey gave him the finger, but she knelt beside the pack and did as Logan said.

"What should I do?" Chase asked.

"You can set up the altar." Logan jerked his chin toward Audrey. "The stones are in her pack."

Chase laughed. "You made her carry a bag full of stones?"

"There are only three stones," Logan answered, too tense to share in Chase's mirth. "One for each of us. Put them in the center of the clearing."

Logan didn't move to assist them, but not because he deemed the work beneath him. Far from it. Logan's days of entitlement were behind him. He knew, however, that young Keepers like Chase and Audrey had long been accustomed to hierarchies. Democracy, discussion, collaboration, consensus: all were viewed by his kind at best as weak, at worst as deadly. If Logan wanted to pull off his new scheme, he could show no doubt and had to take command of his peers.

"Audrey, put the contents of the pouches and vials into the mortar and pestle and grind them into a paste. Then use the paste to draw a circle around the stones, but draw it counterclockwise. That's pivotal."

Audrey sighed, but began emptying dried herbs—and dried things that were much less pleasant than herbs—into the stone mortar. When she uncorked the first vial, she gagged.

"Oh my God, Logan," Audrey choked. "What is this?"

"You don't want to know," Logan answered. In truth he didn't know what substance had turned Audrey's stomach. It was too dark to see what vial she'd opened, but given that it could be bile, asp venom, or the crushed eyeballs of a raven, Logan figured Audrey was better left ignorant. If she vomited into the mixture, the whole spell would be ruined . . . or possibly enhanced, but Logan couldn't be sure.

Chase returned to Logan's side.

"There's a jug of water," Logan said, pointing to the earthen container—thinking to himself that magic was tediously rustic; just once it would have been a refreshing change to see a spell call for a rare vintage bottle of wine decanted through artisanal Italian glass. That sort of thing would have been a snap for Logan to procure.

When Chase picked up the jug, Logan said, "Go pour it over the stones. A continuous stream until the jug is empty, no pauses or breaks."

"You've got to be kidding me." Audrey turned her face away from another vial she'd opened. "This is so gross."

Logan was glad the darkness hid his expressions; it was too much fun watching Audrey squirm not to smile.

She turned to look at Logan. "It's ready. What do I paint the circle with?"

"Your hand," Logan said, struggling not to laugh.

"I. Hate. You." Audrey joined her brother at the stones.

Logan called after her, "Don't forget. Counterclockwise."

On her hands and knees, Audrey painted the circle around the cluster of stones. When she finished, she threw a withering look at Logan.

"It's done. Can I at least wipe my hand off on the ground?"

Logan was tempted to say no, but he didn't want to push Audrey to the point where she'd tell him to screw himself and refuse to help. "Go ahead."

"You could just lick it off," Chase offered.

"Go to hell."

After Audrey had spent a vigorous five minutes rubbing her

fingers against the decaying leaves that littered the forest floor, Logan deemed them ready.

"We've been over this," he said. "Take your places. Once I begin the incantation, there can be no interruptions."

From within his coat, Logan withdrew a dagger.

Audrey made a small, frightened sound.

"You knew this would be part of the spell, Audrey," Logan said.

"I know." Audrey's lower lip formed a pout. "But . . ."

"Ugh." Chase cuffed her shoulder. "Don't be such a wimp. It won't be that bad."

"I don't care about the pain or the blood." Audrey frowned at her brother.

"Then what's the problem?" Chase asked.

Audrey turned a plaintive gaze on Logan. "It's going to leave a scar."

"So?" Logan's brow furrowed.

"I've never had a scar," Audrey replied. "If I so much as skinned my knee, I'd have Guardian blood to heal the wound. My skin is perfect."

"I'm sure the forces of darkness will doubly appreciate your sacrifice, then," Logan said drily. "Now can we get on with this?"

"But—" Audrey held her hands up, gazing at her smooth, pale skin.

"Keep in mind that if we don't cast this spell, those hands of yours will be full of bulging blue veins and wrinkles in a matter of years," Chase added, throwing Logan a wink.

"Fine."

Each of the three would-be supplicants stepped into the circle to stand before a stone. Logan took Chase's hand, turned it over, and carved a triangle into his palm with the dagger. He handed the blade to Chase, who in turn cut the same shape into his sister's palm. Audrey winced but remained silent as she'd been bidden. And she didn't try to make her own slices into Logan's palm overly slow or deep. Her hand shook as she drew the sharp point of the dagger along his flesh, and Logan realized how frightened she was.

Taking the dagger from Audrey's trembling grasp, Logan gave a quick nod and all three of them held their hands, palms facing down, over the wet stones. Their blood mingled with the water from the jug, and Logan began to speak.

"We three supplicants offer our blood on this blind night. Hear our call and let us see beyond this plane. Open beyond and below that we may gain passage to the other, to the Nether."

Logan could barely hear his words due to the roar of blood in his ears. On either side of him, Audrey and Chase were breathing hard, and Logan knew they must be feeling what he was. Power, thick and heavy, like a python curling its way up his calves, constricting as it moved. The force of it made Logan want to fall to his knees, but he did not dare lose control.

Silence covered the forest around them. No birds stirred in the branches. No breath of wind turned leaves over to rustle against the ground.

Then, a sound. Low and steady. Menacing.

A snarl.

"Holy shit." Chase stumbled back, and for a moment, Logan was terrified Chase would step beyond the circle and break the spell. But Chase recovered his balance even as he stared in horror at the shape that had formed from the forest's shadows and now stalked toward them.

"Logan," Audrey breathed in horror. "What did you do?"

"It's all right, Audrey," Logan said, though he was far from sure that was true. He clasped his hands behind his back, afraid that if he didn't they'd begin to shake uncontrollably.

The wolf drew near. It was still snarling but didn't move to attack. The beast's dark fur shimmered with silver, and as it came closer,

Logan saw that its body, though clearly outlined, was partly trans-parent. The wolf was both there and not there. Then Logan's chest clenched.

No. It couldn't be.

Even as his mind rejected the possibility, the wolf shifted forms. A tall, lean figure gazed at Logan with dark, accusing eyes.

Logan cleared his throat and said the only words that came to mind. "Hello, Renier. I wasn't expecting you."

Ren's smile made Logan shiver. "That makes two of us."

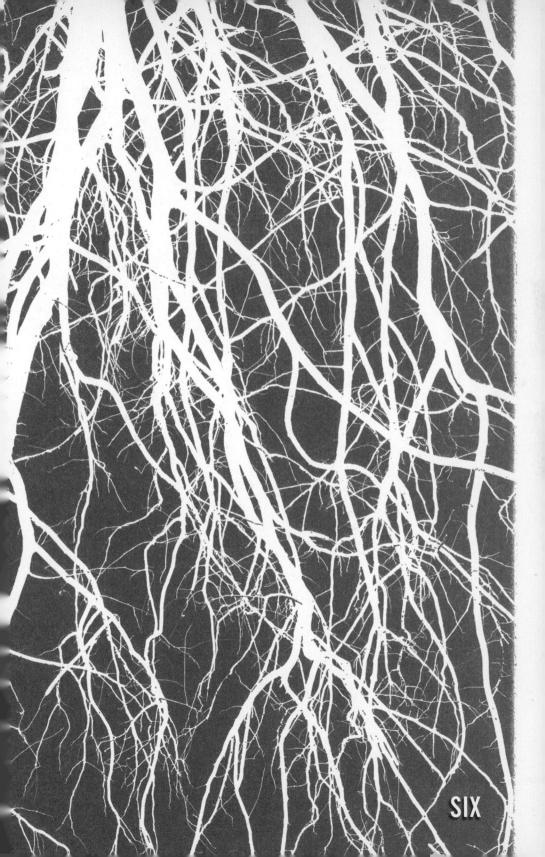

SIX

THOUGH NOT A HARD and fast rule, Adne knew that weaving for her own purposes, and doing so in secret, ran counter to Searcher protocol. She'd never been that reluctant about rule-bending, and sometimes rule-breaking, as she deemed it necessary, but tonight guilt gnawed at her when she began to weave.

Threads of light spooled out from Adne's skeins as she moved, and in a matter of minutes a pattern emerged, then an image. A room full of shelves and boxes.

The Tordis Scribes had declared it foolhardy to relocate Rowan Estate's collection of books, scrolls, and assorted strange occult objects to the Roving Academy. Someone had suggested that it might be possible that one or more of said items could emit magic akin to a beacon, magic that could be traced. While the Searchers widely believed that the remaining Keepers had been cut off from their magical ties, no one wanted to risk revealing the location of the Searcher stronghold.

Thus one of Rowan Estate's drawing rooms had been repurposed as a storage and research area. Scribes came and went from the room, cataloging works and marking them according to subject and relative urgency: what needed to be studied without delay and what could be put aside until more immediate concerns had been addressed.

But even the most obsessive scholars from Tordis didn't crave nights spent in the former lair of Bosque Mar. As a Weaver, Adne knew the schedule of portal openings to and from Rowan Estate, and none of them took place after ten P.M. or before six A.M. And that was why Adne had slipped out of Connor's bed just after midnight and returned to her own room to weave a door that no one else would use or see.

Wiping the fine veil of sweat from her brow, Adne stepped through the portal and immediately closed the door behind her. A rash move, as it turned out, because she was instantly plunged into darkness. The room's lights had been turned out for the night and Adne hadn't given thought to the fact that its temporary state of illumination had been courtesy of her portal.

Fumbling through the darkness, Adne groped along the floor and then the wall until she found a light switch. She flipped the switch without hesitation. The Scribes insisted on keeping the old books and papers stored there in a protective environment, meaning that sunlight was blocked out by heavy drapes drawn over all the windows. The night patrols roaming Rowan Estate's grounds would be none the wiser that a room which was supposed to be empty now had a sole occupant.

The sometime parlor smelled of leather and must. Bookshelves that had been hastily erected were filled with ancient tomes and yellowing scrolls. Adne passed by the scrolls and headed for the shelves that held tall leather-bound volumes.

Logan had stolen several books about the Keepers' history and lineage, but according to the Scribes Adne had struck up casual conversations with, he hadn't taken all of the pertinent volumes.

The books' spines were no help. Their leather bindings might have been exquisite, but they didn't reveal a book's content, so Adne was forced to take one volume off the shelf at a time and scan its pages until she discerned what it was about. The process would have been much less tedious had she been able to get a copy of the Scribes' cataloging system, but asking for those records seemed too likely to invite questions Adne didn't want to answer. As a Weaver, she wasn't supposed to be digging through potentially dangerous books as they were readied for archiving. She also wasn't supposed to be in possession of a box of relics that Logan Bane, for reasons unknown, had deemed valuable.

Connor should have made Adne turn the box over to the Scribes, but he hadn't pressed the issue. Though she knew he'd left her alone about it out of respect, sometimes Adne wished he would confront her and push her to rid herself of the macabre collection. Her obsession with the amulet, rings, and finger bone tucked into the little box was unsettling and often creeped her out. And yet she couldn't bring herself to part with the strange assortment of objects.

She'd even taken to wearing the amulet under her clothing, only taking it off when she went to bed. If Connor saw the necklace, he'd ask questions for which Adne couldn't begin to fathom answers.

Adne's hand slipped beneath her collar. She wrapped her fingers around the gold chain from which the amulet hung. From the moment she'd set eyes on the bloodred stone, Adne had been consumed by the sense that it belonged to her. An impossibility, of course—since this piece of jewelry had been crafted centuries before Adne's birth.

The pull of the stone on Adne's being, however, was undeniable. Powerful as the feeling was, Adne feared it. And she was determined to discover its source.

Releasing the chain, Adne pulled several books from the shelf, set them on the floor, and knelt beside them. Handling the ancient bindings and delicate pages with care, Adne leafed through each book, scanning the pages and hoping that a word or phrase would jump out at her. It wasn't the most practical means of research, but Adne didn't know what else to do. All she had to go on was that her restless nights were linked to the Keepers' history. And that history was documented in these volumes.

The night wore on and Adne's eyes grew strained from hours of staring at page after page of esoteric writings, much of which was barely legible. How did the Scribes bear hour after hour, day upon day of this tedium?

When she knew dawn had to be soon approaching, Adne decided she'd have to abandon her mission. At least for tonight.

She returned three of the books to their shelf. When she lifted the third, something fluttered out from within the pages. Folded, yellowing sheafs of paper landed gently on the floor.

Adne wondered how she could have missed this. Were there pages stuck together that she skipped?

Setting the book on the shelf, Adne bent down and picked up the folded pages. They crackled under her fingers and she winced for fear that they would break apart or tear.

Turning to one of the Scribes' desks that had been brought to the drawing room, Adne carefully smoothed the pages along the wooden surface.

It appeared to be a hand-drawn family tree, which was intriguing enough, but what stole Adne's breath was the inscription at the top of the page.

Sanguine et igne nascimur

Adne reached for her necklace, pulling out the amulet to gaze at the inscription on the back of the stone.

Sanguine et igne nascimur

With her heart tittering against her ribs, Adne stared at the written and inscribed words. This was the link she'd been seeking.

Something in the room stirred and Adne gasped, jumping back from the desk.

But the room appeared to be empty. She was alone.

Nevertheless, Adne stayed very still. When she was certain her imagination had gotten the best of her, she heard it again. Adne shivered at the softness of the sound. It must have been a draft. Old estates like this one always had drafts, didn't they?

The barest breath of a cool wind stroked the back of her neck. She didn't want to admit that she'd heard something more.

Ariadne.

It came again. Still quiet, but more distinct. An accompanying chill slid over Adne's shoulders.

Ariadne.

Adne took the papers from the desk and carefully folded them, tucking them into her coat. Considering that the pages had been stashed in a book, unnoticed thus far by the Scribes, Adne wasn't worried about anyone missing them. She'd return them, of course, but not until she had a better sense of what they were.

She needed to get out of there. The sun would come up soon and the Scribes wouldn't be far behind. She reached for her skeins.

I need you.

Her hands paused beside her hips.

Come to me.

Fingers trembling, Adne drew the skeins from her leather belt.

Come.

Cold that had been making her limbs shake took hold of her bones, but instead of weakening her, the icy sensation began to push away her fear. Her cooling blood felt like a ward against looming danger. The frostiness of her lips and the misting of her breath seemed to serve as a shield.

Without knowing what prompted the thought, Adne mused: *A heart encased in ice can't be broken.*

Adne began to weave. Her movements were smooth, unbroken. A silvery door took shape in the drawing room, casting pools of ghostly light on the shelves. When the portal stood open, Adne gazed through it. Snow covered the ground, its soft sheen enhanced by the predawn light.

All was still.

Come. Now.

Adne stepped through the portal, passing out of the mansion and into Rowan Estate's garden. Snow crunched beneath Adne's boots. The winter night caused no chill, despite the light fabric of her coat. She felt oddly warm, and the source of her body heat seemed to be radiating from the place where the amulet rested against her sternum.

A small object that lay in the snow caught Adne's eye. She closed the portal and bent to examine it more closely.

The rosebud peeked through the snowdrift, barely discernible given that the flower's white hue camouflaged it quite well.

Adne frowned at the rose. "What are you doing here?"

The only possible explanation was that someone had dropped the rose. But why would anyone have been carrying a rosebud through Rowan Estate's garden? Stranger still, the rose's presence didn't trouble Adne so much as a nagging sense that it was the wrong color.

White and still, nearly invisible in the snow, the rose seemed drained of life.

Bloodless.

In blood and fire we are born.

Adne dropped to her knees, reached into her shirt, and withdrew the amulet. Clasping the warm stone in her left hand, Adne stretched her right hand out to hover just above the rose, her palm facing down.

"*Sanguine et igne nascimur.*"

The snow beneath the tight rosebud began to stir. The white rose pushed up toward Adne's palm, and she saw that the flower hadn't been cast aside at all. The rose still clung to its bush, which now poked up through the snow. The dark, twisting wood of the rosebush snaked over the snow, its thick, rope-like branches broken by sharp thorns. The branches curved up and over the white bud.

Adne gasped when suddenly the rosebush wrapped around her wrist and hand. Thorns sliced through her skin and blood dripped from the wounds, falling like raindrops upon the closed white petals of the rose.

Barely feeling the pain of her pierced flesh, Adne was instead transfixed by the rose. As Adne's blood stained the white petals a deep crimson, the rose began to bloom.

In blood and fire we are born.

Somewhere behind her, Adne heard slow, heavy footsteps crunch in the snow. She tried to turn, to see who approached, but her thorn-covered bonds held fast.

The footsteps were closer now. And for the first time since she'd stepped into the garden that night, Adne was afraid.

A spike of adrenaline made Adne jerk back. The thorns tore her skin and she screamed, the wounds suddenly unbearable. Despite the pain, Adne struggled to free herself from the tangle of branches. Not a speck of white remained on the rose beneath Adne's palm, soaked as its petals were with her blood.

Light brought by the rising edge of the sun filled the eastern sky, appearing to set the horizon on fire. Without warning, the rose under Adne's hand erupted into flames. Adne screamed again as the fire seared her palm.

The footsteps halted at Adne's back. A presence loomed over Adne, surrounding her. She would have been able to turn her head to look at whoever stood behind her, but she was too afraid.

"I can take the pain away." A man's voice. Low, coaxing.

Yes. Please, Adne thought, but she didn't say the words aloud. Even so, the flames of the rose became embers. Adne's hand throbbed, but her skin was no longer burning.

"Ariadne," the man said. "I can do more for you. So much more. Let me show you who I am."

Adne didn't want to turn. She didn't want to look. She even shut her eyes, squeezing her eyelids so tight, it made her temples ache. But she felt her head moving, lifting toward the sound of that voice.

"Open your eyes."

Adne shook her head, desperate to resist the command. There was no denying that it had been a command.

"Open your—"

A new sound cut through the night, silencing the stranger's voice. A wolf howled, long and sorrowful. Another voice joined the first. Then another. A chorus of their distant calls reverberated in the winter air.

The pack's song surrounded Adne, filling her ears and easing her frenzied pulse. Their howls carried her to the earth so that snow kissed her cheek. Her hand was suddenly free and she moaned as her burned skin was buried in the cold drifts. A new sound drew close, someone approaching. But these weren't footsteps; they were the quiet padding of paws, nearly silent on the snow. Then she knew no more.

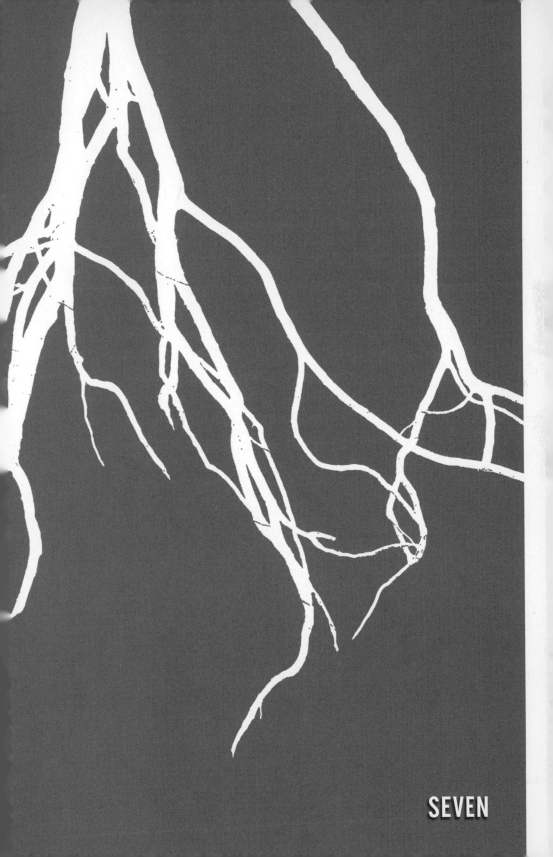

SEVEN

"A GUARDIAN!" Audrey shrieked. "You summoned a Guardian! What the hell are you playing at, Logan? Is this some kind of sick joke?"

"Calm down, Audrey," Chase told his sister, though he was also gazing at Ren in absolute horror. He said to Logan, "I'm sure you can explain what's going on." His voice was calm, but his face had taken on a sickly pallor.

Though his heart beat at a frenzied pace, Logan managed to say, "Of course I can, and I will, just as soon as Audrey stops her hysterics."

"I am not in hysterics!" Audrey flailed her arms.

Fear made her look and act so ridiculous, it actually helped to calm Logan's nerves. "My mistake."

He turned back to the strange, yet so familiar, apparition. At least he hoped it was an apparition. Thinking of what a flesh-and-blood Ren Laroche would want to do to his former master made Logan's skin crawl.

Logan remained silent, returning the Guardian's steady gaze.

"Aren't you going to ask why I'm here?" Ren smiled lazily. The silver flecks in his dark irises flashed with amusement.

With an uncomfortable cough, Logan said, "You're here because I summoned you."

Except that he hadn't. The spell had been intended to open a channel between the earth and Bosque's Nether realm. Manifesting a likely vengeful Guardian hadn't been part of Logan's plan.

Ren laughed. "If that's the way you're going to play it."

"What does he mean?" Chase asked, but Logan held up his hand to silence the other Keeper.

Pondering his next move, Logan didn't take his eyes off Ren, wary of any signs of imminent danger. On the one hand, Logan couldn't risk Chase and Audrey seeing his confidence waver—he had to at least give the appearance of being in control of this situation. The problem remained that Logan had no idea why Ren had appeared in the glen. He needed to play this scene as if he held a winning hand, when in truth he was bluffing.

Lifting his chin, Logan said to the wolf, "You know why you're here."

Still smiling derisively, Ren nodded.

"How do I reach him?" Logan asked, frustrated but not yet disheartened.

At last, Ren's smile vanished. His eyes fixed on Logan's, reassessing the situation.

"I don't want to ask again." Logan squared his shoulders as his confidence reasserted itself. He didn't even flinch when Ren snarled at him.

"I'm the first step," Ren answered. "But placing a single stone won't build the bridge you need to reach the Nether."

"What are you?" Chase blurted out.

Ren snarled again and Chase took a step back.

"Don't frighten my friends." Logan shook his head. "Answer his question."

Ren's jaw tightened with resentment, but he told Chase, "I'm the intercessor."

Logan had to swallow a sigh of immense relief. Chase and Audrey could ask the questions Logan could not. And it was becoming clear that when the spell had brought Ren to Logan, it also forced the wolf to obey him. Now they were getting somewhere.

"What's an intercessor?" Audrey crept up to stand just behind Logan's shoulder. She peered at Ren, curiosity mingling with her fear.

"I can commune with both realms," Ren said, "This one and the Nether."

"How?" Chase sounded skeptical. He watched the wolf as though he expected Ren to shift forms and attack them at any moment.

Logan couldn't blame Chase for his apprehension—after all, when Ren had first materialized in the glen, Logan's mind had filled with visions of Sabine ripping out his father's throat without warning in Rowan Estate's library. For so many nights after that fateful day, Logan's nightmares had been of running through the forests surrounding Rowan Estate, pursued by a pack of howling Guardians.

But those were bad dreams, figments of Logan's imagination. And Logan had been witness to something else that day in the library. Ren's death. Renier Laroche, alpha male of the Haldis pack, had been killed by his "father," Emile. If Ren was dead, he couldn't hurt them. At least Logan hoped not.

Addressing Chase, Ren said, "I'm a spirit. Spirits can move between planes."

Chase mustered the courage to step past Logan and give Ren a closer examination. He began to reach his hand out, but then paused.

With a sigh, Ren said, "Just get it over with."

Chase cautiously stretched his hand out as if to touch the Guardian, but at the point where his fingers should have made contact with flesh, Chase's hand passed through Ren's body as if it were made of air. Delighted with this new discovery, Chase laughed and began to wave his hands through Ren's non-corporeal shape.

"Do you mind?" Ren bared his teeth at Chase. Even lacking substance, the sight of a wolf's sharp canines was enough to send Chase stumbling back.

"You're a ghost?" Audrey asked in fascination. "Seriously?"

"I'm not a ghost," Ren growled at her. "I'm a restless spirit."

"Same difference," Audrey huffed.

"No," Ren replied. "It's actually very different."

Audrey sounded petulant. "What do you mean?"

"Ghosts remain tethered to the world of the living because they can't let go of something or someone from their past." Ren's tone made it plain that he was very much wishing he was still flesh and bone, just so he could attack Audrey. "That's why ghosts are known for haunting. They stay attached to either a person or a place."

"And restless spirits?" Chase prompted.

"Spirits are caught between planes of existence due to the nature of their death," Ren answered. A hint of sadness crept into his voice. "Death that is violent enough to alter the soul so that it can't continue on to wherever most spirits go—like a train that's jumped off the tracks. Instead, spirits exist in the spaces between worlds."

"And you can move between worlds at will?" Logan asked. "All worlds?"

Ren shook his head. "Only those worlds that had purchase on me when I was alive, but because I'm a Guardian, I had ties to this world and to the Nether. That's why I'm a conduit between those realms."

"And that's why you had to answer my summons," Logan continued. The pieces were falling into place now. "Because you're also tied to me."

"Unfortunately," Ren answered with a wry smile.

Logan ignored the insult. All that mattered was that Ren had to obey him; Logan didn't care if the wolf was happy about it.

"Have you been to the Nether?" Audrey asked, a little breathless.

"No." Ren's frown carried a growl with it. "Why would I go there?"

"Because you can," Chase said.

"Have you forgotten what lives in the Nether?" Ren shot back. "Monsters. That's a world of pain and nightmares."

"But you're one of those monsters," Logan said quietly. "Or have you forgotten?"

"I am what you made me," Ren replied.

Audrey pursed her lips, assessing Ren. "If you haven't been hopping between realms, what have you been doing?"

"Watching," Ren said curtly.

"Watching who?" Audrey asked, but Ren snarled at her.

"Enough." Logan folded his arms over his chest. "Now tell me what I want to know."

"Is this really what you want, Logan?" Ren said. "You have a chance to begin again. If you start down this path, there'll be no turning back. By staying hidden, you've stayed safe. You won't be able to hide away anymore. And once the Searchers learn what you're up to, they'll come after you."

Logan felt Chase and Audrey tense up beside him.

"I didn't summon you here to be my life coach, Renier," Logan said. "So stop trying to give me advice."

Ren bristled, but said, "All right. If you want to speak with him, you have to get back what you lost."

"What kind of riddle is that?" Chase complained. "Is he talking about our power? Because that's some kind of messed-up circular logic. Of course we have to get back what we lost, but we can't use the power we lost to get it back."

"Do you have other minions?" Ren asked, casting a reproachful glance at Chase. "Because these two are idiots."

"We are not his minions," Audrey objected.

Logan swallowed his laugh, noting that she hadn't bothered to tell Ren that they also weren't idiots.

"They're just out of practice," Logan answered Ren, then said to Chase, "He's not talking about our power."

"What else did we lose?" Audrey asked, suddenly panicked. Logan knew her mind had gone straight to her bank accounts.

"Not *we*," Logan told her. "He's talking about me. Something I lost."

Ren smiled and nodded.

"What did you lose?" Chase frowned at Logan.

Logan rolled his head from side to side. His neck had begun to pinch with frustration. "A box."

Ren nodded again.

"And do you know where it is now?" Chase asked.

"Approximately." Logan could feel a headache coming on. Those damned useless thieves he'd hired had bungled the job. How was he supposed to get back to Rowan Estate now? The Searchers doubtless had increased their security so as to prevent any further encroachments.

He looked at Ren. "So you've been watching?"

Ren returned Logan's gaze warily. "Yes."

"I can guess who," Logan continued. "Given that seeing your former packmates frolicking through the mountains probably cuts too close to be pleasant."

Ren's stare filled with a hate so visceral that Logan faltered, but Chase spoke up.

"Who else would he be watching?"

Recovering his composure, Logan answered, "His sister."

"His sister?" Audrey asked.

"She's a Searcher," Logan continued, regaining confidence by the second.

"Wait, what?" Chase shook his head. "How is that possible?"

"It's a long, torrid story." Logan smiled at Audrey. "I'll tell you later. You'll love it."

"I can hardly wait," Audrey replied. Now confident that the wolf couldn't attack her, she was eyeing Ren with renewed fascination. "He's a very handsome Guardian, isn't he?"

"He's a ghost, Audrey," Chase reminded her. "You can't take him to bed."

"That's a shame," Audrey sighed. "I'm so bored."

Ren had gone very still, his eyes distant and his body stiff as he waited for Logan's next command.

Logan glanced at Audrey. "Don't worry. You're going to be far too busy very soon to be bored. In fact, I'd wager that your life is about to be more exciting than you'd ever imagined it could be."

Audrey gave a nervous little laugh, looking to Chase for reassurance.

Her brother simply shrugged. "I could use a little excitement. There's only so much fun to be had in Montauk, especially in the winter."

"Good," Logan said to him, then looked at Ren. "You're going to keep watching, but with purpose."

Ren tilted his head. "How so?"

"Find out where the box is," Logan told the Guardian. "I need to know how it's been secured so we can strategize about recovering it."

"It's not secured," Ren answered.

"You already know where it is?" Logan frowned at Ren, who nodded.

"It was never secured because when it was found, one Searcher decided to keep it."

"Who?" Logan asked, though he had a feeling he already knew the answer.

"The person you've already guessed I'm watching." Ren sighed, looking away from Logan. "My sister."

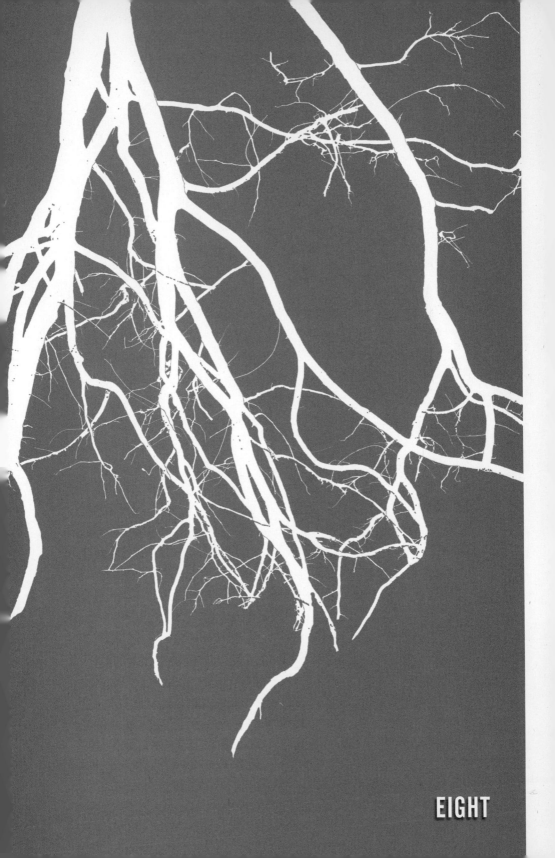

EIGHT

PURGATORY. THAT *has to be it. I've somehow landed in my very own penalty box from hell.*

Ren wasn't sure what he'd done so terribly wrong to merit an afterlife wherein he had to do Logan Bane's bidding, but that was the reality Ren currently faced.

He'd been skulking around Rowan Estate when a bizarre, rather unpleasant sensation had gripped him. He felt a sharp tug, like someone had tied a rope around his waist and pulled hard. The hedges and marble sculptures of the garden had blurred and Ren found himself standing face-to-face with Logan Bane.

The experience had been revelatory. Until now, Ren had been stumbling through his new world as a spirit, improvising, discovering how things worked through trial and error. But from the moment he appeared in front of Logan, Ren's mind had cleared and he could see himself and his place in the world in a way that felt as if someone had taken a blindfold from his eyes.

Ren had thought he was a ghost, but now he knew he was a spirit. He'd thought himself aimless. Instead he discovered he was a messenger.

And with each question that Logan asked, and that Ren didn't expect to be able to answer, the knowledge had simply appeared. It was as though Logan's summoning of Ren created a conduit to the great unknown, filling in many of the blanks about Ren's state of being and the invisible world of which he was a new resident. The downside was that Ren was beholden to Logan to ask the questions. When Ren tried to delve into the mysteries that conversing with Logan revealed, he ran into a wall, unable to get any further than where previous dialogue had taken them.

As much as he hated the idea of being dependent on Logan Bane for anything, a part of Ren wanted to hang around Logan some more just so he could learn about the rules of his current existence.

That was, until he'd heard her cries as clearly as if she'd been standing beside him.

Adne. Something was terribly wrong and Adne was in danger.

Ren was back on the grounds of Rowan Estate before he even thought to worry that Logan might now have him on some kind of mystical leash that would render him unable to move through the world as he'd become accustomed. The thought that his comings and goings probably had some kind of catch flashed through Ren's mind, but was driven away by the scent of blood and smoke.

Adne's blood.

Ren lifted his muzzle and howled his rage at the night sky. In the distance the pack echoed his call. Their voices so familiar to Ren, he never could have failed to recognize the sound.

Coincidence. It had to be. They hadn't been able to hear him before. Why would that have changed?

The other wolves continued to sing a battle song to Ren as he dashed across the snowy ground. At first Ren didn't see Adne, only a huddled shape on the ground over which a tall shadow loomed. As Ren drew closer, the shadow became defined and Ren saw that it was a man. A man he knew.

Startled, Ren skidded to a halt, but he didn't stop snarling.

Bosque Mar turned. "Good evening, Renier."

Ren wanted to lunge at the Harbinger and close his jaws around the Nether lord's neck, but he couldn't seem to move.

"Don't tax yourself, young wolf," Bosque said. "You are here because I willed it to be so, and you cannot destroy that which created you."

Bosque's words only confused Ren, but he stopped growling and shifted forms.

"What are you doing to my sister?"

"Just talking." Bosque glanced at Adne. She lay prone in the snow. And while Ren could still smell her blood and singed flesh, she didn't appear to be harmed in any way.

Despite her lack of visible injuries, Ren said, "Talking doesn't usually involve bleeding."

"You speak of things you can't begin to understand," Bosque told Ren. "I don't wish to hurt Ariadne. Quite the opposite."

"Leave her alone." Ren didn't care what Bosque had to say about his intentions or Ren's inability to attack him. He took a menacing step toward the Harbinger.

Bosque laughed quietly. "Your loyalty to her is remarkable, considering how very recently you learned that you share blood. As to your . . . request, you presume to know what's best for your sister. You don't."

"And you think you know anything about her?" Ren asked.

"I know more than you ever could," Bosque replied. "I've walked between worlds for eons. You've only just begun. Make yourself useful. Show loyalty to me as you do to your sister and I will teach you great things."

He stepped away from Adne and gestured for Ren to approach her. "My business here is finished. I'll leave you to see to her."

Ren almost objected. How could he offer any help to Adne? He couldn't touch her. He couldn't call out for help.

Bosque was gone before Ren could say anything, but the Harbinger's absence brought nothing but relief. Whatever danger Adne might be in now, Ren had no doubt that Bosque posed a far greater threat.

Kneeling in the snow beside Adne, Ren reached out to take her hand. As he expected, his fingers passed through hers as if he wasn't there.

I'm not here. Not really. I'm a restless spirit who walks between worlds. And according to Bosque, I'm a worthless novice at that.

The sudden, creeping feeling that he was being watched took hold of Ren. Frowning, he turned and saw shadows milling about in the forest at the edge of the gardens. A single shape broke from the group and came toward him, passing out of the woods and into the open.

A wolf. A brown wolf with green eyes.

Shay approached cautiously, his ears pinned back and his fur bristling. Ren shifted forms and Shay stopped. His defensive posture eased and he regarded the charcoal wolf with interest.

Reaching out with his mind, Ren hoped that Shay could still communicate the way Guardians had.

Shay, I need you to help Adne. Bosque did something to her.

The other wolf continued to watch Ren, ears flicking in curiosity, but Shay's voice never sounded in Ren's mind.

He's a wolf now, Ren reminded himself. *Not a Guardian. I don't know how it is that the pack came at my call, but they're still wolves.*

Ren padded around Adne, whining to share his anxiety. Shay joined Ren at Adne's side. The brown wolf sniffed at Adne's limp form and nudged her with his muzzle. Adne gave no sign of response.

Shay whined again. He looked at Ren and then at the towering outline of the mansion.

Yes, Ren thought. *He can take her to shelter. Or at least to a place where someone is more likely to find her.*

Ren barked at Shay, then pawed at Adne, showing the brown wolf the way his paw passed through Adne's body without effect. Shay snarled and whined. Barking once more, Ren trotted around Adne and then barked at the mansion.

If holding his breath would have meant anything, Ren would have done it as he waited for Shay's next move. The brown wolf closed in on Adne, bent his head, and carefully grasped her shoulder in his jaws. With slow, steady progress Shay dragged Adne through the garden. Ren followed behind them, encouraging Shay to continue despite the wolf's clear discomfort at being in such close proximity to human habitation. Adne's body made furrows in the snow beside Shay's paw prints.

When they drew close to the mansion, Ren bounded ahead, guiding Shay to the servants' entrance at the rear of the structure. Shay had just released Adne when Ren heard voices. A Searcher patrol was approaching.

Shay heard them too and immediately wheeled around, bolting away from the mansion and back through the garden. Ren watched him go but didn't attempt to follow. He belonged here, with Adne. Once Shay rejoined the pack, they'd return to the mountainside.

Ren waited for the patrol to discover Adne, and when they did, he followed them inside. He listened as the healers from Eydis discussed Adne's condition. He stayed with her until he felt certain that no serious damage had been done to her. The situation perplexed the Searchers as much as it did Ren. Adne was unconscious but otherwise seemed fine. Despite the cold, she didn't even show signs of exposure. Of course, the Searchers were also buzzing about the wolf tracks they found in the garden, but those weren't a mystery to Ren.

Satisfied that his sister was being well cared for, Ren returned to the gardens. He padded through the snow, partly looking for signs of what had transpired before he arrived but mostly lost in his own thoughts.

Ren had learned much that night. Both Logan and Bosque asserted claims on him, but through their spellwork the Keeper and his master had imbued Ren with more power. The Haldis pack had answered his call.

Somehow the magic at work meant the rules of Ren's existence were changing. If he could figure out why and how, he might be able to take control of his own life. Or rather, his own afterlife.

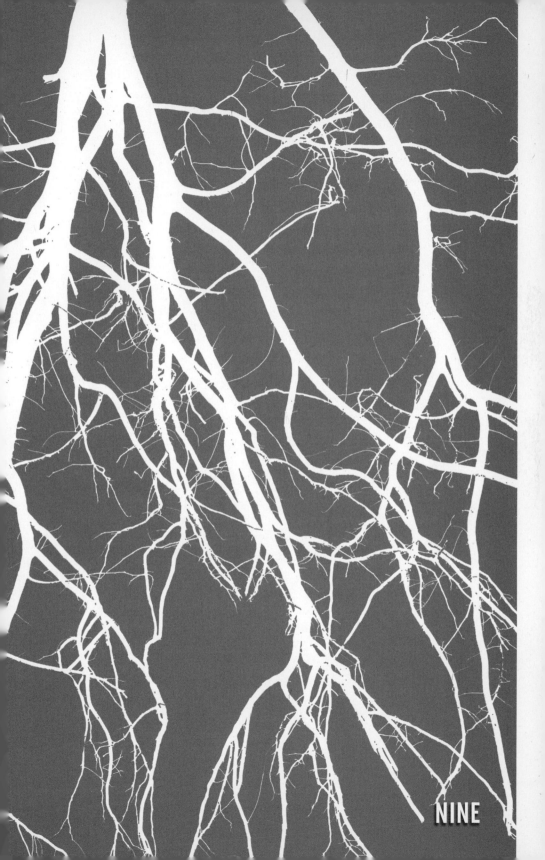

NINE

SARAH'S BREATH fogged the window as she watched the wolf with golden brown fur drag Ariadne's limp body through the snow. When Sarah thought of Shay, she usually imagined the boy she knew, a toddler of three with chubby fingers and wide green eyes that matched his mother's. Sometimes she remembered the Shay who freed her and Tristan from the painting that had been their prison. A tall boy, nearly a man, but with the same eyes.

Sarah never allowed herself to recall her son as a wolf. But that didn't stop her from recognizing him. Though she blocked it out whenever it threatened to surface, the memory of Shay transformed into a beast had been seared into her memory. She didn't want to remember the way he'd bristled at the sight of so many humans near him. How he'd bounded out of the rubble filling the library and into the winter night while Sarah shrieked and sobbed.

Since that terrible day—a day that should have been a triumphant, joyful reunion—Sarah had been returning to Rowan Estate. It wasn't difficult to persuade Weavers to let her come to the mansion with the daily contingent of Scribes and tour guides. A grieving mother, she usually inspired pity, or else she made them uncomfortable enough that they hurried to move her along, making her someone else's problem. Tristan hated it when Sarah didn't return at the end of the night, but Sarah often found it too difficult to leave Rowan Estate. She spent many nights in Shay's room, rarely sleeping, but going through her son's belongings. Trying to recall him through objects, to piece together the years of his life that she'd missed. None of it was enough, and with each passing day the dull ache in Sarah's heart grew sharper, its pain insistent.

Pressing her fingers to the cold glass, Sarah fought the urge to rush downstairs and fling herself out into the winter morning. Shay was here, but he was still a wolf, and Sarah's sudden appearance would surely startle him.

But he's pulling the girl along the ground, bringing her to the mansion. Why would he do that?

Sarah knew enough about wolves to immediately dismiss any suspicions that Shay had attacked Ariadne. The pack's range was well away from populated areas, high on the mountain slopes. Something other than instinct had drawn Shay to Rowan Estate.

He wants to come back. He knows this is where he belongs. It has to be. What else could draw a wild animal to this place?

A surge of hope traveled through Sarah's limbs like an electric charge. She remained at the window, watching as Shay left Ariadne near the mansion's rear entrance. She stayed until the brown wolf bounded away from Rowan Estate, through the garden, and disappeared under the cover of pines.

Though Sarah hadn't known she was waiting for it, she realized this was the sign she'd needed. A sign that Shay hadn't forgotten who he really was. That he wanted to return to his family and that he needed her help to do so.

Filled with a new resolve, Sarah turned away from the glass and went to find a Weaver. She had to get back to the Academy as soon as possible. Anika would help. Now that this had happened, how could she pretend that Shay belonged in the woods with those other beasts? How could anyone deny that the boy belonged with his family?

Her son had saved the world. Yet somehow everyone else has forgotten him. Sarah whispered a promise to Shay: "I'm going to make them remember."

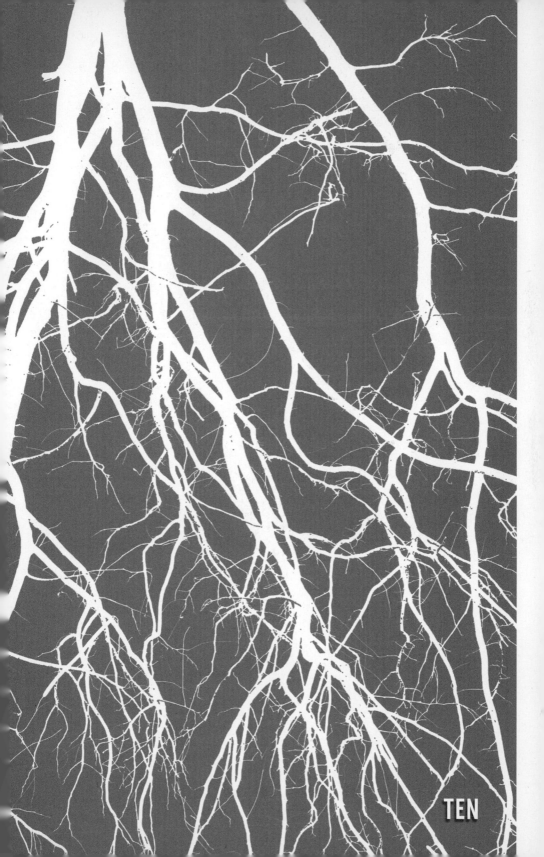

TEN

CONNOR ROLLED over and drowsily stretched his arm out to hook Adne around the waist and draw her against his chest. His seeking hand found only rumpled sheets, long bereft of Adne's warmth. Connor's body tensed, his chest constricting with disappointment. He rolled onto his back and stared at the night sky that seemed to pour down on him through the crystal ceiling of the Roving Academy.

They never talked about it. How often this happened.

The first few times Adne had stirred in the middle of the night, Connor had woken with her, wanting to reassure her that whatever demons had dragged her from a restful sleep inhabited only the dark recesses of her mind and could do her no harm in the waking world.

Presuming that Adne's nightmares must be tied to her grief, having so recently lost both her father and a brother she'd just found, Connor had urged Adne to talk about Monroe and Ren. He'd expected reluctance, but Adne didn't hesitate to share the pain she still felt at Monroe's absence and her sense of failure when it came to Ren's death.

And so they'd talked. And talked. So many nights' sleep interrupted and sunrises greeted with broken memories and tears.

From those conversations, Connor felt confident that Adne was dealing with her grief. At least when it came to Monroe. The blame she wrongly took upon herself about Ren's death remained a touchy subject, and Connor didn't press her too hard on the topic. Adne would deal with that loss when she was ready.

They were talking about it. That was a good first step. It was at least something.

But despite that something, which Connor wanted to believe wasn't a small something, he continued to wake in the middle of the night having lost the lover he'd taken to bed.

Connor tossed out a variety of unsatisfying answers to the puzzle of Adne's insomnia. Perhaps she'd always been a restless sleeper. After all, only in recent weeks had Connor been in a position to make such observations. Or maybe Adne couldn't quite get comfortable sleeping in Connor's room. But anytime he suggested they spend the night in Adne's room, she insisted that she preferred Connor's bed to her own.

If she wants to be in my bed so much, why the hell does she always leave?

Chastising himself for what he deemed a selfish reaction, Connor sat up and rubbed sleep from his eyes. Adne didn't always leave. But more and more nights Connor woke to find her gone.

He wasn't angry about it—admittedly he sometimes indulged a burr of resentment—but Connor was afraid for Adne. Something was off and he couldn't pin down what it was. The more he tried to coax Adne into revealing the source of her restlessness, the more reticent she became.

Throwing the covers back, Connor swung his legs over the edge of the bed. He grabbed the T-shirt he'd tossed on the back of a chair, pulled it over his head, and went to look for Adne.

The halls of the Roving Academy were shadowed and silent as Connor padded through the Haldis living quarters. Even as he approached Adne's door, Connor wondered if he shouldn't turn around and go back to bed. Adne had always been independent. Maybe he was crowding her. And wouldn't stalking after her in the middle of the night push her to seek even more space from him? What if she simply needed to come and go as she pleased? Maybe nothing was wrong at all and Connor just couldn't handle how much he wanted Adne with him. Every day. Every night. Every moment. Every breath.

Standing in front of her door, Connor's fists clenched. He'd begun to suspect that his long avoidance of a romantic entanglement with Adne had been for none of the reasons he'd claimed. Not the seven-year age difference between them. Not that Adne's father had been Connor's commander. Not the risk of loving someone in a life filled with violence and loss.

No. Connor realized that all of those rational explanations crumbled upon close examination. The truth was here. This visceral need that held him hostage; the need for her voice, her touch, her scent. For all that was Adne.

Somehow, despite all his denials, Connor had known that once he let Adne take hold of him—heart and flesh—that it would be like that. That there would only be her for the rest of his life.

If that wasn't scary as hell, Connor didn't know what was.

And now that Adne slipped from his arms more nights than she stayed, Connor had begun to fear that it was too much for her.

"Are you trying to open the door with the power of your mind?"

Connor had been so consumed by his thoughts that he hadn't noticed Sabine approaching.

"Because as far as I'm aware, the Force isn't a real thing." Sabine smiled at him, though her brow was slightly furrowed, revealing concern.

"I know." Connor pushed his hair back from his forehead, giving a little laugh. "It's disappointing, isn't it? I just have to check every so often to be sure."

Sabine kept smiling, but her eyes narrowed. "Seriously, though. What's up?"

Connor ground his teeth. He'd been trying to get Adne to talk about her frequent disappearing acts, but he hadn't told anyone else about it.

"You lose something?" Sabine glanced at the closed door.

Knowing that Sabine wasn't going to let him off, Connor said, "She wasn't there when I woke up. Just want to see if she's okay."

"Fair enough." Sabine shrugged. "But I'm surprised she's not with you. From what Adne's told me, you've got some serious talent between the sheets."

Connor choked a little. He was used to dishing out salacious commentary, but being on the receiving end of those jibes was still pretty new. Though startled by Sabine's remark, Connor nonetheless found it reassuring. At least Adne hadn't passed any complaints on to her friend.

"I do what I can," Connor said, trying to return to form. He wasn't sure he was ready to share his real concerns with Sabine. It wasn't that he didn't trust the former Guardian, but he was protective of his relationship with Adne—letting others in felt risky.

Sabine, however, wasn't one to give up the hunt once she'd caught a scent. "I'm sure you do. But Adne snuck out on you? Does that happen often?"

Sabine was also not one to beat around the bush.

Connor grimaced, which apparently was answer enough for Sabine.

"Really?" Her eyebrows went up.

"I notice you're not in Ethan's bed," Connor shot back.

Sabine laughed. "Ethan knows that I like to prowl at night." Her smile became wicked. "And he loves it when I come back to bed. He doesn't mind at all when I wake him up."

"I'm sure," Connor said drily. He hadn't meant to go after Ethan and Sabine's relationship, which was perfect for both surly Ethan and sharp-edged Sabine. In truth, he was a little jealous. By all accounts, Ethan and Sabine—once sworn enemies—should have the complicated, difficult romance. Instead it was Connor who felt like love was tying him in knots.

The teasing glint in Sabine's gaze faded. "If you're out here in your pajamas, you must be worried. Is something wrong between you two?"

"No," Connor said too quickly, then shook his head. "I mean, I don't know."

Sabine jerked her chin toward Adne's door. "Are you sure she's in there?"

"I have no idea where she is." Connor heard the weariness in his voice and felt the weight of it on his shoulders.

Regarding him with concern, Sabine said, "She loves you. Don't ever think she doesn't. If Adne has a problem, it's not you."

"I know she loves me," Connor told Sabine. "And I . . . there aren't words for what Adne is to me. But—"

"But what?" Sabine put her hands on her hips.

"But . . ." Connor took a step back. Sabine's expression was a little dangerous. "What if it's too much?"

"You're going to have to run that by me again," Sabine said.

"It's just—" Connor scratched the back of his neck, uneasy with the conversation, yet desperate for some relief from the stress of keeping his fears bottled up. "What if it happened too fast? I kept Adne away for so long. I knew what she wanted from me, but I thought I was doing the right thing by keeping my distance. Maybe that was the best course and now I've mucked it up. What if now that she has it . . ."

Connor couldn't finish. His stomach lurched at the thought that after all this time, Adne might regret having pursued him.

"Be careful what you wish for?" Sabine's laugh was harsh. "Bullshit."

"You can't know that," Connor said, slightly injured by her brash reply.

"The hell I can't," Sabine told him. "You had to know that with you and Adne it was going to be all or nothing. Once it happened, that was it."

Connor started to object, but Sabine shook her head. "She doesn't regret it. She has known for years that you belong together. Nothing will change that."

"I guess." Connor shoved his hands into the pockets of his flannel pajama pants.

Sabine laughed again. "When did you get lame, Connor?"

"I am not lame." Connor glared at her, then laughed sheepishly.

"Yep." Sabine nodded. "That comeback proves beyond a doubt that you are in no way lame. Now go back to bed. Despite what anyone says, lurking is not a turn-on."

With a sigh, Connor rolled his shoulders back. He knew she was right. And he was tired.

"Don't you go forgetting who it is you fell in love with, Connor," Sabine continued. "Adne has never needed looking after. She's a survivor—stronger than any of us by a long shot."

"Yes," Connor said quietly. "I know."

"But I'll try to catch up with Adne," Sabine told him. "I've been so busy with Rowan Estate, it's been a while since we've had girl time. If something's off, I'll try to get to the bottom of it."

"Thanks, Sabine." Connor turned away from Adne's door. "Don't wear Ethan out."

"Mind your own business," Sabine hissed at his back.

"You're one to talk." Connor retraced his steps. While his fears hadn't been allayed entirely, he did feel much better. By the time he reached his door and opened it, he half expected to find Adne curled up in bed, awaiting his return.

But the bed lay as Connor had left it. Disheveled and empty. Undoubtedly cold. Connor pushed off the weight of disappointment that tried to drag him back into self-pity. He went to an armoire and took out an extra wool blanket.

Hardly a substitute for Adne, but it was the best he could do. Sabine wasn't wrong, Adne had never been helpless; wherever she was, she could take care of herself. Connor closed his eyes, clinging to that thought and wishing he could understand why now, and never before, he had so much trouble believing it.

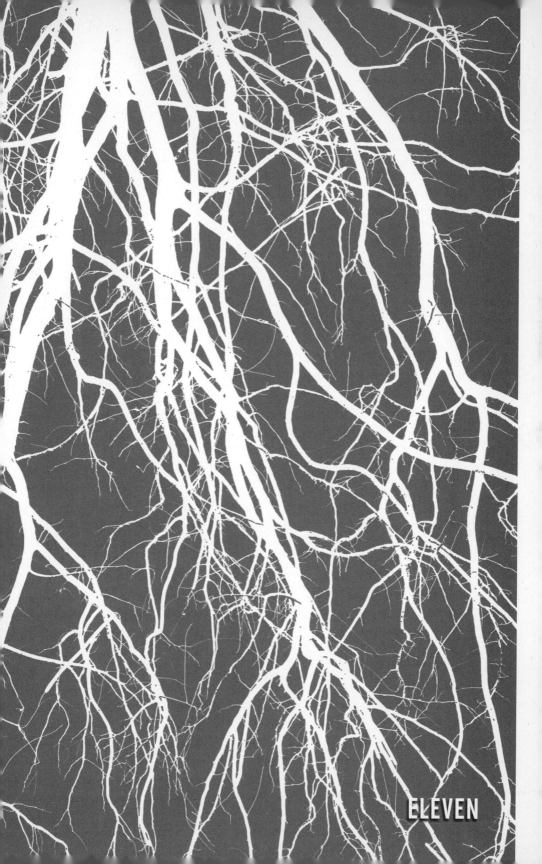

ELEVEN

LOGAN'S VISION BLURRED. He rubbed his eyes for what felt like the thousandth time in the past hour and tried to make the page in front of him come back into focus.

I should have asked more questions. Paid more attention.

His father had lived for over a century. Though he hadn't been born a Keeper, Efron Bane had wasted no time after his ascension. At the sudden, violent end of his life, he'd been one of the most powerful warlocks walking the earth. Logan had taken his father's legacy for granted. As Efron's heir, he'd always assumed that his father's power would be there for the taking.

And there it was again. Regret.

Logan had come to believe that regret was the most unpleasant of emotions. Far worse than grief or melancholy, one became mired in regret as if it were a tar pit, but rather than just slowing and sinking in the muck, regret's dark pool had sharp, toxic spines that pierced the skin and injected its captive with the reminder of missed opportunities, poor choices, and all the wrong roads taken.

Regret: the parasite twisting in his gut, reminding him of all that could have been. Of all he'd failed to become.

Even the spell he'd managed to pull off had been a bust. He managed to call up a Guardian. A Guardian who, spirit or not, probably wanted to tear out Logan's throat just like his packmate had done to Logan's father.

Ren had barely disguised his aversion to serving as Logan's connection to the Nether realm. Whatever magic had chained Ren's will to Logan's command surely chafed at the wolf's neck. It made Logan shudder to speculate about what would transpire should Ren find a way to break that hold.

And that left Logan with what? A reluctant spirit guide and a riddle of a message.

You have to get back what you lost.

Logan didn't doubt the double meaning of Ren's words. Yes, he'd have to get that box of bones and trinkets back, but he also knew that Ren spoke to the loss of Keeper magic itself. That was what had truly been lost. And Ren obviously knew how desperate Logan was to get it back.

Frustrated and demoralized, Logan lifted the heavy book he'd been poring over with the intent of putting it aside for the night in favor of getting a stiff nightcap. As the pages crackled and flipped, however, an illustration on the back inner cover caught Logan's eye.

He'd seen family trees before, but none quite like this. The most elaborate illustrated genealogies he'd seen featured trees blanketed by leaves in shades of jade and emerald, with golden branches filled with blooms and sometimes populated by fauna. The vitality of the scene intended to mirror, or at least project, the good fortune of the family's history.

This tree appeared to be dead. Its enormous trunk and sprawling branches suggested the tree had seen several centuries before it died. In its prime the tree must have been glorious. Why an artist would render such a tree as lifeless eluded Logan.

A gaping hole at the heart of the tree further marred its beauty, but what drew Logan's eye wasn't the wound torn through the ancient wood, but the name inked below the black maw.

Bosque Mar

That couldn't be right. While Bosque ruled the Keepers, he

wasn't . . . human. Logan didn't know what to call Bosque. He'd witnessed his master's horrific metamorphosis from effete gentleman into a creature of nightmares: part man, part insect, all terror.

So why was Bosque's name at the base of this family tree? And what was the Latin inscription beneath his name?

Sanguine et igne nascimur

Something about blood and fire. Logan had taken Latin, but as with all of his studies, he'd been lazy about it. Another regret to add to the ever-growing pile. He ignored the twinge of annoyance with himself and continued to study the image.

The links between marital partners and subsequent generations on this chart weren't simply lines, but rather chain links rendered in crimson ink. Its symbolism made Logan stir with unease.

The blood oath.

It shouldn't have surprised him, but nevertheless Logan felt a cool discomfort crawling up his neck. He'd invoked the blood oath to force Bosque to reveal his true form, making the Harbinger vulnerable to Shay's attack.

And that was how it had ended. Bosque had been exiled to his Nether realm. The Rift was closed.

Logan ran his finger along the curling edge of the paper.

But this is where it began.

"It can begin again."

Logan yelped and jumped off the bed to face Ren.

"What the—" Logan struggled to regain some semblance of dignity. He glared at Ren. "What are you doing here?"

"Bringing the message," Ren answered. "Because you're ready for it." He shot a glance at the open book. "Or at least you're nearly there."

Logan frowned at the wolf. "So you can just show up now? Whenever you want?"

"Pretty much." Ren smiled. "The gate is open. You opened it. I

·can walk through at will." His smile faded. "Though I have to go where I'm told at times as well."

"Like now?" Logan's heart had finally stopped ramming his rib cage.

Ren nodded. "Like now."

"Who sent you?" Logan reached for the book, pulling it to the edge of the bed so he could get a better look at the illustration.

"Do you really have to ask?"

Logan's eyes flicked to the name at the base of the tree. His throat closed up.

It can begin again.

Was this real? Could Bosque really be sending him messages from another world?

"If this is a trick—" Logan peered at Ren.

"What?" Ren gave a rough laugh. "You'll kill me? You're a little late to the party for that, Logan."

Logan didn't acknowledge the futility of his threat.

Ren grimaced. "Do you think—if it were my choice—that I would spend any moment of my afterlife, or whatever this is, hanging around you?"

"You make a good point," Logan replied.

Ren shrugged. "You have the message. Can I go?"

"That's it?" Logan asked, feeling a renewed surge of frustration. "Cryptic one-liners are all you can give me?"

Baring sharp canines, Ren answered, "I'm just the intercessor. I go where I must and say what I've been told to say. From what I can gather, you're the architect of this scheme as well as its constructor. All I can do is confirm that you have the design and components right." Ren's eyes grew distant, then he glanced at the book again. "I can tell you that you've found the key."

"And is there a lock?" Logan asked.

When Ren answered with a smirk, Logan said, "Never mind. Just get out of here."

"With pleasure."

Logan wanted to shoot back an insult, but Ren had vanished.

Wonderful. I have a creepy ghost Guardian who can pop into my life without warning.

None of Logan's plans were unfolding as he'd anticipated. And yet, for all the unpleasant surprises, he couldn't say things were going badly. He'd made progress. Logan stretched out on the bed to take a closer look at the book.

So this is the key.

His eyes scanned the page. *But where's the lock?*

"Well, let's start with what we have," Logan murmured.

Bosque Mar's name was the largest inscription on the page, but the blood chain connected him to a second, only slightly smaller name inscribed near one of the tree's roots.

Eira

Logan knew Eira had been the first Keeper—he'd seen her name in Keeper ancestries plenty of times—but in this genealogy her name was linked to Bosque's. In fact, the rest of the family names on the tree were familiar to Logan. Though, in keeping with its strange form, this particular chart had been created in an inverse pattern from most genealogies. The oldest generation, Eira and Bosque, seemed to be at the bottom of the page, the base of the tree. Which meant . . .

It didn't take Logan long to find his own name. It was one of only two names at the uppermost branches of the tree: *Logan Bane* and *Seamus Doran.*

What the—

Logan forced his gaze to return to the bottom of the page and then he traced the lineage charted on the tree slowly and carefully. He started with his side of the family first.

He recognized his grandparents' names, Cavan and Josephine Bane, but in this ancestry Josephine's maiden name was included. And it was Mar.

Not ready to accept the implication, Logan kept reading. Cavan and Josephine had a daughter, Marise. Logan's mother. A mother who'd died in childbirth and he'd never known. His father's name, Efron, was scribbled next to his mother's almost carelessly. Logan knew too well why that was. Though he'd rarely spoken of it to Logan, all the Keepers whispered about Efron's unlikely rise to power. After all, he'd been elevated at the whim of Marise, whose desires couldn't be denied because she *was* directly descended from Eira's original line.

And Bosque's. Eira and Bosque's. Logan swallowed hard as he corrected his thought.

No wonder his family had been accorded so much power. If this chart proved truthful, it meant that Eira hadn't simply sworn an oath to Bosque and received his power in return; she'd also borne his children.

Logan's grandmother was Bosque and Eira's daughter, but they'd also had a son. Fial Mar.

And Fial Mar's son was named Tristan.

The traitor.

The traitor because he'd fallen in love with a Searcher named Sarah Doran, forsaking his heritage and his kind. They'd married. They'd had a son: Seamus.

Shay Doran is my cousin. And Eira is our great-grandmother.

Logan stared at the chain linking Eira's name to Bosque's for a long time.

Bosque Mar is my great-grandfather.

Was it even possible? And if it was true, then why the secrecy?

When Efron had ordered Logan to shepherd newcomer Shay Doran around the school and Vail, calling him Bosque Mar's "nephew," he'd known it had been a hoax. What did it mean if all along not only Shay but also Logan himself were related to Bosque?

Logan turned over his hand to gaze at the scar on his palm. My blood. Bosque's blood.

You've found the key.

Is this what Ren meant? The key is my lineage?

A fist tightened around Logan's heart.

I betrayed him. We share blood and I'm the one who made it possible for Shay to close the Rift. The two remaining descendants of Bosque and Eira Mar and we're the ones who sent him back.

Regret.

Logan didn't know if he could take much more of it. He traced the shape of the scar with his fingertip.

"I don't know about you, but mine's been kind of itchy."

Logan looked up. Chase stood in the doorway with his laptop.

"I think that means it's healing," Logan said. "What's on your mind?"

"This." Chase walked over and opened his laptop.

Logan quickly closed the book and pushed it away, making space for Chase to sit. Whether truth or fiction, Logan needed to know more about his real ancestry before he was willing to share its existence with anyone else.

Chase positioned the computer in his lap, angling the screen so Logan could look over his shoulder.

"'Historic Rowan Estate,'" Logan read from the screen. "There's a website."

"Apparently they're giving guided tours." Chase smirked.

"I didn't realize the Searchers were that strapped for cash," Logan murmured.

Chase shook his head. "I don't believe they are. I'm guessing that they've opened the mansion up to the public so that it doesn't present too tempting a target for thieves of occult relics."

"Is that a criminal specialization?" Logan asked, half smiling. "Occult theft?"

"You should know."

"I'd bet I'm the exception," Logan told Chase as he peered at the screen. "So they've made Rowan Estate into a historic landmark. What's next: spelunking expeditions through Haldis Cavern?"

Chase laughed. "You have to give the people what they want."

"So are you showing me this for a reason?" Logan asked. "Or are you just trying to reassure me that the Searchers are too busy bringing in the tourists to come looking for us?"

"I thought I might take a long weekend, see what this tour is all about," Chase replied casually. "Do you know that I've never been west of the Mississippi?"

Logan waited for Chase to laugh, but when the other boy held him with an unwavering gaze, Logan frowned. "You're not serious."

"I'm very serious," Chase said. "I'd take Audrey, of course."

"What the hell are you and your sister going to accomplish by going to Vail?" Logan couldn't deny that he was intrigued, but he was also irritated. If Chase viewed this trip as a weekend romp with a dash of adventure, he hadn't begun to grasp how dangerous the Searchers were.

"Stop looking at me like that." Chase made a disgusted sound. "I know what I'm getting into."

"Convince me." Logan felt a little like they were playing a game of chicken, each waiting for the other to flinch.

Chase's expression of irritation mirrored Logan's. "Fine. We're spinning our wheels here. You summoned that ghost, who said you have to get what you lost. And whatever that is—you could fill me in anytime, by the way—it's with the dead Guardian's sister."

"Ariadne," Logan offered. He felt a twinge of guilt. Chase and Audrey had taken him in without hesitation, yet he too often treated them like petulant children who had the gall to interfere with his game. Unbidden, Logan's mind conjured the great dead tree.

Maybe the arrogance of authority is in my blood.

Whether that quality was a boon or a flaw remained to be seen.

Chase took Logan's one-word affirmation in stride. "This Ariadne, then. We need to find her."

"We do," Logan said, nodding slowly. "But there's no reason that she'd be at Rowan Estate."

"You're right, of course." Chase smiled. "But it's the only place we have access to the Searchers. It's the only way we might be able to find someone who knows where she is."

Logan couldn't help but laugh dismissively again. "You and Audrey are going to waltz into Rowan Estate, kidnap a Searcher, and interrogate him or her? I had no idea you had such a wealth of special intelligence talents between you."

"You're doing it again," Chase said with a reproachful gaze. "Just let me finish."

Biting his tongue, Logan gestured for Chase to continue.

"We'll just keep our eyes and ears open," Chase told him. "Find out what we can about what the Searchers are up to, and if we can locate this Ariadne, all the better."

When Logan didn't offer immediate comment, Chase said, "You're not wrong. We may go and find nothing at all. But you can't get anywhere near Rowan Estate and we have to start somewhere."

"That's a good point," Logan said. "We do have to start somewhere."

And maybe Ren can give us a little help. Logan didn't know what the rules were regarding the wolf's movements, but if he could shadow Chase and Audrey without being noticed, it might give them a major advantage. If anyone would be able to locate Adne, it was her brother. He'd already admitted to watching her.

"Sorry for giving you a hard time." Logan flopped onto his back, gazing at the ceiling. "It's a good plan. Better than anything I've got."

"Here to help." Chase leaned on one elbow, eyeing Logan's supine form. "You want to go to bed?"

"I know it's late, but I'm not tired." Logan frowned, glancing at the leather-bound tome that was half shoved beneath one of the pillows. He didn't think he could bear reading any more that night.

"I didn't say anything about sleeping." Chase closed his laptop and set it on the nightstand.

Logan gazed at the other Keeper for several moments.

"Well?" Chase asked.

"Close the door."

TWELVE

SABINE SMILED when Ethan stirred beside her. This was her favorite moment of the day. No matter the number of hours she'd spent roaming the night before, Sabine always woke before Ethan. She'd never been much of a sleeper.

She lay on her side, letting her gaze roam over the slope of his shoulders. She waited as Ethan turned over. He always followed the same pattern. First he rolled onto his back and snuck a sidelong glance at Sabine to see if she was awake. When his eyes met hers, she'd smile, and then he'd reach for her.

The first kiss of the day would be slow, sweet, wonderful.

Ethan had just slid his hands beneath Sabine's silk chemise to touch her bare skin when frantic knocking startled them both. But it wasn't quite knocking. Pounding was more like it.

"Stay here."

Frustrated as she was by the interruption, Sabine nonetheless enjoyed the view as shirtless Ethan strode across the room to open the door. He'd barely turned the knob when Connor burst in.

"Get dressed."

"Good morning to you too," Ethan grumbled. "What the hell, Connor?"

"Get dressed now," Connor said, and Sabine noticed the pallor of his face.

She slipped out from under the covers and crossed the room, not caring that she wasn't really dressed.

"Sabine!" Ethan apparently did care. He even blushed a little, but Sabine just gave him a reassuring kiss on the cheek.

"I have more clothes on than you do," she said before she turned to Connor. "What's wrong?"

"It's Adne," Connor said.

"What about Adne?" Ethan asked.

"I don't know," Connor answered, raking his hands through his hair. "They won't tell me. I just know she's at Rowan Estate and something happened to her."

"Are they opening a portal in Haldis Tactical?" Sabine frowned, surprised Connor wasn't already at Rowan Estate.

"Yes." Connor grimaced. "Anika sent me to get you."

Ethan and Sabine exchanged a look, then Sabine said to Connor "She didn't want you to see Adne without us."

"That's not what it is," Connor replied. "At least she's saying that's not what it is." Connor shoved his hands into the pockets of his duster. "They need you to look at something."

"Me?" Sabine found that surprising. The Searchers trusted her, for the most part, but some of them still regarded her presence warily. Centuries of violence between Guardians and Searchers had a way of leaving a lasting impression.

"Before you ask what, I don't know." Connor pivoted on his heel and headed for the door. "Just put some clothes on and meet me in Tactical."

He slammed the door shut before either of them could speak.

"This isn't good." Ethan folded Sabine into his arms. She let herself lean against him, enjoying the warmth of his bare skin and his familiar, alluring scent—which had always reminded her of river stones and early frost.

Sabine cast a longing glance at the rumpled sheets on the bed before she pulled away. As much as she was sorry for the interruption, Sabine knew making sure Adne was all right had to take precedence over romance.

They dressed quickly and quietly, neither Ethan nor Sabine attempting to speculate about what had transpired at Rowan Estate. Nor did they speak of other things for the sake of distraction. It was one of the qualities Sabine appreciated the most about her relationship with Ethan. They were both comfortable with silence.

When Sabine and Ethan arrived at Haldis Tactical, a small cluster of Searchers awaited them. Anika stood facing off with a trio of men. Sabine was sorry to see the Arrow's rather haggard appearance and her defensive stance. An anxious-looking waif of a girl stood slightly apart from the tense group.

Winning the war against the Keepers was the greatest achievement an Arrow could have hoped for, but the new peace wasn't without its troubles. Though Sabine had tried to keep a respectful distance from the politics of the Roving Academy, Ethan had become entangled enough that Sabine heard much of what transpired behind the closed doors of Haldis Tactical. And most of it wasn't good.

Without a singular focus, the Searchers struggled to find a new purpose in the world. Anika was doing her best to hold things together, but she'd met with some resistance from those of her peers who had a different vision for their future.

The nature of the Searchers' victory created part of the problem. Sabine had been inside Rowan Estate's library along with Calla Tor and her father, Stephen—the Nightshade alpha—as well as Adne, Shay, Ethan, and Connor. Meanwhile, the other Searchers had remained outside on the estate grounds, battling both the Guardians who'd remained loyal to the Keepers as well as the menagerie of Nether creatures summoned to fight on behalf of their masters.

Until the moment that Shay banished Bosque Mar into the Nether, Searchers were fighting and dying on the other side of the mansion's walls.

With so many casualties, it wasn't surprising that new players would rise to fill the vacuum of authority. But from what Ethan had told Sabine, it sounded as though their perpetual politicking and jockeying for power had only made Anika's role more difficult. Even now the sound of bickering filled Haldis Tactical.

"How did she get there?" A man whose face featured a long, pointed nose and whose salt-and-pepper hair was clipped severely close to his scalp held Anika with an accusing glare.

"I've already told you, Holt." Anika kept her tone even, but her shoulders were tight with anger. "Ariadne is a Weaver. We don't know *why* she went to Rowan Estate, but *how* is obvious."

Sabine glanced at Ethan, who gave a brief nod to confirm her suspicions. She hadn't encountered Holt before, but she'd heard plenty about him—and what she'd heard was usually laced with unflattering adjectives. Having taken the place of the Pyralis Guide, another casualty of the war, Holt had quickly earned a reputation for his ambition and his caustic attitude toward Anika's leadership.

"It's not obvious when Weavers are meant to be regulated," Holt objected. "I don't care what she did in the war. That's the past and it's time we all moved on. She shouldn't be getting special treatment."

"No one is getting special treatment," Anika said. "And our primary concern at this moment is Ariadne's welfare."

"Her welfare wouldn't be an issue if she followed the rules," Holt shot back. "But I'm sure she believes herself above them. Monroe always coddled that girl. It's no wonder she's such a spoiled brat."

Connor took the front of Holt's shirt in his fists. "Watch yourself, friend."

Holt shoved Connor away without missing a beat. Whiny as he might seem, Holt obviously had muscle to spare. "And here would be Lolita's great champion, come to rescue her."

Ethan grabbed Connor's shoulder and hauled him back before he could throw a punch.

"That's enough!" Despite her war-weariness, Anika's voice was still cold and hard as steel, easily silencing the room.

"Holt, we can discuss your concerns when the Guides meet this evening," Anika said. "Now isn't the time."

"Your will, Anika," Holt replied stiffly. "Who am I to question the Arrow's judgment?"

He cast a snide glance at Connor, who was still being firmly held in check by Ethan, before he left the room. Two other Searchers trailed after Holt, and Sabine could only assume they shared his opinions. She grimaced. Anyone who made a habit of gathering cronies had to be bad news.

Ethan let go of Connor. "Holt couldn't be more of an ass. Don't let him get to you. He's not worth it."

"That's easy for you to say," Connor growled.

"It's not," Ethan said. "But we won't do Adne any good by brawling."

"It didn't have to be a full-on brawl." Connor cracked his knuckles. "I would have settled for getting one good punch in . . . at least for the time being. And I don't see how it would hurt, since no one will tell me what the hell happened to Adne."

He shot a bitter look at Anika.

"You'll be with her soon enough," Anika sighed. "Mikaela, please open a door to Rowan Estate."

The fidgeting girl drew long silver skeins from her belt and began to weave. Though Mikaela had seemed skittish in the face of conflict, as she pulled threads of light through the air, she became utterly possessed by her spellcraft.

Though Sabine had witnessed it many times, the Weavers' art nevertheless filled her with awe in a way no other magic did. Living among the Searchers had afforded Sabine the opportunity to observe many things about her former enemies, but the truth that struck her most deeply was this: Throughout her life as a Guardian, she'd witnessed Keeper magic time and time again. Their conjurations and summonings had been masterpieces of terror. But not once in all her years serving the Keepers had Sabine felt wonder.

And that was the essence of what separated the two sides of the Witches' War. The Nether magics of the Keepers relied on fear and domination. The elemental magics of the Searchers manifested in creation and possibility. It was hardly surprising, then, that to draw upon one of these competing sources of power meant forsaking the other.

Watching as the multihued strands of light combined to reveal the hazy image of Rowan Estate's interior, Sabine found it hard to understand what could compel someone to give up the beauty of the elemental for the grotesque of the Nether. Then again, Sabine couldn't see the Keepers' power as anything but repulsive. She knew too intimately its corruptive nature.

"You'll be met on the other side of the portal," Anika told them. "If you'll excuse me, I have other business to attend to."

"That's it?" Connor blurted at the Arrow. "You raise the alarm, tell me nothing, and then don't even bother to see this through—whatever the hell it is?"

"Connor." Ethan's voice had a warning note, but Anika lifted her hand to pacify him.

"Of course you're upset," Anika told Connor. "And I'm very worried about Adne. I'll be kept informed about the situation and take any necessary steps as we learn more. But you have to understand, there are other things . . ."

"Sarah, wait!"

Sabine turned as a dark-haired woman with a tear-streaked face rushed into the room. Sarah Doran. The sight of Shay's mother tied a knot in Sabine's throat. The look of haunted grief that Sabine remembered from her meeting with Sarah in the Rowan Estate library was still there, but a new expression half covered her sorrow.

There was a wild light in Sarah's eyes and a feverish flush to her cheeks.

The man who'd shouted after Sarah as she ran into Haldis Tactical was Tristan, Sarah's husband and Shay's father. He threw an apologetic look at Anika and grasped Sarah's wrist.

"Sarah, let's talk about this," Tristan urged in a whisper, glancing at Sabine and her companions. "Be reasonable."

Sarah ripped her arm free and kept walking until she stood inches away from the Arrow.

"All I want to do is tell Anika the truth." Sarah glared at Tristan. "Stop acting like I'm crazy. I know what I saw."

"What's going on?" Anika looked from Sarah to Tristan.

"He came back," Sarah told Anika through a breathless smile. "He came back to the mansion. He wants to come home."

"Sarah—" Tristan started, but Anika held up her hand to cut him off.

"Who came back?"

"Shay," Sarah said. "I watched him bring that girl to the back door. He dragged her through the snow."

"Wait, what?" Connor's skin went chalky. "Are you talking about Adne?"

Sarah threw a cursory glance at him. "I'm sure she's fine. Shay wouldn't hurt her. He's not a monster. I know it."

Sabine moved so she stood face-to-face with Sarah. "You saw Shay? At Rowan Estate?"

"In the garden." Sarah nodded. She turned back to Anika. "Don't you understand what this means, Anika? We have to help him."

"Sarah," Anika replied in a curt voice, "this isn't the time. We should discuss this in private. Go to the kitchen and get some coffee. I'll join you in a few minutes."

"Fine." Sarah pivoted around and left the room, leaving Tristan to gaze after her.

"I'm afraid I'm losing her," Tristan said to Anika. "She's getting worse."

"You think she's lying?" Connor asked. "That she just imagined seeing Shay?"

"How could it be otherwise?" Tristan rubbed his bloodshot eyes. Sabine wondered how many sleepless nights Shay's father had passed since his return to the Roving Academy. "She can't accept that Shay isn't coming back."

"I don't disagree on that last point," Anika told him. "But Sarah might not be lying about having seen a wolf."

"What the hell are you talking about?" Tristan shot Anika a hostile look.

"Go after Sarah," Anika replied. "I'll explain in a bit."

Frowning, Tristan gave a brief nod and left them.

"What was that about?" Ethan asked as Anika drew a long, shuddering breath.

"I wish I could say I knew," Anika answered in a clipped tone. "Strange things are afoot. You'll understand what I mean when you get to Rowan Estate. It's better if you see for yourself."

Anika didn't wait for anyone to answer. She drew herself up straight and walked with purpose from the room.

"You heard the lady." Connor jerked his chin toward the portal. "Let's go."

Sabine followed Connor through the light-filled door. Her skin prickled in the charged air for a few seconds and then she stood in the immense foyer of Rowan Estate. The moment Ethan arrived at her side, the portal winked closed.

"I guess Mikaela isn't joining us?" Sabine said, noting that the Weaver had closed the portal from the Academy side.

"She's a pretty new Weaver." The answer came from the top of the stairs. A woman with shining black ringlets and bright blue eyes looked down at them. "Still finding her feet. It'll be a month or two before she's ready for the field."

"Tess!" Connor bounded up the stairs and caught her in a tight embrace. "What are you doing here? I thought you were still breaking down the Denver hideout."

"I was." Tess smiled at him. "And it's broken down. Anika gave me a new assignment, starting now."

Sabine and Ethan reached the top of the stairs as Connor asked, "New job, eh?"

Tess nodded. "I'll fill you in later. You should go to Ariadne now. Shiloh will take you there." She gestured to the young man standing beside her. He had the bearing of a warrior, strong-set shoulders and watchful eyes. His dark hair curled gently at his ears and the nape of his neck, and the pale blue of his irises contrasted sharply with the caramel shade of his skin.

"Shiloh just completed his Academy trials," Tess told them. "He'll be joining Haldis as a Striker."

"Welcome aboard," Ethan said, offering his hand.

Shiloh nodded, returning the gesture. "It's an honor to be part of the team."

He gave Sabine a curious look. She'd seen it before.

"Yep." Sabine smiled a bit dangerously. "I'm the one who used to be a Guardian."

Shiloh had the decency to blush, which made Sabine like him.

Looking to Connor, Shiloh said, "I'll take you to Ariadne."

He gave a quick nod to Tess and then led Connor toward the east wing of the mansion. Sabine started to follow, but Tess caught her arm.

"You'll get to see her soon enough," Tess said. "But there's something else we have to deal with."

Without further explanation, Tess descended the stairs. Sabine and Ethan followed her through the ground floor of Rowan Estate. Sabine knew this route well. Tess was leading them toward the kitchen.

When they reached the cavernous space of ovens, cooktops, and copper pots and pans, Tess didn't pause but instead went right to the back door. Opening the door, Tess stopped before stepping outside.

"That's quite the draft you're letting in," Ethan said, but Sabine heard the nervous edge to his voice. "You do remember that we pay the heating bills for this place now?"

Tess gave him a wry smile that quickly faded. "This is where they found her."

"What are you talking about?" Sabine asked. She looked at the snow outside the doorway and saw it—the impression left there by a body. "You mean Adne? Who found her? What was she doing outside?"

"The morning patrol found her," Tess answered. "She was unconscious and just outside this door."

"Is she okay?" Ethan asked.

Sabine bit her lip, as worried as Ethan. In this weather it wouldn't take long for hypothermia to set in. What could have sent Adne out in the cold?

"The Eydis Elixirs were able to bring her body temperature up," Tess told them. "And from what they could discern without speaking with Adne, their best guess is that she wasn't at the door very long—which is a damn lucky thing."

Ethan frowned, gazing at the dented snow. "What the hell was she doing?"

"I don't think we'll find out until she wakes up," Tess told him. "But that's not the only thing I'm concerned about."

Tess pointed to the snow just beyond the shape Adne's prostrate form had left. "Sabine, tell me what you see there."

Sabine looked at the place Tess indicated. Her heart knocked hard against her ribs. Before the place Adne's body had come to rest was a trail in the snow.

"Someone dragged her here," Sabine said quietly.

"Not someone," Tess replied. She pointed again and Sabine saw them. In the snow beside the drag marks were unmistakable tracks. Wolf prints.

"Oh my God," Sabine breathed. Had Adne been in trouble and had the Haldis pack, sensing it, come to her aid? Was that even possible? "Sarah was right."

"Are those . . ." Ethan stopped speaking and stared at the tracks.

"What do you think, Sabine?" Tess asked quietly.

Sabine shook her head slowly. "I have no idea. It doesn't seem like the pack would range this close to a populated area. Wolves don't like humans. But Sarah said she saw Shay."

"And these aren't ordinary wolves," Ethan said. "That matters, doesn't it?"

"Except they are ordinary wolves now," Sabine replied. "For all intents and purposes the closing of the Rift means that Guardians are one hundred percent wolf."

Tess nodded. "That's what I've been given to understand. But is it possible that they could have some residual memory? Shay in particular? Right before the Rift closed, we all knew he was the wild card. I think most of us were surprised when he ended up a wolf."

"Sabine." Ethan looked at her. "You've seen the pack more than anyone else. Have you noticed anything about Shay? Anything not wolfy going on there?"

Sabine thought about her trips up the mountainside. The hours she'd spent watching the wolves near Haldis Cavern. She'd seen them and they'd seen her. At times she'd believed the pack knew her. Knew that she once belonged with them. But Sabine wasn't entirely convinced that belief was any more than wishful thinking. A cold comfort drawn from the past.

And Shay hadn't seemed any different from the other wolves. He was their alpha. They were his pack. All seemed right in their world.

"Not that I noticed, but I guess anything is possible," Sabine said.

"What happened here when the Rift closed . . . it was new. I don't think anyone can know the full ramifications."

"I suppose not," Tess sighed.

"Are you okay?" Ethan rested his hand on Sabine's shoulder.

She nodded, though her pulse still hummed in her veins, not quite frantic, but faster than she liked. Sabine let herself lean against Ethan, but turned her head toward Tess.

"Not that I mind," Sabine said, "but how is it that you're the one asking all these questions? Is that your new job? Head Inquisitor?"

Tess laughed, rubbing the back of her neck as though abashed. "I'm not quite sure what Anika was thinking, but when the Arrow asks you to step up, you say yes."

"Sounds important," Ethan said.

"I'll say." Tess nodded. "I hope you'll keep not minding me being in charge, Sabine, because I'm your new Guide."

THIRTEEN

SHILOH WASN'T much of a talker, Connor found, and it was driving him a little nuts. Not knowing what had befallen Adne left Connor at his wits' end. His only means of distracting himself was his usual fallback—easy banter. But with Shiloh it seemed that banter was neither usual nor easy.

"You're a fan of the classics, I take it?" Connor asked, attempting yet another foray into conversation.

"I'm sorry?" Shiloh kept a brisk pace as they walked through Rowan Estate's east wing.

"Warrior archetype," Connor answered. "Tall, dark, silent. You fit the bill. I can respect that."

Shiloh didn't answer.

"Good for you, not breaking character," Connor muttered.

When they stopped in front of a door, Connor swore under his breath in relief.

Shiloh gave a quick rap on the heavy wood. A robed woman, one of the Eydis healers, answered his knock.

"Is it all right for us to come in?" Shiloh asked.

Screw all right, Connor thought. If the woman objected, he was determined to blow right past her.

Even so, he was glad when she nodded and stepped aside to let him pass. Connor had been telling himself all morning that no matter what he saw when they brought him to Adne, he'd stay calm. He managed . . . sort of.

Connor didn't shout or cry, but he did run to the bedside and grasp Adne's hand before asking anyone if it was okay to do so. Her fingers were cool in his grip, but not frigid. He knelt beside the bed, trying to gather as much information as he could by just looking at her.

She was far too pale. That was clear. Adne's skin was always fair, but the blush of life that painted her cheeks was missing. She looked cold. Like time had frozen her in place.

It occurred to Connor how sick stories like Snow White and Sleeping Beauty were. There wasn't anything romantic or hopeful in this scene. Anyone who loved a person and found them in a state like this wouldn't feel heroic or courageous. Connor only encountered a near-overwhelming despair.

"What happened to her?" He managed to croak out the words.

"We're not certain," the healer answered. "The morning patrol found her outside the mansion, unconscious, and we haven't been able to wake her. But I can assure you that she's out of immediate danger."

That news brought Connor some comfort, but not much. Physically, Adne might be stable, but something else plagued her. Something that had driven her to Rowan Estate in the middle of the night. But what?

Adne's fingers twitched in Connor's grasp. She started to murmur and Connor thought she was waking, but her eyes remained closed.

"She's been restless like that on and off," the healer told Connor. "We can't make sense of her words."

Connor stood up and bent over Adne, listening as she spoke in a quiet, breathless tone.

"Ren . . . Ren . . . Don't let him take me. Please. Don't let him take me. Ren."

Connor dropped Adne's hand and took a few steps back.

The despair he'd been feeling gave way to dread.

"Do you understand what she means?" the healer asked.

Connor didn't want to answer.

It's nothing. Of course she'd be having nightmares about her brother. Bad dreams. Hallucinations after exposure. That's all it is.

Rational as his excuses were, Connor knew they were lies.

"Oh God, Adne." Sabine halted in the doorway, gazing at her friend. Tess and Ethan stood in the hall just behind Sabine.

Clearing his throat, Connor could only manage to mimic the healer. "She's out of immediate danger."

Sabine crossed the room and took up Connor's abandoned post, kneeling beside Adne and taking her hand. At Sabine's touch, Adne grew restless again, mumbling.

Frowning, Sabine leaned closer. Connor had to stop himself from grabbing Sabine and hauling her away.

After a moment, Sabine pulled back and looked over her shoulder at Connor. "Is she saying what I think she's saying?"

Connor ground his teeth, wishing he could deny it. Sweat broke out on his brow and his pulse became frenzied by panic. He felt utterly helpless and he couldn't bear it.

Tess came into the room and whispered quietly to the healer. The robed woman nodded and quickly left them, closing the door behind her.

"Tell me why you're so upset, Connor." Tess gave him a measured look.

With a rough laugh, Connor gestured to Adne. "I'd say it's obvious."

"That's not it," Tess replied.

"You'd better fess up," Ethan told Connor. "She's the boss of us now."

"What?" Connor frowned at him.

Sabine sat on the edge of the bed. "Tess is our Guide now."

"Since when?" Connor threw a startled glance at Tess.

"Since this morning," Tess answered. "So if you don't mind . . ."

Connor hesitated, looking quickly at Shiloh. The new Striker hadn't uttered a word since they'd arrived in Adne's sickroom. Not that he seemed ever likely to be a big talker.

"Shiloh is part of the team," Tess said, following Connor's gaze.

"One big happy family, are we?" Connor muttered. When Tess gave him a withering look, he held up his hands in surrender. Yet he couldn't bring himself to repeat Adne's words. "Sabine heard it too. She can tell you."

Tess lifted her eyebrows, turning to Sabine.

"It sounded like she thought she was talking to Ren." Sabine shrugged. "She's been saying his name."

A shadow passed through Sabine's eyes. "But there's something else."

"What's that?" Ethan asked, frowning at Sabine's worried expression.

"'Don't let him take me,'" Sabine answered. "She also says, 'Don't let him take me.'"

"Who?" Ethan shifted his weight, uneasy.

Sabine shook her head, looking to Connor.

"I don't know," Connor said. "I have no idea what she's talking about."

"Tell him about the tracks," Tess said to Sabine.

"What tracks?" Connor looked at Sabine sharply.

"Odd as it seems," Sabine told him, "it looks like a wolf dragged Adne from the middle of the garden to the back door of the mansion."

"A wolf?"

"There were wolf tracks in the snow alongside the drag marks," Ethan said.

Connor felt worse by the minute. "Are you trying to tell me that Adne was out in the garden in this weather, she passed out, and a wolf brought her back? Was it Shay? You mean Sarah Doran really saw him?"

"None of us know what really happened, Connor." Sabine managed a pretty wolf-like snarl. "But there were wolf tracks in the snow."

"But they weren't Ren's tracks." Ethan crossed his arms defensively when they all fixed him with incredulous stares. "I'm just putting it out there. There were wolf tracks and now Adne's talking about her brother."

"Renier Laroche is dead." Sabine's voice was brittle. "Emile killed him. We saw it happen."

Tess nodded and said gently, "I'm sure that if a wolf somehow came to Adne's aid, then in whatever state of confusion she experienced, it might have dredged up memories of her brother."

Though Connor didn't find much reassurance in the image of a wolf clamping its jaws around Adne and pulling her through the snow, it was at least helpful that Tess's explanation about why Adne would be saying Ren's name made sense.

"Connor." Sabine looked at Adne, who'd gone still again. "I know you've been worried about her. Is there anything else we should know?"

Connor tensed, reluctant to speak about Adne without her knowledge. It felt like a betrayal.

"If you want us to help her, we need to know what's really going on," Sabine said. "If there *is* something else going on."

Dropping into a chair as the weight of his fears took over, Connor said, "She's been having nightmares. Nightmares and headaches."

"Nightmares about what?" Tess asked.

Connor shook his head. "She doesn't like to talk about them. I've always assumed they were about Ren and Monroe. About their deaths. But now I'm not so sure."

"I'm surprised she won't tell you about them," Sabine said. "That's not like her."

"I know." Connor rested his head in his hands. Sabine had said what he'd been afraid to: Adne had never held anything back from him. Not ever. But now he felt like he barely glimpsed what she was thinking and feeling.

"Maybe she feels guilty."

They all looked at Shiloh in surprise.

"I don't mean to intrude," he said, uncomfortable with their sudden focus on him.

"You aren't," Tess told him. "Please go on."

Shiloh threw an apologetic glance at Connor. "I don't know Ariadne, but from what you've said, she sounds very loyal. Maybe her nightmares make her feel disloyal and she's afraid to tell you that."

"How would dreams make her feel disloyal?" Ethan asked.

"The other thing she's been saying, 'Don't let him take me,'" Shiloh replied. "That sounds to me like she can't stop herself from being taken. She needs someone else to intervene. And, no offense, but she was calling out for her brother. Not for you."

An uncomfortable silence settled over the room.

Knowing the others were waiting for him to speak, Connor finally sighed. "Well, it's a theory."

"If I may . . . ," Shiloh began, looking to Connor for permission.

"Have at it, man," Connor told him. How much worse could this theory get?

Shiloh nodded his thanks and turned to Sabine. "She might be more willing to talk to someone else. A girlfriend?"

"Girl talk?" Sabine laughed. "You don't know me either, friend."

Shiloh ducked his head, blushing.

Seriously? Connor was beginning to have doubts about this guy. *Was he going to ask a monster's permission before chopping its head off?*

"You're not giving yourself enough credit, Sabine." Ethan grinned at her. "You can do girl talk, I'm sure."

"I suppose." Sabine nodded.

"Good," Tess said. "When Adne recovers, I'll want her supervised, but not too obviously. Sabine, why don't you train her to lead tours—but draw the training time out so you can chaperone her while we get to the bottom of this."

"She won't like being told what to do," Sabine said. "Or having me look over her shoulder all the time."

"I think she'll take it in stride." Tess glanced at Adne. "She'll expect consequences for weaving without permission. The assignment will be her probation."

"My tours are punishment now?" Sabine raised an eyebrow. "Thanks for the vote of confidence."

Ethan had covered his mouth, pretending to cough, but it was clear he was laughing pretty hard.

"Is this why you never come to see me work?" Sabine asked, her smile curving wickedly. "I guess we'll be talking about punishments too."

Tess cleared her throat. "All right then. I really should get the healer back in here."

"What should I do?" Connor was almost afraid to ask. His estrangement from Adne was out in the open now, and Connor felt both dejected and vulnerable.

"The best thing for you is to stay busy," Tess answered. "And I'll be taking care of that." She looked from him to Ethan. "In fact, I have work for both of you."

"Does it involve overtime?" Ethan asked, grinning at Sabine. "Because I think my domestic bliss might be in jeopardy."

"It probably will, given the nature of this business," Tess said. "Anika's decided it's time for us to go back into the field."

"To do what?" Ethan frowned. "I thought the war was over."

"It is," Tess said, sounding a bit wary. "But after the theft in the library, the Arrow has been under a lot of pressure to make sure our future is secure."

"How does one secure a future?" Sabine smirked. "That sounds awfully meta to me."

"I agree." Tess nodded. "And I don't think Anika is completely happy with this new strategy, but like I said, she's been under a lot of pressure."

"Holt and company?" Connor asked.

"Yes, Holt, but unfortunately there's a growing emphasis on *company*," Tess said. "While Anika is busy trying to hold everything together, Holt has all the time he wants to bring people to his way of thinking. Anika is conceding on this issue because she hopes it will keep him from interfering in other areas of the Academy."

"So what does Holt want us to do?" Connor stood up, straightening his duster.

"He wants us to round up the Keepers."

FOURTEEN

ADNE WAS AWAKE for a long time before she opened her eyes. She stayed hidden behind the dark veil of her eyelids, afraid to face the world.

What am I going to tell them?

There were no good answers to the questions she would have to face. No explanations to justify her actions.

And just as she'd known they would be, a little crowd of worried Searchers huddled around Adne's bed when she finally opened her eyes.

"There's my girl." Connor bent and kissed Adne's cheek. "How are you feeling?"

"Okay." Adne tried to smile at him, but her frantic pulse was distracting her. *He'll want to know what happened. They all will. I don't even know what really happened.* "How long have I been out?"

"A few hours," Connor answered. "We think . . . no one is sure when exactly you lost consciousness . . ."

He watched Adne's face, waiting for her to fill in the empty space, but Adne just nodded, unwilling to answer the questions Connor didn't ask.

Her friends were polite, of course, expressing their concerns over Adne's well-being before diving into the interrogation she knew was coming. Propped up in bed, Adne tried to answer each question truthfully, but vaguely, and soon she could see frustration registering on her friends' faces.

I don't have a choice. They would never understand.

Adne snuck a glance at her hand. Her skin was smooth, unblemished.

I remember thorns and blood and fire.

Closing her eyes, she too easily recalled the ripping of her skin, the burning of her flesh—but it had all been in her head. How could it have seemed so real?

Agony wasn't all Adne remembered. She could still hear heavy footfalls in the snow. A voice with an entrancing low, rich timbre.

It wasn't real. None of it was real.

Except the wolf.

When Adne had made it clear she'd said all she was going to about that strange night—which wasn't much at all—Sabine had told her about finding wolf tracks beside the drag marks where her body had been hauled through the snow. But when Sabine had asked if Adne remembered a wolf in the garden, Adne had kept silent.

Days had passed, and life had returned to its usual rhythms, and Adne held the truth back.

I heard them howling.

"Adne?" Sabine's voice pulled Adne from her thoughts. "Did you want to add anything?"

Adne wasn't surprised to find the entire tour group staring at her, waiting for her answer. Sabine probably was equally unsurprised that Adne hadn't been paying attention to the narrative as the tour progressed through Rowan Estate.

"No, thank you," Adne answered, making sure to smile at the tourists.

It had to irk Sabine that she'd been assigned the worst apprentice ever. Adne couldn't believe otherwise. But Sabine never showed irritation at Adne's shiny new absentmindedness, and Adne presumed that Sabine's kindness was a sign of concern.

Adne's own lack of annoyance upon being reprimanded for her nighttime excursion to Rowan Estate and subsequent assignment to assist Sabine with the tours derived from her own fears. Though Adne sensed her punishment was intended to be of the "be careful what you wish for" variety, Adne didn't mind the days confined to Rowan Estate and kept under Sabine's guard. The night in the garden had frightened Adne enough that she welcomed Sabine's vigilance . . . at least so far.

And at least enough that she felt guilty about being such a poor tour guide, more of a burden to Sabine than anything resembling helpful. Adne had a hard time keeping on task, whether it was during the actual tours or studying the history and anecdotes necessary to keep visitors entertained. Most days Adne could barely recall things about Rowan Estate that she should have known offhand. There didn't seem to be room in her mind for any of it.

Since the incident (that was what Tess called it when doling out Adne's punishment), there were only two things that Adne could concentrate on for sustained periods of time: the hazy memories of what transpired in the garden and the contents of the papers she'd found just before something or someone had beckoned her into the winter night.

Adne studied those papers when she was supposed to be memorizing the tour scripts. While other facts and stories slipped in and out of her mind, unable to find a resting place, Adne had no trouble committing what she'd discovered in those old pages to memory.

Perhaps the exception could be accounted for because of the unsettling information scrawled across the yellowed paper. Or maybe it was because Adne was certain that information had profound implications, but she wasn't sure what those implications were.

I should tell someone.

That thought crossed Adne's mind at least twice an hour, but it was always chased away by that low voice.

This is a secret. It's our secret.

Adne repeatedly justified her silence about the pages by assuring herself that anything they might have once revealed was made obsolete by the Rift's closing.

It didn't matter that all Keepers were not created equal.

It didn't matter that the Harbinger's bond to this world had been manifested physically as well as magically.

It didn't matter that the Searchers' salvation, the long-awaited Scion, shared the same blood as the bringer of their doom.

All of that was past. What Adne knew would someday feature in the footnotes of a history book or as obscure trivia about the Witches' War.

As she rationalized the keeping of these secrets, one crack in her resolve remained.

Logan, too, carried the blood of the Harbinger. And Logan had hired thieves to ransack Rowan Estate's library.

Logan was hunting for something. And Adne couldn't help but wonder if she'd found it. Even if she had, she didn't know why Logan would risk exposing himself to the Searchers. He must believe there was something to gain by tapping into the origins of the Keepers.

But what?

The tour group began to move along the hall, and Adne tried to listen with interest as Sabine described the estate's art collection. This part of the tour was utter fabrication given that Bosque's paintings of captured Searchers in torment had been disposed of and replaced by greatest hits of the Dutch masters and landscapes by William Sonntag. But Adne only managed to focus for two paintings before something turned her head toward the far end of the hall.

The sound was so quiet, Adne considered for a moment that she'd simply imagined it. Only for the sake of curiosity, Adne took a couple of steps in the direction from which the noise that might not have been a noise came. She heard it again.

Muffled, but plaintive, with a keen edge that could not be silenced.

Adne glanced at Sabine, who was directing the herd of tourists into the next room. Determining that she could slip away for a few minutes without causing alarm, Adne stayed toward the back of the group, and when the last visitor had entered the conservatory, Adne quickly walked in the opposite direction.

Keeping her footsteps light, Adne followed the strange sound. It pulled her down the hall as if she held a string that someone on the other end was slowly winding up. The sound led her around a corner into a hallway whose rooms were hidden behind closed doors.

Still following the noise, Adne approached one of the doors and pressed her ear up against it.

A shaking breath. A choked-off sob.

Someone was inside. And they were crying.

Adne didn't knock. Instead, she turned the doorknob and slowly pushed the door open.

The weeping stopped suddenly.

"Who's there?" a woman's tremulous voice called out.

Adne peeked her head into the room. Her throat closed up when she recognized the questioner.

Sarah Doran's eyes were bloodshot, her face chalk white. She was kneeling on the floor beside an open steamer trunk, and her arms were wrapped around what appeared to be a baby's blanket.

"Oh, Ariadne." Sarah squinted at Adne, and some of the hostility left her voice. "I don't mean to be rude, but is there a reason you're here?"

Letting herself into the room, Adne approached Sarah cautiously. "I'm helping with the tours."

"The tours." Sarah's face scrunched up. "How quickly they've forgotten this was someone's home."

Adne began to frown, but then she noticed the room's features. Unlike the opulence of Rowan Estate's other rooms, this bedroom was simply appointed. And it looked as though someone was still living in it. A hooded sweatshirt was casually thrown over the chair beside a desk that was piled with books. The closet door was open and Adne saw boys' clothes hanging inside.

"This was Shay's room." Adne spoke aloud without intending to and instantly regretted her words.

"I take it you never visited him here." Sarah's reply had a cold edge to it.

Adne bristled, feeling she hadn't earned a reproach from Shay's mother. Of course she hadn't visited Shay at Rowan Estate; she was a Searcher, not one of his classmates from Vail.

"No," Adne answered slowly, reminding herself that Sarah wasn't trying to give offense, she was grieving her son. "I never came to Rowan Estate while Shay lived here. I think only Calla did."

"The wolf girl."

Sarah's words were so rough with anger that Adne could only nod.

"She had no right . . ." Sarah's voice trailed off as her eyes closed. Tears ran unchecked down her cheeks.

Edging closer to Sarah, Adne whispered, "Had no right?"

"To take him." Sarah broke down into a fresh round of sobs.

Adne wanted to defend Calla but wondered if that might make things worse. She didn't know what to do. Had Sarah and Tristan requested that Shay's room be left intact so they might have a chance to get to know their son through the artifacts of his life at Rowan Estate?

"I don't understand," Sarah continued raggedly. "No one does. I've spent hours with the Scribes, with Anika. No one can explain to me why my son is gone."

"He's not exactly gone." No matter the circumstance, Adne didn't want to just leave the poor woman. She had to offer Sarah some sort of hope. "He's with the pack. And Calla loves him. I think they'll be happy together."

Apparently that was the wrong thing to say.

Sarah drew a hissing breath and glared at Adne. "I am his mother. Do you think some girl he'd known a few months could ever care for him as much as I do?"

"I just meant . . ."

"He was three years old." Sarah's voice was thick. "And I would have been able to accept those lost years if he were here now. We could have been a family again, but we had only moments before—"

Unable to continue, Sarah bowed her head. She didn't make a sound, but her shoulders shook violently and somehow her silent weeping was much more terrible.

Sarah's right. It shouldn't have happened. It goes against everything we know about Guardians. Shay's mother had been human, a Searcher. Yet somehow Shay had willed himself to remain a wolf even after he'd closed the Rift, thereby returning Guardians to their natural state. According to those rules, Shay *should* have remained human. He hadn't.

Adne thought of what she'd discovered about the Scion's lineage. To have the power of the Nether coursing through his veins must have affected his ability to control the outcome of his transformation, even if subconsciously.

A murmur caught Adne's attention. At first she thought it was simply a return of audible evidence of Sarah's weeping, but then she realized Sarah was speaking.

"I'm sorry?" Adne took a step forward, daring to rest her hand on Sarah's shoulder. She drew a quick breath of relief when Sarah looked up at her with pleading, not hateful, eyes.

Sarah grasped Adne's fingers, crushing them in a desperate grip.

"No one will listen to me. Not Anika. Not even Tristan. No one understands how wrong this is. I can't bear it."

Adne returned Sarah's grip, hoping to provide some reassurance that someone was listening to her . . . even if grief had driven Sarah to ranting.

"I know how hard it is to lose family," Adne said quietly. "I lost everyone. The war took my mother first. Then my father. And finally my brother."

The image of Ren's wolf lurking in the shadows of Rowan Estate flashed through Adne's mind, but she quickly pushed it away. Her mind had proven untrustworthy of late, but a comforting idea formed in Adne's thoughts. Maybe her nightmares and visions weren't the corruption of insanity but merely a side effect of her grief.

"Forgive me, dear," Sarah said. "I mean no harm in this. Of course I'm sorry for your losses, but don't you see that it's not the same?"

Adne withdrew her hand from Sarah's, which took some effort.

"Don't be angry." Sarah stood up and faced Adne. There was a wild resolve in her eyes that Adne found unsettling. "I don't mean that my grief is more than yours, only that your family was killed in the war. My Seamus isn't dead. He was taken. And it was wrong. I know he wants to come back to us . . . I saw him."

Her tone became accusing. "I saw him with you."

"With me?" Adne's mind filled with the memory of wolves' howls. "Shay was the wolf who saved me?"

Sarah's eyes widened and Adne held her breath, regretting the slip.

"You remember?" Sarah asked. "You remember that Shay came to you?"

Adne shook her head. "I don't remember Shay—I just remember hearing wolves."

I thought I remembered Ren.

"Surely you understand why I have to help Shay." Twisting the blanket in her hands, Sarah continued, "All that Tristan and I sacrificed for the cause, and this is our reward? I won't abide it."

Adne inched back toward the door as the implications of Sarah's words sank in. If Adne had feared for her own sanity, in this moment she was much more worried about the fragility of Sarah's mind.

"Maybe I should take you back to the Academy," Adne offered.

Sarah's lip curled in disgust. "To my so-called friends? The ones who offer embraces and condolences but won't help me?"

"Help you do what?" Adne didn't want to ask but felt she had to. Whatever mad road Sarah was determined to walk down, Adne thought it best that someone knew about it.

"Get my son back."

That's impossible.

Adne didn't say it. It wouldn't help anything, and from the way Sarah had been going on, Adne figured other Searchers had already tried to tell Sarah the same. All Adne could do was find someone who was close to Sarah and hope they could help her get over this delusion.

"Who are you?" Sarah asked sharply. She was looking past Adne into the hall.

Adne turned to see a tall, slender girl with pointed features and silken hair the shade of mink.

"I'm sorry, I think I'm lost. I was with the tour," the girl answered.

Adne frowned, knowing the tour should have reached the opposite end of the mansion by now. This girl was clearly one of those visitors who thought it clever to slip away from the group and snap pictures of the off-limits sections of the estate.

Glancing at Sarah, Adne said, "I should take her back. Will you be okay?"

"Sarah!" A man's voice sounded farther down the hall. "Sarah!"

Adne watched Sarah stiffen. Her mouth drew into a thin line of resolve as a man with golden brown hair pushed past the wayward tourist and into the bedroom. Tristan threw an apologetic glance at Adne, and took Sarah by the shoulders.

"I thought we agreed that you wouldn't come here alone," Tristan said in a low voice. "It isn't good for you. Anika and I both think—"

Sarah pushed Tristan's hands away. "I'm tired of you and Anika telling me what to do, Tristan."

"He's my son too," Tristan told her.

"Then act like you care," Sarah shot back. "Believe what I've told you instead of looking at me like I'm insane. Help me instead of standing in my way."

Adne winced at Sarah's lashing words and then the lines of grief that tightened around Tristan's eyes.

Tristan turned to Adne. "Could you please excuse us?"

Adne nodded, relieved to get out of the room and away from that horrible scene. She grabbed the girl from the tour group by the elbow and towed her down the hall.

"What was wrong with that woman?" the girl asked.

Ignoring her question, Adne said, "Let's just get you back to the tour, okay?"

"I was just curious." The girl pouted. "All that history in the tour was boring. I prefer the drama of the present. It seemed like a good story was developing back there."

"That's not a story," Adne replied. "That was a private conversation that you had no business overhearing."

"You don't have to get in a snit about it," the girl said.

Adne wondered if she had the authority to kick this girl off the tour and send her on her way to wherever she'd come from. But that probably wouldn't go over very well with Sabine. So Adne settled for reprimanding the vagrant.

"You shouldn't wander away from the group," Adne told the girl. "It's not safe."

"So the stories about this place are true?" The girl gave a nervous laugh. "Ghosts in the closets and monsters under the stairs?"

"Something like that," Adne muttered. She heard Sabine's voice in one of the rooms ahead and quickened her pace.

Adne had already seen a ghost and she didn't want to think about it. As for the monsters, they were supposed to be gone, but Adne was beginning to fear they'd only been slumbering.

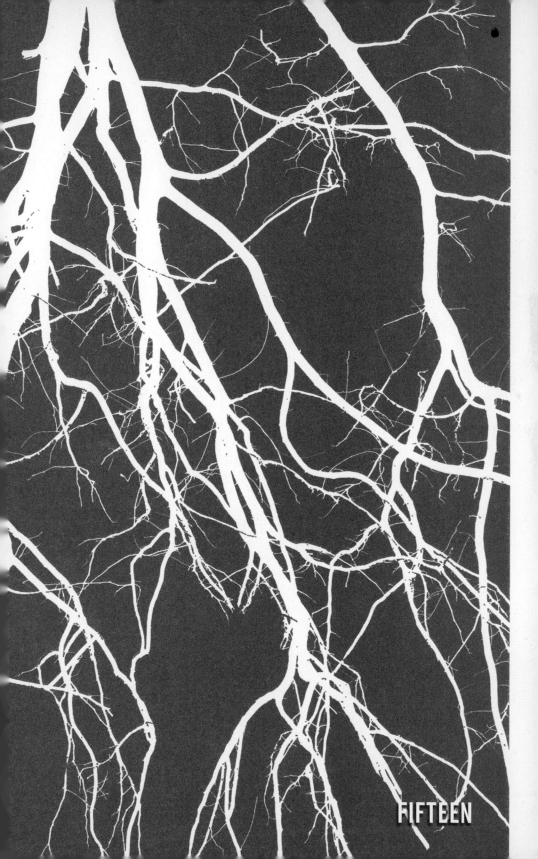

FIFTEEN

LOGAN KNEW HE must have felt elation at some point in the not too distant past, but it seemed like that kind of joy had eluded him for years. The giddiness that suffused his being now was intoxicating. After three days in Colorado, Chase and Audrey had returned with news. Good news. At last.

Chase popped the cork and Audrey held out her glass. Champagne foamed up and spilled over the rim.

"Be careful!" Audrey shook droplets from her fingers.

"One does not take care when one celebrates with abandon," Chase replied, filling his glass, then Logan's.

"That's easy for you to say," Audrey replied. "You're not wearing silk."

"I had my doubts about this plan of yours," Logan told them, raising his glass in a toast. "But I have to admit, you were brilliant."

Logan didn't add that he'd spent the seventy-two hours of the twins' absence second-guessing the wisdom of their trip to Rowan Estate. He hadn't slept for the past two nights, his mind too full of all the ways that the excursion into hostile territory could go horribly wrong. In all of Logan's imagined worst-case scenarios he ended up dead with self-righteous Searchers gloating over his corpse.

Audrey flashed her perfectly white teeth at him. "Of course I was." She rewarded herself with a sip of champagne.

"You mean *we*," Chase added. "We were brilliant."

After sticking her tongue out at her brother, Audrey said, "I don't mean *we*. I'm the one who found her."

"And I'm the one who came up with the plan in the first place," Chase replied.

"Let's just all agree that we make a good team," Logan cut in, hoping to avoid a round of bickering between brother and sister.

"Go team." Chase lifted his glass. "Not to compromise our ability to savor this moment, but do we have a plan for what happens next?"

"I was already brilliant," Audrey said. "My work is done."

"Good to know we can count on you to see the whole thing through, Audrey." Logan smirked. "But to answer Chase's question, I have an idea. I wouldn't call it a plan . . . yet. But as far as ideas go, it's not a bad one."

"Care to fill us in?" Chase settled back into the leather club chair, throwing one leg over its arm.

"What Audrey has done is identify the weak link in the Searchers' armor," Logan answered. "We have to exploit it."

"Agreed." Chase sipped his champagne. "And how can we do that?"

"Sarah Doran feels betrayed." Logan leaned forward, setting his glass down. "She needs to believe someone out there is on her side."

Audrey laughed. "Do you really think she'll take up with three Keeper orphans? If I'm remembering correctly, the man . . . or creature . . . or whatever Bosque is that you're trying to bring back kidnapped her child and imprisoned her in a painting for fifteen years."

"It's not as if we're going to bring her in on our plan." Logan shot an irritated glance at Audrey. "All we have to do is convince her that we're the key to bringing her son back."

"Is that something we can do?" Chase asked. "Bringing Shay back."

"I have no idea," Logan said. "I'm guessing not, but again—that's not something Sarah has to know."

"Exploiting that woman's grief isn't a bad strategy," Audrey added, nodding. "From the way she was acting at the estate, I'd guess that suggesting the possibility of getting her son back will be too tempting to resist. Even if some part of her doesn't believe us, I think she's well past the point of reason. Dangle the right carrot and she'll bring you the box."

"Let's hope so." Chase finished off his glass and poured another. "Are you up for another tour, Audrey?"

"Audrey isn't going back to Rowan Estate," Logan said. "None of us are."

Logan stood up and went to the fireplace. Taking the small pouch of herbs out of his pocket, he tossed it into the flames. The burning herbs produced a cloying sweetness that turned Logan's stomach, but he swallowed the bile that tried to climb up his throat.

His ploy was a tad overdramatic, but Audrey and Chase were still impressed by such things and Logan needed to keep them enthralled and obedient.

For a minute, Logan was afraid the spell hadn't worked, but then Audrey shrieked. Her glass shattered on the floor.

"Damn it, Logan." Chase had jumped up on the chair as if a mouse had entered the room instead of the wolf that sat silently in the corner, watching them. "Can you give us some warning before you pull a stunt like that?"

"He can't hurt you," Logan replied coolly, pretending that the very sight of Ren—even in spirit form—didn't make his bones ache with fear.

"True," Ren said after he'd shifted into his human visage. "But tragic."

"I think that answer is justification enough for me to remain afraid of him," Chase muttered.

Logan ignored his friend and offered the wolf a flat smile. "I have a task for you."

"Wonderful." Ren folded his arms across his chest. "I live to serve. Well, maybe 'live' isn't the best choice of word."

"Do you know who Sarah Doran is?" Logan asked.

Ren flinched at the name, but he nodded.

"And can you find her?" Logan continued. "Speak with her?"

"Yes." His answer carried a growl with it. "Why?"

"I'd like to set up a meeting with Shay's dear mother," Logan told him. "It seems we may have a common cause."

"I find that very unlikely." Ren reached out as if to touch the petals of an orchid that decorated a side table. He watched his own fingers pass through the plant.

"I guess restless spirits lack imagination," Logan said. "Tell her that I'd like to talk to her about Shay."

"Is that all?" Ren wasn't looking at Logan, but his tense bearing informed Logan that the wolf was desperate to find a way out of this scenario.

Logan smiled, ready to lay down his winning hand. "Ask her what she'd do to see her son again. The boy, of course, not the wolf."

Ren shot a hateful glare at Logan. "What the hell are you talking about?"

"Bringing Shay back," Logan replied. "I thought that much was obvious."

"You can't do that," Ren snapped. "It's impossible."

"Are you sure about that?" Logan continued to smile. "Has becoming a spirit gifted you with omniscience?"

Ren didn't answer, but his lips drew back, revealing sharp canines.

"You won't be lying to her, Renier. It's just a matter of semantics," Logan said with a smile. "Emphasize that it's only a slim possibility if you prefer. Tell her how dangerous and risky magic this powerful will be. Say that it might not work at all. As long as you deliver the message, I'll be happy."

After glaring at Logan for a long moment, Ren finally bowed his head. He turned away, but Logan called him back.

"There's one more thing."

"What?" Ren kept his back to Logan.

"The Harbinger. I think it's time I spoke with him directly," Logan said. "You're a fine messenger, but I'm tired of the riddles."

Ren pivoted to face Logan, his fists clenching. "Did you really expect I'd make this easy for you?"

"That's what I thought." Logan walked in a slow circle around the Guardian. "You're giving me the bare minimum, aren't you? Anything you can withhold, you do."

"What do you think?" The malice in Ren's gaze was answer enough.

"I think it's time to cut out the middle man," Logan replied. "I can deal with Bosque directly. You're better suited to other work, I believe."

"If you can," Ren shot back. "You're an infant when it comes to magic."

"Every child learns to walk on his own eventually," Logan said. "I do appreciate your concern, though, Renier."

Ren shifted to his wolf form, snarling at Logan.

"Yes, yes." Logan waved him off. "Your complaint is noted. Now run along and find Sarah."

Ren gave a harsh bark of protest, but then he turned and loped away.

Logan let his body relax. Despite Renier's uncooperative attitude, he'd answered Logan's questions exactly as the Keeper had hoped. That meant Logan's work wasn't done for the night.

"My goodness, Logan." Audrey gave a breathy laugh. "I didn't know you had it in you."

"Good show. Very good." Chase nodded, teetering in the chair a bit, and Logan noticed that Chase had managed to finish off the first bottle of champagne and start in on another one within the short duration of Ren's visit.

Guardians must truly frighten him. Even dead ones.

Logan tucked away that bit of information. He'd never know when he might need to substitute intimidation for charm.

"We all did good work today." Logan gestured to the second champagne bottle. "Keep celebrating. I'll catch up when I get back."

Audrey paled slightly. "You weren't serious, were you? About summoning Bosque Mar? I thought you were just winding up the wolf."

"I was serious." Logan maintained his easy manner, though the prospect of facing the Harbinger was hardly appealing. But it had to be done.

"I'll come with you." Chase jumped up, wobbled, and then fell back into the chair. "Be your wingman."

"I . . . I suppose I should come too?" Audrey said, though she made no move to get up off the chaise longue.

"I don't think speaking with Bosque requires a wingman, Chase," Logan said. He didn't need to make a poor impression by bringing a half-in-the-bag Keeper and his partly terrified, mostly annoying sister along. "If things go well, we'll move on to introductions. The first time, though, I'm going to say requires a solo act."

"You sure?" Chase asked, but he was already reaching for the champagne bottle.

Audrey just looked relieved.

"Back in a bit." Logan went through the French doors onto the veranda and descended the steps to the path that would take him to the beach.

For a midwinter night, the shore was strangely windless. Waves languidly reached for the shore only to draw slowly back again. Even without the wind, cold air bit into Logan's skin, and his breath crystallized in front of his face.

The notion of summoning Bosque had been playing out in Logan's mind for some time. He couldn't believe that contact between Conatus and the Harbinger had exclusively been through an intercessor. The more Logan learned about the origins of the Keepers, the more convinced he became of that. If Eira's relationship with Bosque had been only about opening the Rift so that her followers could access the Nether's magic, Logan might have been persuaded otherwise. But knowing that Eira and Bosque were Logan's own great-grandparents made it seem impossible that there had been any real distance between them.

Logan took his shoes and socks off and walked to the edge of the water. The touch of the waves on his bare skin was like cold fire, but that was part of Logan's plan. Spellwork relied so much on intention. Logan knew he couldn't hesitate, couldn't doubt his ability to summon Bosque. Even Logan's fear had a purpose in this magic. While he couldn't succumb to it, Logan could channel his dread into the spell—making it part of his intent; acknowledging and moving beyond that fear signified Logan's determination and reflected the strength of his will.

At least he hoped so.

Drawing a knife from his coat pocket, Logan used the blade to reopen the wound on his palm. He watched crimson droplets fall into the sea foam at his feet.

Logan closed his eyes, willing Bosque to appear. He supposed some incantation or another existed, but he'd decided against hunting for one in the books he'd retrieved from Rowan Estate. Logan had learned how to invoke dark spirits that way, and all he'd earned himself was a surly Guardian spirit guide.

No. This time it's about pure intent. My will and my will alone.

"I must confess, Logan." The low voice was so close that Logan lurched sideways. "I didn't believe you had it in you."

Bosque stood, or rather hovered, a foot away from Logan. He appeared to be walking on the water, but Logan knew that while Bosque was here, he was also not here—whether to call him an apparition or a projection, Logan wasn't sure.

He also didn't know how to respond to Bosque's comment.

No hesitation.

"I thought it best if I spoke with you." Logan forced himself to speak with confidence, though he felt little. "I have no doubt you already know why I've summoned you here."

With a shrug, Bosque said, "You regret the loss of your power."

"I do . . . ," Logan replied. "But it's more than that."

"How so?" Bosque's casual tone was more chilling than the waves that numbed Logan's bare feet.

Logan drew himself upright, looking directly into Bosque's eyes. "We are kin."

A smile graced Bosque's lips. "Ah. You've delved into your past."

"I have." Logan nodded. "And I'm taking steps to make amends for my great folly."

"I'm aware of that," Bosque said. "You've made good use of the wolf. Another unexpected success on your part."

Logan bowed his head. "I know I've been a great disappointment to you in the past."

"More than a disappointment, Logan." At Bosque's sudden anger the water beneath his feet became turbulent. "You violated the blood oath, the sacred vow taken by your great-grandmother that gave me passage into this world. Your legacy is sullied."

Logan was silent for several minutes.

He had to be brave or all of this meant nothing.

"And yet you're here," Logan said, raising his eyes to meet Bosque's.

Bosque gazed at Logan and then began to laugh. "You do have some of her mettle after all."

Logan could only assume Bosque meant Eira. "I'm glad to hear it."

"And you've navigated the obstacles I put in your way with competence," Bosque added.

"That you put in my way . . ." Logan frowned. "I see. I take it the wolf was a test?"

"Renier proved a serviceable messenger, but I knew he'd resist the task, presenting you with an obstacle." Bosque smiled. "I admire persistence, and I needed to know if you were serious . . . or just playing at power, as the boy I knew would have."

Logan cringed at the reproach. He wondered if Bosque would ever regard him as worthy of forgiveness. "I was arrogant and foolish, but I've changed."

"It's not that easy, Logan," Bosque said. "You betrayed me. I haven't forgotten. I'm not inclined to ally myself with one so treacherous."

Logan dropped to his knees. Icy water soaked through his jeans, making him so cold, he didn't know how long he could bear it. "I beg your forgiveness. I didn't understand who you truly are. What I did . . . it was the worst mistake I've ever made."

"Words," Bosque said. "Words are not enough."

"Tell me what to do." Logan bowed his head, hoping to appear obsequious but not wretched. "Whatever you require to prove my loyalty, it's done."

"Make an offering," Bosque told him. "If I deem it worthy, you will once again be in my favor."

"An offering?" Logan twitched, feeling uncertain. Bosque wouldn't tell him what to offer, that was obvious, but Logan didn't know how he was meant to determine what would be worthy.

Glancing up and meeting disapproval in Bosque's gaze, Logan quickly said, "I will make an offering worthy of you."

"We'll see." Bosque reached out as if to touch Logan's face.

Though Logan never felt the contact of Bosque's hand on his skin, a sudden warmth surged through his body, driving away the terrible cold of the winter sea.

Then Bosque was gone and Logan was standing beside his shoes. His feet and legs were completely dry, as if he'd been watching the waves at a distance and had never touched the water.

Logan picked up his shoes and turned back toward the house. He decided he would make coffee so that Chase would sober up.

They had work to do.

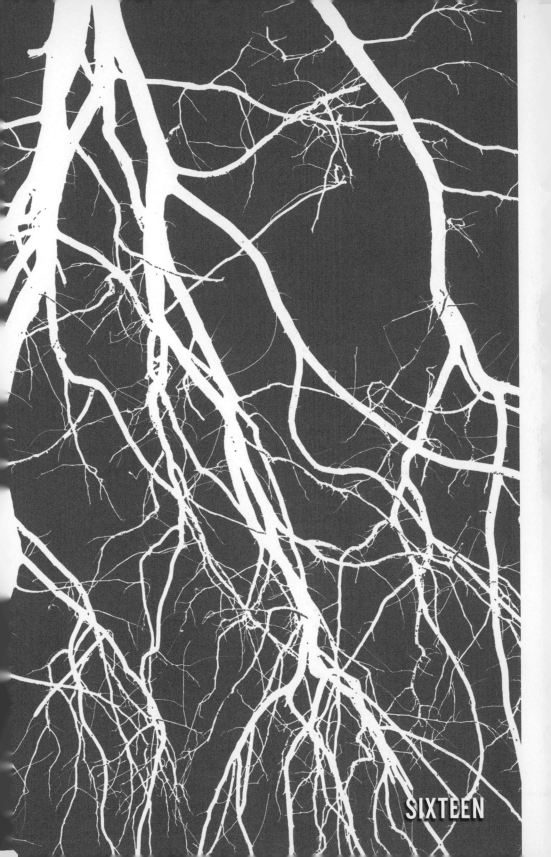

SIXTEEN

ADNE DIDN'T WANT to resent the new Weaver, but she couldn't help it. Mikaela had just begun to spin and twist when Shiloh sprang forward, tackling the girl.

Mikaela yelped as she hit the floor. Her silver skeins rolled across the room, well out of reach.

"Hold!" Tess was perched on the back of a chair, her feet resting in its seat. "Adne. Comments?"

Put me back on active duty, Adne thought, but said to Mikaela, "The task of the Weaver requires awareness and sensibility on multiple fronts. You're focused on creating the door, but you can't be oblivious to where you are and what's happening around you."

"Ethan? Connor?" Tess asked. The other two Strikers were watching with Adne from the side of the room. "Anything to add?"

"To be fair," Connor said as he watched Shiloh help Mikaela up, "in the field she'd have Strikers protecting her, not attacking her."

"That's true. But the point of this session is that we don't know what will happen in the field," Tess corrected him. "Strikers always try to protect the Weavers, but Weavers must be able to defend themselves should the Strikers fall."

Mikaela nodded, though she looked shaken as she went to collect her skeins.

Amateur, Adne thought, then chided herself for indulging such pettiness.

"Again." Tess nodded to Shiloh.

Shiloh ducked behind one of several tall obstacles that had been placed around the room for this exercise. The lights were dimmed as well, allowing the Striker to move with stealth as Mikaela began to weave.

This time, Shiloh waited until Mikaela's portal was nearly complete. He didn't tackle the Weaver, but crept up behind. When he grabbed Mikaela, she screamed.

"Oh, please," Adne muttered.

"Hey!" Connor shot her a questioning look, surprised by Adne's harsh tone. "Go easy."

Defensive, Adne whispered, "I don't think she's even trying."

"Not everyone can be a *wunderkind* like you." Connor tried to smile, but Adne could see that he was disappointed by her lack of compassion for the younger Weaver.

Mikaela faced Tess, looking crestfallen. "I'm sorry."

"No apologies," Tess replied. "That's why we're training. Don't be too hard on yourself, Mikaela. It's like this for everyone."

Adne didn't remember it being like this for her, but maybe she just wasn't willing to admit that she'd been a novice once. She also couldn't pin down why she felt such a visceral dislike for Mikaela. Adne could recognize the skill with which Mikaela wove portals despite her current inability to anticipate attacks. Though a slip of a girl, Mikaela moved with strength and purpose. Never hesitating, never losing the rhythm of her dance.

Mikaela began to weave again while Shiloh disappeared into the room's shadows. Adne could see the source of the problem, and it was directly related to the grace of Mikaela's weaving. Mikaela utterly closed herself off to the world as she pulled threads to create a door. Adne understood the allure of that technique. Opening a door to another part of the world was giving oneself over to the pulse of the earth itself. A Weaver touched something so much greater than the experience of an individual. Amid the dance, the Weaver knew infinite paths and innumerable places. All that existed was possibility. Adne knew nothing more beautiful. But if Mikaela wanted to sense an impending attack, she would have to stop giving in to that glorious abandon.

It was obvious Mikaela hadn't put up any such barriers when Shiloh dropped from the rafters onto the Weaver's shoulders.

"Take a breather, Mikaela," Tess said. She turned to Adne. "Do you and Connor want to demonstrate? Maybe that would be helpful."

"I'm game." Connor glanced at Adne, lifting his eyebrows.

"Sure." Adne drew her skeins, wondering if there was any chance that, should she perform well enough, Tess would just reinstate her as the Haldis Weaver.

"Ethan," Tess said to the other Striker, "since Adne's an old hand at this, why don't you join in as well."

When Adne looked at Tess with a frown, the Guide smiled at her. "You want a challenge, don't you?"

Adne laughed, and felt a bit smug when she noticed Mikaela's wide eyes upon her.

Ethan and Connor huddled up to plot Adne's demise. She waited with her hands on her hips.

"Any time now," Tess called out to the Strikers.

Connor gave Tess a thumbs-up, and he and Ethan dashed to their hiding places.

Adne was nearly ecstatic with anticipation. She hadn't realized how hobbled she felt, having been taken off the team. She could still weave, but only with another Searcher looking over her shoulder. Though it was just for training, this was the first time since the night in the garden that Adne felt like herself. She was in her element and she was about to show Tess why this was exactly where she belonged.

"Go ahead, Adne," Tess said.

Closing her eyes, Adne began to move. Her limbs bent and curved as her body dipped and turned. Though she wasn't watching, Adne could feel the threads of light spooling out from the ends of her skeins. Seeing the pattern unfold wasn't important; sensing the connections between the here and the there was everything.

Weaving was the means to an end, a way to travel in an instant from point A to point B, even if those two points were in opposite hemispheres. The magic of opening portals relied on pulling threads from many sites to create the path.

Everything was connected, one infinite pattern that Weavers tapped into. The fabric of the universe. But Adne had discovered she could do more.

Beyond weaving the door, Adne saw always the other potential paths she could create. The roads not taken. She caught glimpses of people and places she could reach. And she'd learned to hone her skill so that she knew how her immediate surroundings fed into those paths.

And with her eyes closed, she could see Ethan and Connor moving through the room, because the Strikers, like every living being on the planet, were threads in the world's pattern. As they closed in on her, Adne sheathed her skeins.

Ethan came at her first. Side attack. He dove at Adne's legs, hoping to knock her down. Adne propelled herself into the air, flipping over while Ethan sailed underneath her. Recovering from his miss, Ethan rolled onto the balls of his feet. The flicker of his gaze to a point just behind Adne gave Connor away.

She whirled around as Connor rushed at her. Surprise registered on his face as Adne met his advance with a roundhouse that hit directly in the center of his chest. Connor went flying back.

Adne pivoted just in time to meet Ethan's next attack. As he grabbed for her, she lifted onto her toes and pirouetted past him, landing a hard blow to his back with her elbow as she turned. Ethan grunted in pain but swung around to strike at Adne once more.

Blocking his first punch, Adne retaliated with a knee that only missed Ethan's groin by an inch when he jumped back.

"Hey!" Ethan yelled at her in surprise.

Adne hit him in the jaw with enough force to send him reeling.

"Adne!" Connor was behind her. She wheeled on him.

He put his hands up, but Adne lunged and they both went tumbling along the floor. When they stopped rolling, Adne was on top of Connor. Her vision had become a sea of red. Her pulse was shrieking as blood sped through her veins, on fire. How dare they try to take away her power?

Kill him.

Adne didn't remember drawing the silver spike, but her skein was suddenly in her hand and she was raising it up.

Make him bleed.

She brought the skein down.

Mikaela screamed and Adne froze.

The pointed tip of the skein stopped just short of Connor's left eye.

"Adne, what are you doing?" Tess was running over to them.

Adne pushed herself up, backing away quickly.

His voice. She'd heard his voice. Bosque had been in her head.

Connor was propped up on his elbows. He was staring at Adne, his expression confused, wary, and a little angry.

"You all right?" Ethan offered Connor his hand, but Connor didn't take it. He kept his eyes on Adne.

Tess reached them. She looked from Connor to Adne.

"What was that?" Tess asked. "What were you thinking?"

Adne couldn't tell them. They'd take everything away from her. How could they not?

Shiloh and Mikaela crept up to stand behind Tess. The two newest members of the Haldis team were both watching Adne as if she were a venomous snake about to strike.

Drawing her second skein, Adne took both the spikes in one

hand and then violently cast them aside. The metal clattered along the floor, ringing bright and sharp with each impact.

"I'm showing you how it's done."

Adne turned her back on them and walked from the room. She kept her back straight and her pace measured, so they wouldn't know she was running away.

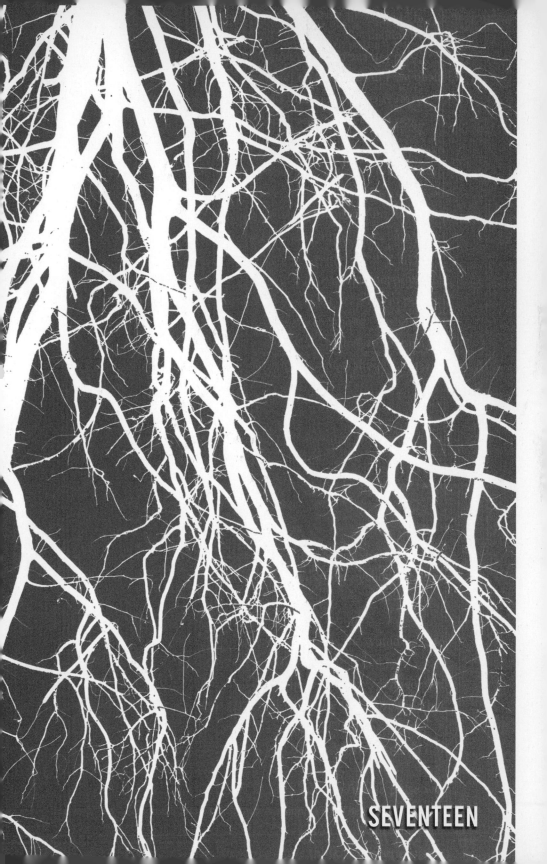

SEVENTEEN

CONNOR COULDN'T help but glance over his shoulder as he walked with Ethan toward Haldis Tactical.

"I should stay here."

"The hell you should." Ethan cuffed Connor across the back of the head. "You need to get out and get your mind on something else. Seeing you glum is downright scary."

"But Adne—" Connor rubbed the base of his skull. Ethan didn't cuff gently.

"Adne is with Sabine," Ethan cut him off. "You won't do her any good by hovering over her every second."

Connor wanted to disagree, but he couldn't. If anything, his vigilance seemed to make Adne feel worse. She wouldn't talk about why or how she'd ended up in the gardens outside Rowan Estate. Not to Connor. Not to anyone.

Tess tried to assure him that Adne was likely acting out after having repressed too much grief for too long, but Connor wasn't convinced.

"You're thinking about it," Ethan said. "Just stop. Stop thinking about it all the time. You're turning yourself into an old man."

Connor grunted by way of answer. It was easy enough for Ethan to throw placations at him. Sabine, who by all accounts should be having the harder time adjusting—not that there was anything wrong with the girl, but she *had* been a wolf—had taken to life with the Searchers as if she'd been born into it.

"Tell me this, my mopey friend," Ethan said, hefting his crossbow. "Does it or does it not feel good to have your weapons strapped on again?"

That drew a grin from Connor. "It does."

Going to the armory had been oddly comforting. At last there had been something familiar, something that had once been routine to distract him from the unpredictable and largely unpleasant shape of his life of late.

"Then just focus on that." Ethan nodded in approval. "We're going to get the bad guys again 'cause that's what we do."

"That *is* what we do." Connor felt a little bit of swagger infuse his gait. It felt good.

By the time they reached Tactical, Connor was practically his old self again.

"Ethan! Connor!" Tess waved to them. "Over here!"

Tess stood with Shiloh and Mikaela. The sight of the wallflowerish Weaver made Connor's gut clench. He couldn't miss the horror etched on the girl's face after Adne's attack. A look that said: I never want to become that. Mikaela's expression had made Connor want to throttle her and shout to the world that Adne was nothing but good, that she hadn't become anything other than the extraordinary woman she'd always been. But Connor couldn't shout that or do anything. He didn't know what to believe or feel anymore.

With Adne out of commission, Mikaela would weave the portal for their mission. Connor tossed an uneasy glance at Ethan. Timid as she was, Mikaela hardly seemed ready for the field. But Ethan just shrugged in reply. They hadn't talked about what happened with Adne. Neither had Tess tried to push Connor into sharing his thoughts about the episode. All of Connor's friends were treating him with kid gloves. He didn't blame them.

Though he might be resentful of it, Connor knew Ethan's nonchalance about the new Weaver wasn't misplaced. If Tess or Anika had deemed Mikaela fit for the mission, then she was. Still, she wasn't Adne and that was the long and short of it. Connor wanted Adne here, not Mikaela. But that wasn't going to happen today, maybe not tomorrow, maybe not for many tomorrows, and Connor needed to deal with it.

Taking a quick survey of the room, Connor noted that the Searchers had formed up according to faction. The Pyralis team appeared to be happily allowing Holt to lord over them. Eydis's team was mostly new faces—the hideout in Mexico had been wiped out by the Keepers' attack; Connor's chest tightened at the memory of losing his friends. Pascal was still leading the Alps-based Tordis team, but he looked to be the only veteran surrounded by very young, newly minted warriors from the Academy.

I could make the same observations about my own team.

Ethan, Connor, and Tess had been around Haldis for a while, but Shiloh and Mikaela were new. In the past year they'd lost Stuart, Kyle, Lydia, Isaac, and Monroe. Connor wondered if maybe he'd been too quick to dismiss Tess's theory about Adne and grief. They were all probably due a lot more grieving than they'd allowed themselves.

"Your attention!" Anika stepped into the center of the room. "Thank you for gathering and for your patience. After much debate and discussion, the Guides have concluded that we are needed in the world once again. We've spent the past weeks regrouping and have started rebuilding, and while that work continues, your purpose has always been to be in the world, defending it."

A murmur of approval passed through the group.

"As we make the transition from pursuit of the Elemental Cross to safeguarding the world from occult intrusions, we must be patient, both with our individual selves and with one another." Anika gestured to the four groups in the room. "The Guides have deemed it wisest to continue using the Striker teams as before to promote continuity within each unit."

Connor leaned over to Ethan. "Considering how few of the old teams made it through the war, do you really think continuity is possible?"

"Just go with it," Ethan murmured. "She's doing the best she can."

Chastised, Connor shoved his hands into his coat pockets. He hadn't meant to insult Anika. He'd been feeling good when he and Ethan entered the room, but as he waited for deployment, his doubts had crept back in, souring his mood. The complaint had been borne out by his own frustration and a nagging sense of betrayal. It wasn't that Connor felt Adne was betraying him. His resentment went well beyond that.

The war was over. His side won. He and Adne were together and he'd thought they were in love.

This was the part of life where things were supposed to be rainbows and unicorns, but somehow that wasn't happening. Happily ever after, it turned out, was total bullshit, because Connor was miserable.

"While many of the Keepers perished at the closing of the Rift due to the simple fact that they were long past a natural human life span, there are Keepers who survived," Anika told them. "We haven't yet determined the level of threat any remaining Keepers pose. It is your task to assess that threat."

Anika waited until the buzz of reaction died down before she spoke again. "We've been able to trace the location of some Keepers by following the one asset they still have: their money. Your Guides have your team assignments. After you've gathered the intelligence we need, you'll return here for debriefing. Are there any questions?"

The room was tense with energy, but silent.

"Remember," Anika said, "this mission is strictly recon. We have to assess the state of any remaining Keepers before we move against them. Unless you are in immediate danger, do not engage."

Though the majority of the teams nodded in assent, a few grumbles and snickers could be heard from Pyralis. Holt didn't even bother to hide the smirk on his face.

Anika ignored her detractors. "I look forward to your reports."

A low roar filled the room as the teams broke off to discuss their missions.

"So I hear this Guide person has our assignment." Connor winked at Tess. "Must be some kind of hot shot."

"Montauk," Tess replied.

"What's a Montauk?" Ethan asked. He turned to Shiloh. "Do you know what a Montauk is?"

Shiloh stared at Ethan, trying to figure out whether he was serious.

"It's a where." Tess laughed, sparing Shiloh. "In the Hamptons."

"I thought the Hamptons were a hotel chain," Connor said, scratching his chin.

"Different Hamptons," Tess answered, and said to Shiloh, "These two grow on you. I promise."

Shiloh just nodded.

"Pssst, Connor," Ethan said very loudly, "I think our new Striker is a robot."

"Does that mean he has lasers?" Connor replied. " 'Cause lasers would be very cool. And deadly. Deadly is always good."

Tess shook her head, laughing but exasperated. "Forget what I said, Shiloh, just ignore them."

Shiloh nodded again, but he cracked a little bit of a smile.

"I saw that." Connor pointed at him. "I saw it."

"Mikaela," Tess said to the girl who'd been watching the exchange with wide eyes. "Will you please open a door so I can kick these hucksters out of the room?"

Mikaela sprang, literally, into action, jumping and whirling as she pulled threads to weave a portal. The moment the door took its full shape, Connor plunged forward.

"Tallyho!"

"We're spies this time." Ethan was on his heels. "Spies don't say 'tallyho.'"

"What do spies say?" Connor asked.

Shiloh said softly, "Nothing."

Ethan and Connor exchanged a glance.

"I'm not wrong," Shiloh added. "That's why they're spies. The stealth. Also, ninjas. Ninjas can do stealth. And they also say nothing."

"He's pretty good," Ethan said to Connor.

Connor nodded. "Definitely stuff we can work with in there."

"Stop corrupting my new recruit," Tess said as she emerged from the portal.

Mikaela followed the Guide and closed the door.

"So this is Montauk," Ethan said, checking out their surroundings. "Looks nice."

"It looks like woods," Connor said.

"Nice woods, though," Ethan replied.

"If you like woods."

"All right, that's enough," Tess told them. "I know you have lost time to make up for, but we also have work to do."

"Yes, sir," Ethan said. "Or do you prefer ma'am?"

"Or Unflappable Director of the Lost," Connor offered. "It's just a fancier way of saying 'Guide.' Has a nice ring to it."

Tess rolled her eyes. "There's a house a half mile due east of here. That's where our targets are located. I'll survey the grounds. Connor and Ethan, take the house. Shiloh, you're with the Weaver."

Shiloh nodded.

"I knew he was going to say that." Ethan grinned at Connor. "You owe me five dollars."

"Get going." Tess shoved Ethan in the direction of the house while she headed south into the woods.

Connor and Ethan picked their way through the forest, maintaining an appropriate silence now that the mission was under way. The forest ended abruptly. A perfect line of trees demarcated the beginning of what Connor guessed was a perfectly manicured lawn when it wasn't covered with snow.

Ethan whispered, "Is that a house? Really?"

"Not terribly cozy looking," Connor replied, "is it?"

Though enormous and undoubtedly appointed with every amenity a person could want, the harsh angles of the glass-and-steel structure seemed cold and uninviting.

"Our job should be pretty easy." Ethan pulled out a pair of binoculars. "Most of the exterior walls are just giant windows."

"I'm okay with easy," Connor said, grabbing his binoculars. "What exactly are we supposed to be looking for?"

"Suspicious activity."

"And what constitutes suspicious?" Connor asked. "I mean, besides if we see them standing in robes, chanting. Is a goat randomly wandering around suspiciously?"

"Do you see a goat?" Ethan stood up. "Where?"

"I meant in theory."

"I don't think we need to mess with goat theories." Ethan lifted his binoculars again. "Okay, got someone. Female. I'm guessing she's about twenty."

"I see her." Connor tracked the girl as she walked through her living room. She settled onto a sofa and began to read a magazine. "Can you see what she's reading? Is it suspicious?"

"Shut up."

"Hey." Connor elbowed Ethan as another person enter the room. "She has a friend."

"Male," Ethan said. "Same age, I think."

"Are you saying this stuff because you want me to write it down?" Connor watched the boy pour himself a drink. "Well, now I'm thirsty."

The boy sat down and began a conversation with the girl.

"Are we supposed to have fiber optics so we can listen to this?" Connor asked.

"This mission is all about keeping Holt in check by addressing his complaint, while not really giving in to his demands." Ethan put his binoculars down. "We aren't spies, Connor. We're warriors. And the war is over." He waved toward the house. "Look at them. Without magic they're just spoiled kids with big bank accounts. They're nothing to do with us."

Connor didn't answer. He was staring through the binoculars at the third person who had entered the living room.

"Connor, are you listening to me?"

"Ethan, look."

"What's wrong?" Ethan crouched beside Connor.

"Just look."

Logan settled on the sofa beside the girl. The three young Keepers seemed to share an easy rapport.

"Tell me that's not Logan Bane." All the humor had left Connor's voice.

"Shit."

"Exactly." Connor put away his binoculars. "All right, let's go."

"Go where?" Ethan frowned at him.

"Grab him," Connor answered. "Logan isn't just a kid with a big bank account."

Ethan shook his head. "We can't grab him. Not without Anika's say-so."

"You think Anika wants Logan roaming free?" Connor objected.

"Of course not," Ethan said. "But there's a precedent here. Anika specifically stated no engagement on this mission. We did our recon.

We know Logan is here. We have to report that. Then Anika will send us right back here to pick him up."

"What if he's gone?" Connor asked.

"He won't be." Ethan nodded toward the house. "He looks comfy, don't you think? He's here for the long haul. He'll never see us coming."

"But—"

"If we take Logan without securing an order from Anika first, Holt will have a free pass to flout her authority," Ethan said. "We can't risk that."

"All right. I'm on board." Connor threw a regretful glance at the house. "Let's go find Tess."

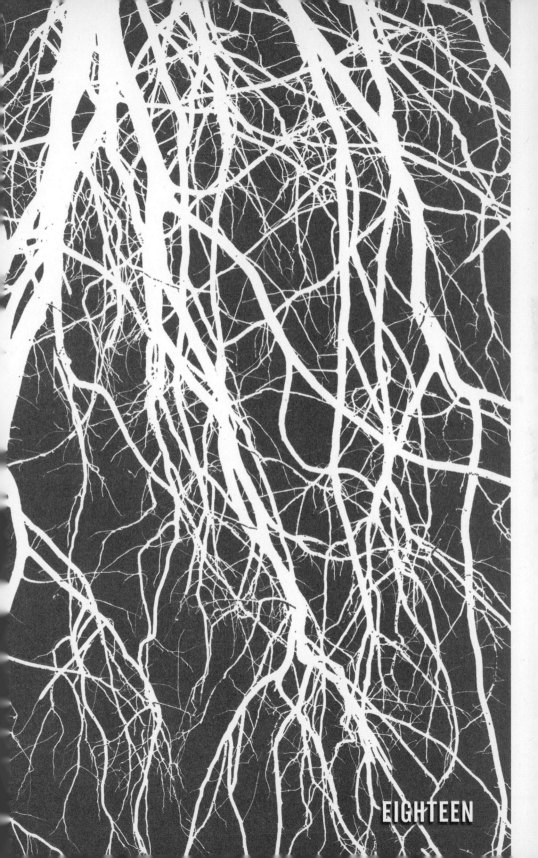

EIGHTEEN

ADNE FOUND SABINE waiting for her at the top of the grand staircase with a welcoming smile that made Adne sigh with relief. After the freak show that had taken place in the training room, and after she'd been forced to slink back to that site of her shame once the others had gone to retrieve her discarded skeins, Adne hadn't known where to go other than Rowan Estate. Sabine would be there, and since she'd been leading tours all day, she didn't know what had happened at the Academy. Thus, Adne decided that volunteering to drone on about history and architecture was much better than facing her friends. She wasn't ready for that. She didn't know if she ever would be.

"Nice job," Sabine said. "You only made up the answers to five questions."

"Sorry about that," Adne replied. "But can you really blame me for that last one? Who asks where baby gargoyles come from?"

"I was being serious." Sabine laughed. "I think five is the new lowest number of BS answers for a first-timer guiding a tour."

"In that case, thanks . . . I guess," Adne said.

Sabine slung her arm over Adne's shoulders. "All right, my dear, you're off the clock now and our boys are preparing for that mission—so we have to take this opportunity for a girls' night out very seriously. What sounds fun?"

"How about a hike?" Adne blurted, and felt her heart clench as she waited for Sabine's reply.

"A hike?" Sabine cast a wary glance at Adne. "You do know it's the end of the day? There's maybe an hour of daylight left."

Adne looked down at her feet. "They'll be out at night."

"Oh, Adne." Sabine let out a sigh. "Don't ask me to do this."

"Why not?" Adne straightened, locking Sabine in her gaze. "I know I'm on lockdown because of what happened here, except that no one really knows what happened, not even me. Sabine, crazy things are happening and they're happening to me, and I am not okay. I need to know what the hell is going on."

Sabine didn't flinch from Adne's outburst, but Adne was horrified by it.

"I'm sorry," Adne whispered. "I shouldn't have said anything."

"Don't be," Sabine replied. "I wish you would say more."

Adne wanted to tell Sabine how afraid she was. How she dreaded sleep because of the nightmares that inevitably came with it. How she worried that she might be losing her grip on reality, but that if she wasn't in fact going crazy, then the truth of what was happening might be much, much worse. She wanted to say all of this and more, but she couldn't let go of the secrets that she'd been holding on to so tightly.

Instead, Adne said, "Don't you want to see for yourself?"

"I'm not following." Sabine's brow furrowed. "See what?"

"Shay," Adne said. "Sarah told us that she saw Shay dragging me through the garden and back to the mansion."

Frowning, Sabine replied, "I've seen Shay. He's a wolf. Nothing has changed."

"What if something has changed?" Adne countered. "I think we need to go up to Haldis."

"Adne, even I try to make my trips as infrequent as I can manage," Sabine said with reluctance. "If a wolf pack thinks its den is compromised because they scent too many humans, then they'll abandon it. They'd leave and I don't know if we'd see them again."

"One trip," Adne pressed. "That's all I'm asking."

Sabine gave Adne a long look, then said, "I guess we're going to need warmer clothes."

The air on the slope near Haldis had a bite to it, as if it resented Adne and Sabine's presence. As they climbed the snowy mountainside, doubts began to plague Adne.

What am I even doing up here? And why did I drag Sabine into this?

Mired in her own thoughts, Adne yelped in surprise when Sabine grabbed her arm.

"Shhhh." Sabine pulled Adne into a crouch beneath a huge pine. "I think it would be best if I scouted ahead. I'll come back for you if the pack seems docile enough."

Already indebted to Sabine for joining her on this madcap expedition, Adne just nodded. Sabine crept into the thick of the trees and vanished from sight. Alone, Adne watched her breath curl like smoke toward the treetops.

"Adne."

Putting her back to the tree trunk, Adne glanced around what appeared to be a silent forest. The whisper of her name had come from right behind her, but now that she was looking, she saw no one.

"You shouldn't be here."

Adne whirled around, following the sound of the voice, but again there was no one.

"It's not safe here."

Adne turned again. "Who's there?"

No answer.

Pressing her cheek against the rough tree bark, Adne closed her eyes.

There is nothing. There is no one there. You can't trust your mind anymore.

When another low sound rumbled at Adne's back, she ignored it. But it came again, this time more distinct, and there was no mistaking it for an imagined voice. The snarl was slow and menacing and very, very close.

Taking care to move ever so slowly, Adne turned around.

Calla's golden eyes were locked on Adne, her pristine white coat only marred by the crimson splashed across her muzzle. The blood was so fresh, Adne saw drops of it fall from Calla's jaws onto the snow-covered ground.

"We should get out of here," Sabine said as she emerged from the woods at Adne's back. "The pack has a fresh kill and that means they'll be territorial. And I don't know . . ."

When she reached Adne's side, Sabine froze.

"Where Calla is?" Adne finished for her.

"Damn." Sabine took Adne's hand. "Let's try to back off. She might not see us as a threat if we get far enough away from the kill."

"How far is far enough?" Adne asked.

Sabine didn't take her eyes off the snarling she-wolf. "It depends on how pissed off Calla is."

"She seems pretty pissed off." Adne mimicked Sabine's measured steps away from Calla.

"She does, doesn't she?"

Calla stalked after them, keeping her head low and her fangs bared.

"Do you still speak wolf?" Adne asked, heart climbing up her throat. She'd seen Calla's muzzle bloodied before, but never as the target of the wolf's menace herself.

"Do I still speak wolf?" Sabine snapped at her. "You've got to be kidding me."

"Just throwing ideas out there," Adne said in a tight voice. "I thought that was better than 'you got a bloody steak in your pocket?'"

"Connor has been a very bad influence on you."

"Noted."

They were still backing away, but Calla's snarls were only growing louder. Hackles raised, Calla hunched down, her limbs tightening, ready to propel herself at the intruders.

She's going to kill us.

A blur of movement split the shadows and Calla gave a yelp of surprise. Snow filled the air in a sparkling cloud as Shay skidded to a stop directly between Calla and the two girls.

Shay barked at Calla, a sound that was sharp but not harsh. Calla replied with a dismissive snarl. Shay barked again and then trotted to the alpha female. Ears up and demeanor friendly, Shay licked some of the blood from Calla's muzzle. Calla shook her head and snapped at Shay, obviously confused by her mate's behavior. Shay barked once more, put his head to Calla's chest, and pushed her back.

Startled, Calla jumped away from him and gave a sharp growl that to Adne sounded almost like a question. Shay replied with a bark and wagged his tail. Casting a final, resentful look at Adne and Sabine, Calla pivoted around and disappeared into the brush.

"I don't know what the hell just happened, but I'll take it," Sabine murmured.

Shay peered into the forest where Calla had fled, as if making sure she wasn't doubling back for another strike. He glanced over his shoulder at Adne and Sabine, watching them with intelligent green eyes.

"What do we do now?" Adne whispered.

"Why are you asking me?" Sabine replied. "I thought I made it clear that there is no wolf-whispering potential on my part."

Shay looked back at the forest, and that was when Adne saw him. Barely distinguishable from the shadows, Ren was nonetheless there, watching them. Shay tilted his head, ears flicking while he gazed at Renier.

"Sabine," Adne said in a strained voice. "Look."

"Look at what?" Sabine was still watching Shay.

"Where Shay's looking," Adne answered, "in the woods."

"I don't see anything," Sabine said. "He probably just heard something in the underbrush. He has much better hearing than we do."

Adne's pulse stuttered. "Are you sure you don't see anything?"

Ren was looking right down at her. His eyes glittered in the moonlight.

"Do you see something?" Sabine asked. Her tone told Adne that, without a doubt, Sabine didn't see Ren. But Adne could, and she strongly suspected that Shay could as well.

"No," Adne said quickly. "I just thought because he's looking at the woods so intently."

"Wolves do that," Sabine said. "Can we get out of here now? I don't want to press our luck. Shay might think we're okay, but Calla could decide to come back with reinforcements."

"Okay."

Sabine was already trudging away. "I guess we answered that question. Sort of."

"Sorry?" Adne asked.

"Something is different about Shay," Sabine answered. "He's not acting like a wolf would—that's what Calla did. But he *is* still a wolf, not a Guardian. I don't understand why he'd be compelled to protect us."

As they retreated down the slope, Adne threw one last look behind her. Shay had turned to face them again. The golden brown wolf was sitting on his haunches, watching them leave. In the woods behind Shay, the other wolf was gone, and instead a boy stood there.

Adne felt her throat close as Ren raised his hand and waved goodbye. She didn't know how it was possible or what it meant, but Adne was certain that her brother had just saved her life.

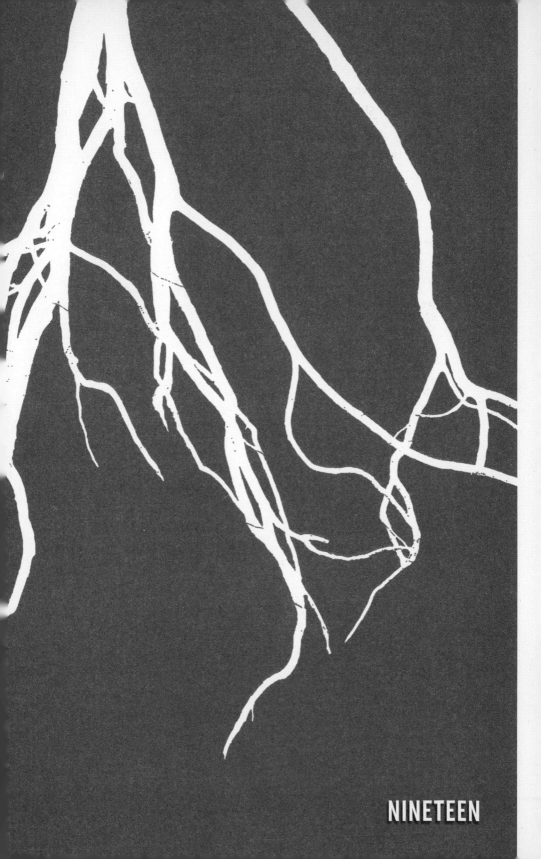

NINETEEN

REN STILL HAD a hard time feeling at ease with his ability to move through the world without being seen. That was why he preferred spending most of his time in wolf form, running through the woods. Hidden among the trees, Ren could forget that he was less than a shadow in this world, that he was seen only by those who tapped into the magic that had kept him on this plane after he'd died.

As he made his way down one of Rowan Estate's long halls, Ren felt more like a ghost than ever. The labyrinthine mansion was the kind of place a ghost belonged. Ren didn't want to belong at Rowan Estate.

He'd wandered these halls many times while keeping an eye on Adne. But those visits had been on his terms. Tonight Ren was little more than Logan Bane's errand boy, hardly a role to be relished. It wasn't as if he slunk off, tail between his legs, to do Logan's bidding.

From the moment Logan had sent him after Sarah Doran, Ren had been fighting the command to no avail. Resisting didn't cause Ren pain, nor did he feel like someone else was in control of his mind and body. He simply couldn't stop himself from going to find Sarah.

Though Logan wouldn't hesitate to name himself the executor of this power, Ren suspected that his inability to resist the Keeper's commands had a different source.

You are here because I willed it to be so and you cannot destroy that which created you.

The more Ren thought about it, the more convinced he was that his existence as a spirit had been devised and continued to be manipulated by Bosque Mar. Ren didn't know why Bosque would have determined that the alpha Guardian was the best choice for the role. Perhaps the Harbinger expected that Ren would blame the Searchers for his untimely end, and desire vengeance because of it. But Ren had a creeping feeling that Bosque's selection had far more to do with Ren's tie to Adne.

I don't wish to hurt Ariadne. Quite the opposite.

Ren knew there were far worse things Bosque could do to Adne than physically harm her. He swore to himself and to his sister that he would do everything in his power to stop Bosque from fulfilling whatever plans he had for Adne.

To that end, Ren had begun to test the boundaries of his spirit form. Ren found that he could manipulate Logan's commands in small ways. For example, he had the ability to put himself in the same room with Sarah, but instead Ren had traveled to Rowan Estate's grounds, taking his time to enter the mansion and make his way through its dark halls. He'd even been able to make a detour to Haldis before carrying out Logan's wishes.

Ren sensed that he would only be able to take these acts of rebellion so far, though. For example, he was pretty sure that if he'd tried to arrive at Rowan Estate via a cross-country excursion, some unseen force would have prevented it. Even knowing that in his current state his life wasn't completely his own, Ren found hope in being able to exert his will at all. It meant that while he was being kept in check by Bosque's power, there were limits to what the Harbinger could control as well. Ren simply needed to find as many ways to exploit those weaknesses as he could.

As Ren approached the room where he knew he'd find Sarah, his wolf senses were overwhelmed by a surprising but familiar scent.

Shay?

Quickly dismissing the notion that wolf-Shay had somehow ended up inside the mansion, Ren crept forward, poking his muzzle inside the door. Ren didn't need the room's décor, the comic books, or the clothes that still hung in the closet to confirm that he'd just entered Shay's bedroom. Shay's scent pervaded the air. Beneath it Ren caught another scent that he knew well. Snow.

Calla.

Without thinking, Ren snarled.

Sarah had been sitting in a chair beside the bed, staring off into space, but at the sound she jumped up and gave a cry of alarm. Steel flashed in her hand and Ren growled again at the sight of her dagger.

I'd forgotten that she's not just Shay's mother, she's a Searcher. And Searchers are trained to kill Guardians.

Sarah stared at Ren. Though she didn't sheath her dagger, she drew a long breath and shook her head.

She thinks she's only imagining that I'm here.

Ren took a cautious step into the room. Now that he'd adjusted to the predominant scent in the room, he could distinguish what about Sarah's scent was similar to her son's and what was different. Sorrow clung to Sarah Doran like a thick fog, but Ren also smelled the acrid touch of madness in her grief.

If I wasn't a spirit, I'd be in danger here.

Any wolf knew better than to cross a mother and her young. Humans weren't as different from animals as they thought.

Ren shifted forms and Sarah gasped, but Ren noted that her grip on the dagger didn't waver.

"You . . . you can't be here." Sarah's voice shook.

She's afraid, but not of me. She's worried she's losing her mind.

"I can't disagree with you there," Ren said. "My being here is an impossible thing. But it's where I find myself these days, despite my former beliefs about what's possible and what isn't."

Sarah frowned at Ren. "You're a Guardian."

"I was a Guardian," Ren answered. "But the Guardians are no more."

Sarah's jaw clenched and Ren smelled a new wave of grief pouring off her.

"I died here," Ren said simply.

"You're a ghost," Sarah said, shaking her head again. She laughed, but it sounded like she was on the verge of tears. "Of course. I would want to see ghosts, wouldn't I?"

"You're not crazy," Ren told her. *At least not when it comes to me.*

Sarah looked at him sharply. "Excuse me?"

"You don't think I'm really here, so you're afraid you've lost it," Ren said with a shrug. "That's understandable, but it doesn't change the fact that I am here."

When Sarah shifted her weight, clearly unconvinced, Ren said, "If your mind conjured up a ghost, wouldn't it be Shay? He's the one you want to see. You don't even know who I am."

"My son isn't dead." Sarah finally sheathed her dagger. "Why would he be a ghost?"

"Good point." Ren nodded.

"But *you* died here." Sarah regarded Ren differently now, examining him as if she could turn up clues about his appearance. "In this room?"

"No," Ren replied. "In the library."

"When?" Sarah asked.

"The same day you were freed from Bosque's prison." Ren sighed. "The last battle of the war."

Sarah's eyes narrowed. "Wait, I . . . I think I saw your body."

"It would have been this body." Ren shifted into his wolf form and Sarah took a moment before she nodded.

Ren shifted back. "I'm Renier Laroche."

"You were the other alpha," Sarah said quietly, then her voice sharpened. "You were supposed to be with them. With her. If you were there, he wouldn't have a place. He would have stayed."

Ren had to fight back a snarl. "That's not how it works."

"I don't care how it works." Sarah glared at him. "You're the Guardian. You should have been the one who turned into a wolf and ran off into the mountains."

"You don't know how much I wish it would have been that way," Ren murmured.

Sarah didn't hear him. Still angry, she said, "So why are you here, Renier? Have you come with a message from beyond to tell me my son is at peace? Are you supposed to be some kind of wolf angel who brings me comfort?"

The image of a wolf with wings and a halo jumped into Ren's mind and was so ridiculous that he actually burst into laughter.

Sarah stared at him, incredulous.

Collecting himself, Ren said, "I'm sorry. But . . . a wolf angel?"

"I just . . ." Sarah tried to sound indignant, but quickly deflated. "I suppose that would be unlikely."

"Pretty much," Ren said. "But I'm a wolf spirit, and I would have told you that's unlikely too."

"Why are you here?" Sarah asked.

"I do have a message for you." Ren gritted his teeth. *A message I don't want to give.*

Sarah watched him expectantly.

"It's about Shay." Ren saw Sarah's face blanch, then light up, then pale once more.

He didn't want to say anything else. He wanted to lie. To keep Sarah away from Logan and his machinations. But he couldn't.

"I was sent to you by someone who wants to help you," Ren said.

"Help me how?" Sarah twisted her fingers together.

"Help you get your son back." Ren growled at the hateful words, and Sarah took a step back, frowning.

"So it's really possible?" Sarah asked. Ren watched a flurry of emotions cross her face and he could see that, despite her outbursts and her clinging to Shay's memory, she hadn't ever believed he would return to her.

Ren struggled with his answer. "I don't know. I'm only bringing the message."

And there it was, exactly what Logan had said. Semantics. It wasn't much, but it was all Ren had. He wouldn't promise Sarah anything. He wouldn't attest to the truth or falsehood of Logan's message. He would simply deliver it.

Sarah sank onto the edge of the bed. "Who sent this message?"

"Logan Bane."

Ren felt a spike of satisfaction when Sarah stiffened. "Bane? A Keeper?"

"The son of Efron Bane," Ren answered. "The heir to the pack that now occupies Haldis Cavern."

"His legacy was undone by the war." Sarah nodded, then her brow furrowed. "But wait. That name . . . Logan . . . didn't he help to bring the Harbinger down?"

"He did," Ren told her. "He's been having some regrets about it."

He was surprised he could say that. Ren found himself smiling.

"But," Sarah said slowly, "he must want something. Something from me?"

"Right now he just wants to meet you," Ren replied. "To talk."

"Can I trust him?" Sarah asked.

"Absolutely not," Ren answered without missing a beat.

Nice. Apparently neither Logan nor Bosque could force him to lie about who they were. This was getting better and better.

"Then why should I meet him?" Sarah stood up, folding her arms across her chest.

"I can't tell you what you should or shouldn't do," Ren said, wishing it were otherwise. "I'm only here to give you the message. And there's one more thing."

"What?" Sarah asked, dread creeping into her eyes.

"Logan needs a demonstration of your intent," Ren answered. "To show him that you want to collaborate and that you're not going to just hand him over to the other Searchers."

"Tell me what that means," Sarah said.

"You need to bring him something," Ren told her. "A box that was taken from him. It's carved from ebony wood."

"A box?" Sarah frowned at Ren. "Where is it?"

"Ariadne has it," Ren answered, wishing he could lie. "It's in her room at the Academy. What's in the box is what matters: a pendant, a small piece of bone, and a pair of rings. Make sure you have them all."

Sarah sat down on the bed, then stood up again. She buried her fingers in her hair, bent her head, and moaned.

"Are you okay?" Ren asked. He didn't have a playbook for this part of the game.

Sarah kept her head bowed, but she nodded.

After a few minutes she looked up. "I'll do it. God help me, I know I shouldn't, but I want to."

Don't do this, Ren thought. *Please.*

But he said, "I can tell him that. Just bring the box and its contents when it's time to meet him."

"How will I know when and where?" Sarah asked. Ren hated the spark of hope he saw in her eyes.

Damn you, Logan. I hope you rot in hell for this.

"I'm sure he'll send me back with that information," Ren sighed.

Sarah nodded.

Ren felt a sense of completion and suddenly he knew he was free to leave. And he wanted nothing more than to get out of there. Without so much as a parting word to Sarah, Ren shifted into wolf form and vanished.

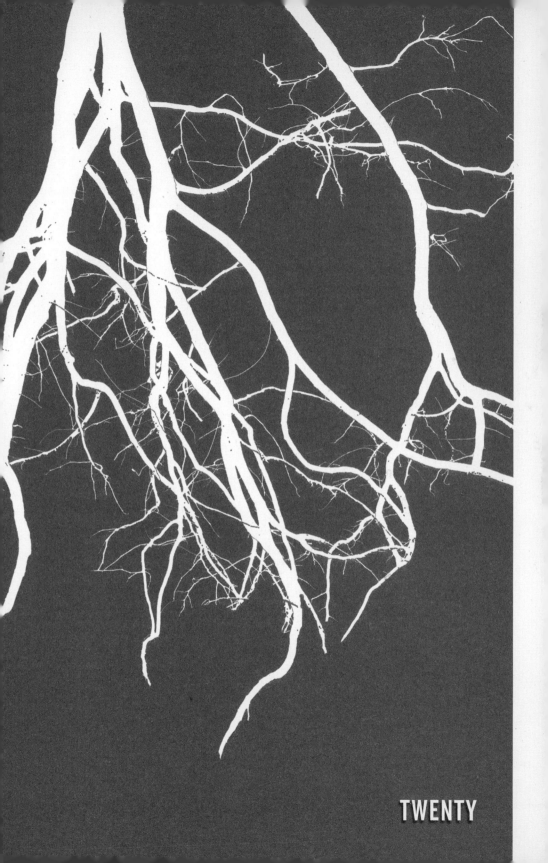

TWENTY

LOGAN HAD NEVER rehearsed conversations in front of a mirror before, but he'd felt compelled to as he devised a strategy for getting Audrey to take a walk alone with him. It wasn't easy to make himself sound convincing. Aside from Chase, Audrey's general relationship to other people was bare tolerance, and that included Logan. Logan doubted that Audrey ever would have agreed to let Logan stay in Montauk, much less drag her and her brother into the depths of occult malfeasance, without serious pressure and cajoling on Chase's part.

Logan had maintained doubts about Audrey's reliability in all of this. She was easily frightened and manipulated, likely to change her stated opinion about something or her allegiance as quickly as doing so worked to her benefit.

Just like he used to do.

He couldn't deny it. Logan was sensitive to the fact that much of his rancor toward Audrey derived from how much she reminded him of the petulant boy he'd been for most of his life. Coddled, arrogant, and completely divorced from the history of blood that had bought his expansive lifestyle.

He hated Audrey for holding up such an ugly mirror of his past every day. And Audrey wasn't oblivious to Logan's opinion of her. But, as with everything else in her life, Audrey didn't give a damn about anyone's thoughts but her own.

That made Logan's task tricky.

As he descended the stairs to the living room, Logan wasn't certain he'd be able to pull it off. At least it hadn't been difficult to get Audrey alone. Logan had sent Chase into town to track down a bottle of Dalmore 50, which Logan insisted was the only thing he would drink. And only a Keeper would actually regard such a request as a perfectly reasonable thing. It didn't matter that it was the middle of the night. Chase's family had enough sway in Montauk that when Chase called ahead, the shop owner would be waiting to open exclusively for him.

Audrey sat on the chaise, examining her nails.

"I think I need a new manicurist," Audrey told Logan, as if he cared. "This one can't seem to get the gloss on the polish right."

"Audrey." Logan sat in the chair to the right of the chaise. "I was hoping to talk with you about something."

"Sounds serious." Audrey continued to inspect her manicure.

When Logan didn't reply, Audrey dragged her gaze away from her varnished nails. "Ugh, Logan. Is it serious? Don't we have enough going on?"

"I'm sorry," Logan said, and Audrey's eyes narrowed in suspicion. He was laying it on too thick. Changing tack, Logan continued, "I'm sure the replacement of your manicurist deserves your time far more than our shot at immortality."

"Well, you don't have to be so dramatic about it," Audrey huffed. "What do you want to talk about?"

"Can we take a walk?" Logan asked.

"It's freezing out," Audrey objected.

"Wear a coat," Logan shot back. "Look, I don't want Chase barging in on us. I need to talk to you alone."

"Oh my God, Logan, I thought you said this was about immortality." Audrey's mouth twisted in revulsion. "Did I hear you incorrectly? Because I don't care what you do, but I do not want to hear about any boy drama you're having with my brother. That's not my job."

"Don't worry, I don't kiss and tell." *God, I really, really hate you.* "Let's go down to the beach." Logan stood up. "And I'll tell you what's going on."

With a lengthy show of sulking and an endless stream of complaints, Audrey donned a coat and finally let Logan open the terrace door for her so they could make their way to the shore. When Logan's feet sank into the sand, he felt a charge of anticipation. It was time.

"Okay, Logan, I came outside. We're on the beach. Now, why am I freezing my ass off out here?" Audrey rubbed her arms for effect.

"You won't be for long," Logan answered. "It's just . . . he wants to speak with you. And just you. Not Chase."

"Who wants to speak with me?" Audrey frowned at him.

When Logan simply watched her, waiting, Audrey's eyes grew large.

"You mean *him*?" she gasped. "But why?"

"Maybe it's all that brilliance you've demonstrated," Logan snarked. "All I know is that he asked to see you."

"How can that . . . how is it possible?" Audrey began to fidget. "He's cut off from us now. Isn't he?"

"He's confined to his realm, yes," Logan said. "But with the proper rites, I can speak with him. I've done it once. And if you agree, I'll summon him now."

"Now?" Audrey gaped at Logan. "Right now?"

"Yes, right now." Logan had already been edgy, and as usual, Audrey was getting on his nerves. He pointed at the bright moon overhead. "It's the appropriate time of night to do this kind of spell-work."

Audrey stared at him, and Logan decided she looked like a dumb cow chewing cud.

"Well?" Logan asked.

"Uh . . . I . . . um . . . okay." Her voice had gotten very small, and Logan almost felt guilty about the cow thing. "Logan, can I ask you something?" Audrey sounded shy, almost embarrassed to be speaking.

"Of course," Logan replied, though he was impatient to get on with the summoning.

"If we can really do this . . . I mean get our powers back," Audrey said, "can we have Guardians again?"

"God, Audrey," Logan scoffed. "Why would we—"

"I don't mean the awful ones, like that mean one you summoned who doesn't want to help us and only does it because he has to," Audrey told him. "I just thought we could have some of the nice ones back. The ones who liked us."

She kicked at the sand, unable to meet Logan's puzzled gaze, but Audrey didn't need to say anything more. The picture painted itself vividly as Logan watched her squirm in the discomfort of her unintentional confession.

The only one around to pay Audrey compliments and offer her adoration, even if it was most likely feigned, had been her pet Guardian . . . Joel, Chase had called him. The spoiled girl was lonely and she wanted her forced friend back. How sad . . . and pathetic.

None of them liked us, you stupid child. If Joel had known about the rebellion before he was transformed into a wild wolf, he no doubt would have slit your throat while you slept.

"I'm sure you'll be able to have whatever you want," Logan said quietly. "That's the beauty of being a Keeper. Isn't it?"

Audrey offered a little smile and nodded.

"May I continue?" Logan asked her.

"Yes," Audrey said. "Go ahead."

"Good." He drew the knife from his coat pocket and Audrey gasped again.

"What's that for?"

"It's for cutting," Logan answered drily. Without hesitating, he drew the blade in a swift stroke, tracing the scar on his palm.

Though he wasn't looking at her, Logan heard Audrey whimper as he held his palm out. His blood rained onto the sand, mingling with the waves that lapped the shoreline.

"Don't worry," Logan said without turning to face Audrey. "You don't have to use the knife."

As he spoke the words of the incantation that would summon Bosque, Logan's skin prickled with fortune's fickle nature. He'd uttered the same phrases to call Bosque to Rowan Estate, knowing it might lead to the downfall of the Harbinger, handing victory to the Searchers. Now he invoked the same magic with opposite purpose— to restore instead of destroy.

He didn't need to do it this way. Logan had already established that he could call upon Bosque by blood and will alone. But tonight he needed to give Audrey a show.

The retreating waves pulled Logan's blood into the sea, and soon the water's surface began to stir. A small patch of ocean seethed and boiled as a shape rose from beneath the dark waters.

"Logan." Audrey grasped his hand, but he shook her off.

"Show a little dignity," Logan whispered harshly.

The silhouette of a man, obscured by the night, came toward them. Logan could sense the fear emanating from Audrey, but he ignored it, focusing on Bosque. Logan was a little surprised when Audrey fell to her knees before he did.

At least she has enough sense to show deference.

Logan knelt beside Audrey as Bosque's features were revealed by the moonlight.

"What have we here?" Bosque's gaze immediately fell upon Audrey.

"A fellow Keeper," Logan answered. "Audrey and her brother have aided me in my quest to reach you."

My quest? Really? Logan didn't think he'd ever said anything more lame.

"I see." Bosque regarded Audrey curiously.

She lifted her face, casting a timid glance at the Harbinger. "How are you . . . sir?"

Well, that was much worse that what Logan had said. It would make what was coming easier . . . maybe.

"Intrigued," Bosque answered Audrey. He returned his attention to Logan. "You summoned me."

"I did." Logan found it strange that his pulse wasn't racing. Instead it rolled through his veins, heavy and insistent as a dirge. "I'm ready to continue the conversation we'd begun."

The barest hint of a smile appeared on Bosque's mouth.

That was all Logan needed.

Logan grabbed Audrey by her hair, jerking her head back. He drew the knife across her throat, the cut so deep and swift that surprise had hardly registered on her face before she bled out in the sand. It was fast. It was easy. Logan felt a surge of triumph.

"A worthy offering." Bosque gazed at Audrey's limp form. "You've managed to impress me, Logan."

Bowing his head, Logan said, "Thank you."

"Worthy, yes," Bosque continued. "But it will not be enough."

Logan barely stopped himself from shouting an objection. He clenched his fists and maintained his submissive posture. "I don't understand."

"To cross over, I must be invited," Bosque said, his voice quiet enough that the waves almost muffled it. "By someone of this earth."

Daring to look up, Logan asked, "And I don't qualify?"

Bosque regarded Logan with disdain. "You especially."

"Because of my blood," Logan said.

"Yes." Bosque nodded. "But no Keeper will be able to complete the rite. Anyone who swore a blood oath to me while I walked this realm does not have the power to open the Rift. Only one tied to the earth and its power can wound this world enough to give me passage."

"It was Eira who opened the Rift in the beginning," Logan said.

"A knight of Conatus," Bosque finished Logan's thought. "And only one such as she can repeat the task."

The brief flare of triumph Logan had felt after winning Bosque's approval was drowned in fresh disappointment.

"There is someone." Bosque's voice reached Logan through the noise of his self-pity.

Logan couldn't hide his disbelief. "Who?"

"The girl called Ariadne." Bosque said her name softly, with near reverence.

"Adne?" Logan blurted, then hurried to cover his outburst. "Forgive me, but . . ."

Bosque tilted his head, gauging Logan's reaction. "Yes?"

Taking a deep breath, Logan said, "I can't think of anyone who has more reason to hate me."

"I find it hard to believe your charming nature didn't win her over," Bosque said smoothly.

Logan took the insult with chagrin.

"Her feelings toward you are irrelevant," Bosque continued. "She has the power required to bring me into this world. It is Ariadne you need and Ariadne alone."

When Logan continued to sulk in silence, Bosque said, "Are you so blind that you can't see I've already given you what you need to win this girl?"

Logan looked at Bosque and frowned.

"You so easily came to the right conclusion in the case of Sarah Doran, yet you stumble blindly around the matter of this girl." Obviously irked, Bosque spoke in a curt tone. "Ariadne hates you because what she loved was taken from her. Give it back."

Logan almost laughed. *God, I am a moron.* "Renier."

This time Bosque's smile was indulgent. "See about it. Don't delay."

"I won't." Logan glanced at Audrey's lifeless body and didn't quite manage to stifle his sigh.

"You're worried about her brother?" Bosque seemed to pull the thought from Logan's mind.

"Yes," Logan admitted. "It could be a problem."

It will be a problem. God only knows why, but Chase liked his sister.

"A solution will soon be at your door," Bosque told Logan.

"Really?" Logan frowned. "How so?"

"You might not sound so eager when I've told you what it is," Bosque said. "The Searchers. They're coming for you."

Alarm jolted through Logan's body. "What?"

"Even now they're nearing the house," Bosque continued. "Go into town, get your friend, and flee. Blame the girl's death on your enemy. Now go."

Nodding mutely, Logan turned and ran.

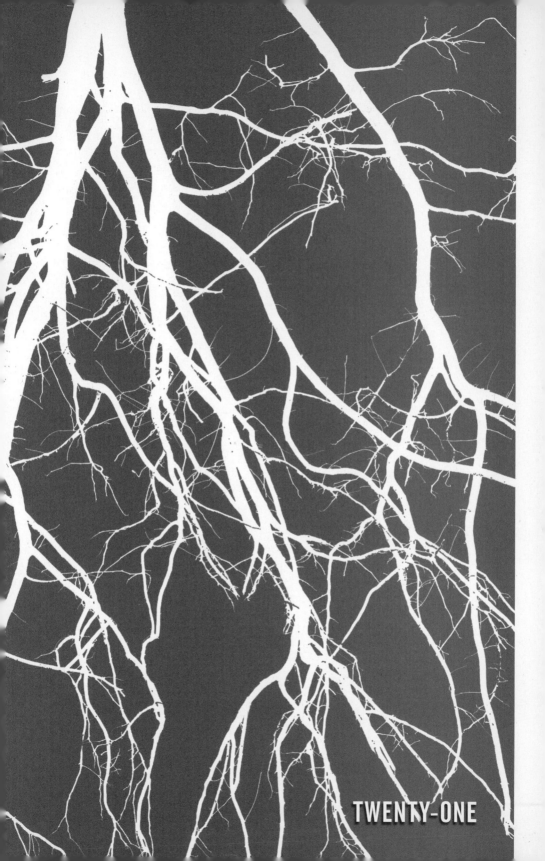

TWENTY-ONE

IT WASN'T THE mission Connor had in mind. He'd envisioned coming back to Montauk with Ethan and Shiloh, snatching Logan, and getting the hell out of there. Quick, clean, done.

Three teams felt like overkill. Over-overkill.

Of course Holt had demanded a piece of the action for his Pyralis team. The newly composed Eydis team felt the necessity to prove themselves. Since the Haldis team had identified the target, they were obliged to lead the strike. Fortunately, Pascal had sense enough to insist that Tordis didn't need to be an act in this circus.

Connor grudgingly admitted that the benefit of having three teams on the mission was that they were able to surround the house while his team went in, greatly decreasing the chances of any of the Keepers giving them the slip. And they were after all three Keepers, since Holt had spent a good fifteen minutes berating the rest of the group about the dangers in leaving Logan's "accomplices" behind.

Holt had a point, but Connor had trouble putting the two socialites he'd observed in the same class as Logan. Before today, the other young Keepers hadn't been so much as a blip on the Searchers' radar. They were the vein of Keepers that didn't have run-ins with Searchers. They enjoyed the wealth and power bestowed by their fealty to Bosque Mar, but that was about as far as it went.

By the time the new mission had been settled on, Connor was kicking himself for not having just strolled up to the house and dragged Logan out of it. Instead it was three hours later and Connor was watching Mikaela weave a door to Montauk for the second time that night.

At least this door was closer. Connor stepped through the portal and onto the snow-covered lawn.

Sensing Ethan and Shiloh at his flank, Connor said, "Let's go."

Mikaela closed the door behind them. This time she would remain in the safe confines of the Academy. They only needed one Weaver to get back and it had been decided that a more experienced Searcher was better suited to that task.

The trio moved quietly and swiftly up the stairs and onto the terrace. The lights were on inside the house, but the living room was empty. With Shiloh and Ethan covering him, Connor went to the door and was surprised to find it unlocked. He waved for the other Strikers to follow him inside.

Though Connor didn't see anyone, the house had signs of being recently occupied. Unfinished cocktails sat on the coffee table. Music filtered through speakers surrounding the room.

It's the middle of the night, Connor told himself to counteract the sinking feeling in his stomach. *They're in bed.*

Signaling Ethan and Shiloh to secure the main floor, Connor made his way up the stairs. He searched the master suite and two bedrooms, finding them all empty.

He's gone. Damn it all. He's really gone.

Deflated, Connor headed back downstairs.

Ethan was waiting in the living room. "Anything?"

"No," Connor answered. "They're not here."

"We should search the grounds," Ethan said. "I sent Shiloh to call in the other teams."

Evidence of Ethan's words arrived in the unpleasant form of Holt.

"What do you mean they're not here?" Holt stormed into the living room. "I thought you had good intelligence about this place."

"We did." Connor checked his temper. He didn't want to give Holt the chance to place the blame on Anika.

"Then can you explain why three Keepers would up and leave their house at two in the morning?" Holt had the sort of face that became tomato red when he was upset. From the current shade of Holt's cheeks, Connor discerned that he was very, very upset.

"Holt!" One of the Pyralis Strikers came running into the room. "We found something."

"Show me." Holt grabbed the Striker by the elbow and was out the door immediately.

Ethan half groaned. "We better follow him."

Connor nodded and they went out into the night.

A group of Searchers, and it appeared to be most of the teams, had gathered on the beach.

"Do you think they're having a clambake?" Connor joked, but he couldn't shake the bad feeling that rattled his bones.

"No threat?" Holt had apparently seen whatever there was to see and now pushed his way through Searchers to confront Connor and Ethan. "All Keepers are monsters."

"We need a little more information before we can agree or disagree with you," Ethan answered. He rather indelicately knocked Holt out of the way.

Connor followed Ethan into the small crowd. They were looking at a body.

The girl's throat had been cut deeply and cleanly. No doubt she'd died within the space of a minute. And Connor recognized her.

Ethan said it first. "She was in the living room."

"I know." Connor turned away, not wanting to see the girl's glassy eyes for another second.

"Do you agree with me now?" Holt thrust himself in Connor's path.

"Haven't decided," Connor told him. "That girl was with Logan and another boy. My money was on her being one of them. Her being dead on the beach doesn't quite add up."

"What more do you need to know than that she's dead?" Holt argued. "Obviously murdered."

Connor couldn't deny that. The girl had died violently. What Connor didn't understand was why.

What are you up to, Logan?

Holt gave up on Connor and returned to the beach. Ethan fell into step beside his friend.

"What do you make of it?"

Connor just shook his head.

"I know," Ethan said quietly. "I know."

Behind them, Holt's voice rose to compete with the waves hitting the shore. Connor couldn't make out what he was saying, but he didn't expect he'd want to hear it anyway.

Loud voices rose to answer Holt's shouting. The shouts became a chant, and Connor turned around.

"What the—"

He grabbed Ethan's arm and jerked them both out of the path of the sudden onslaught of Searchers tearing up from the beach. Paying no mind to Connor or Ethan, the mob surged into the house. The sounds of breaking glass and smashing objects joined their frenzied cries.

Ethan started toward the house, but Connor held him back.

"That's a riot, friend," Connor said. "Better not get in its way."

"Are you telling me you're okay with that happening?" Ethan glared at him.

"Far from it," Connor replied. "But going in there now would be like trying to calm a rabid dog by petting it. We'll deal with this, but not now."

While a sizable group of Searchers had taken up with Holt in destroying the house, Connor was reassured to see others hanging back. When he spotted the Weaver from Eydis, Hernan, among them, he quietly rounded up Shiloh and Ethan.

They couldn't stop the violent rampage now, but they didn't have to watch it happen.

Hernan quietly opened a door and the silent objectors passed through it one by one.

Connor stood watch over Hernan until only he, Ethan, and Shiloh remained.

"You should come with us," Connor told the Weaver. "Once Anika has been updated, we'll send a team back to deal with this."

Hernan shook his head and pointed at the house. "My brother has been taken in by that madness. I won't leave without him."

"I understand," Connor said.

Ethan went through the door, but Shiloh paused beside Connor.

"When we don't have a war to fight, is this what we become?"

Connor didn't have an answer, but as Shiloh passed into the portal, Connor was overcome with the feeling that the walls of his world were being pulled down on top of him. And there was nothing he could do to stop it.

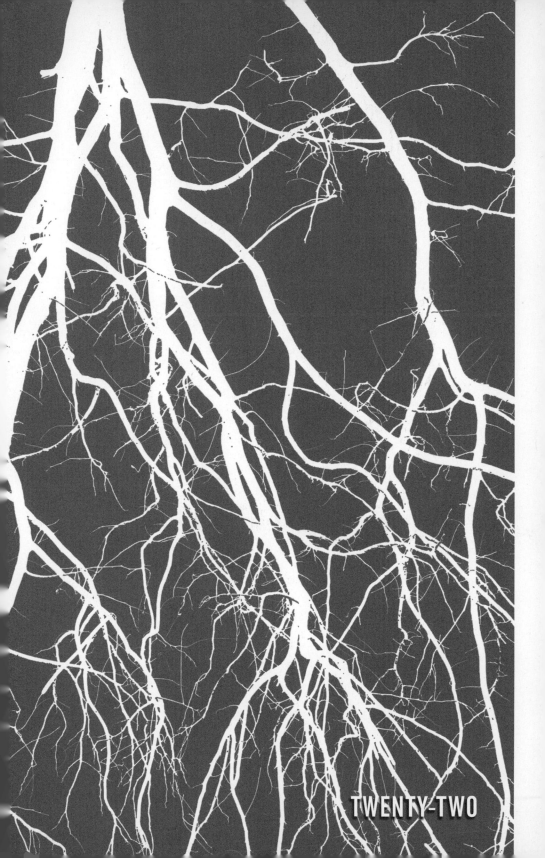

TWENTY-TWO

IN ALL THE TIME Adne had known Connor, he'd been at war, but this was the first time she'd ever seen him beaten down by a mission. His face was world-weary and his every movement stilted by frustration. At least he was telling her it was about the mission and nothing else. He didn't bring up the training session. Neither did she.

"It's not your fault he got away," Adne told Connor. "Logan's always been slippery. Saving his own skin is his raison d'être."

"I know that," Connor said, shrugging off his duster. "I don't even know if we should bother chasing down Keepers. In fact, because it's what Holt wants us to be doing, I'm kind of convinced it must be a terrible idea. And given the way he ransacked that house tonight, I'd almost be afraid to see him catch up with a Keeper. But I can't help thinking . . ."

"What?" Adne knew Connor too well not to notice that he'd cut his thought off prematurely, which meant he was hiding something.

Connor shook his head. "It's nothing."

"The nothing is bothering you," Adne replied. "Just tell me."

With a sigh, Connor smiled at her. "No secrets with you."

Adne swallowed what felt a stone lodged in her throat, but she forced herself to nod.

"We found a girl," Connor said. "The same one we saw with Logan and the other Keeper boy during the reconnaissance mission."

"So you didn't come back empty-handed after all," Adne said. "You know what they say, a bird in the hand."

Connor went very quiet.

"That was my attempt to cheer you on," Adne offered, frowning at him.

"She was dead, Adne," Connor said, his expression bleak. "We found her on the beach near the house. Her throat was cut."

Adne's heart thudded, her pulse suddenly loud in her ears. "What do you think happened?"

"Nothing good," Connor answered.

"You think it was Logan," Adne said. "But she was a Keeper, like him. Why would he kill one of his own? And since when does Logan have the guts to kill someone? I thought he hired people to do that."

"He does." Connor rubbed his temples and Adne noticed how tired he looked.

I haven't been helping with that, Adne thought. *I probably bring him more worry than comfort these days.*

"Or at least he did," Connor continued. "I don't know what happened, and without having Logan here to question, there's no way for us to find out. What I do know is that I have a very bad feeling about all of this."

Adne agreed but she didn't trust herself to say so. She could barely hear her own thoughts over the roar of blood in her head. It was making her dizzy.

Connor stripped off his shirt, revealing hard muscle and scars won by years as a Striker. Suddenly uncomfortable, Adne turned away.

What the hell is wrong with me? She'd wanted Connor more than anything for the last two years, and now he was hers. Had her feelings been nothing more than childish infatuation? Had winning him been the only real goal, and now that she had him, had her interest waned?

The thought made Adne's skull ache.

It can't be that. I can't be that horrible.

Adne forced herself to turn around. While she'd been looking away, Connor had stripped off his jeans and donned a loose-fitting pair of pajama pants. Adne let her gaze roam over him slowly, taking in the lines of his body, reminding herself of how good it felt to hold him, to be close to him, to feel how much he wanted her whenever he took her in his arms.

"What's that look about?" Connor asked, noticing Adne's perusal.

"I love you." Adne walked up to Connor and rose up on her toes to place a gentle kiss on his mouth.

Connor's arms went around her back, holding her against him. "Lucky me."

He bent his head and pressed his lips to hers. His kiss was soft and Adne could taste his sadness. She wanted to take it away.

Connor broke off their kiss and pulled back to look at Adne's face. His eyes were searching, and Adne knew he was cautious about where to go from here. Guilt stung Adne's heart. His hesitation was her fault. She'd been more and more reticent when it came to intimacy.

Determined to repair the damage she'd done, Adne ran her fingertips over Connor's collarbone, then down his chest and stomach. When she slipped her hand beneath the waistband of his pants, she murmured, "I think you should carry me to the bed now."

"Is that what you think?" Connor gave her a teasing smile, but his voice had grown hoarse.

Adne nodded.

How had she never noticed the softness of these sheets?

Adne would have sworn the bed linens were simple cotton; tonight they felt like silk on her skin. But the slide of the sheets over her body was nothing compared to touch of her lover's hands.

He placed his palm against her abdomen gently, but even so, Adne was aware of his immense strength. She felt an unfamiliar flutter deep within her.

"He is well," her lover's voice rumbled, low and rich with pleasure.

Though cocooned by happiness, Adne couldn't help but feel something was wrong. Her lover's voice, though familiar, wasn't what she'd expected it to be.

Or was it?

She knew him. Knew his touch.

Did she?

"He?" Adne teased. "How can you possibly know?"

The twinge of unease came again. Her own voice sounded off as well. And the words—both hers and his—didn't make sense. What were they speaking of? How could she not remember?

"My love." Adne couldn't see his face, but she could hear that he was smiling. "If I could share my vision with you, I would. But you can trust that I speak the truth. The child is male."

The child? Adne's head was swimming, but she answered in that voice that wasn't her own.

"Are you pleased?"

"You never need ask such a question," he replied. His fingers touched her lips. "Male or female, my blood flows in our child's veins. That blood binds me to this world. It is our legacy."

"Yes," Adne replied. She didn't understand. What legacy?

Her lover bent over her. She felt the warmth of his breath on her cheek. His weight pressed down on her. The sensation set fire to her veins and Adne was overwhelmed by need.

She wanted to tell him. To say his name.

But she couldn't remember it.

How was that possible?

His hands were tracing the shape of her body.

Why couldn't she remember?

His lips touched her ear. "You are mine."

"Yes," Adne said again.

Who are you?

His hand cupped her cheek, turning her face. Adne parted her lips, anticipating his kiss.

Then a much more terrible question filled her mind.

Who am I?

His mouth covered hers and Adne couldn't breathe. The desire heating her limbs fled, chased away by a cold hollowing of her bones.

With the little air left in her lungs, Adne screamed.

"Adne! Adne!" Connor gripped her shoulders.

Adne flailed, trying to free herself. She could still feel the other man's weight, taste his breath.

"Adne, please!" Connor's voice was on the edge of breaking. "You're going to hurt yourself."

His voice still whispered to her, tempting her.

Remember me.

Amid her violent struggle, the sound of Connor's voice reached Adne, breaking through the mesmerizing tones of the stranger's words.

That voice. She knew that voice.

Adne went limp in Connor's arms.

"I'm Ariadne," she whispered.

"What did you say?" Connor gathered her slumped body against his chest.

The fog of the dream began to melt away and Adne saw Connor clearly. The horror in his eyes made her chest cramp.

"I—" She looked away from him. "It was nothing. A dream."

"That wasn't nothing, Adne," Connor said. "I thought you were having a seizure."

"It was a nightmare." Adne groped for a lie. "I dreamt I was drowning. It was horrible, but it wasn't real. I'm okay now."

Connor didn't answer. He held her tight and Adne could feel the rapid beating of his heart.

"I'm sorry I scared you," Adne said. She hesitated for a minute. "Maybe I should go."

Connor tensed. "Is that what you want?"

"When was the last time you got a decent night of sleep?" Adne asked. "I'm pretty sure I'm making you miserable."

"You could never do that," Connor replied, but he sounded pretty miserable.

"Look." Adne wriggled out of Connor's arms and off the bed. "I'm not going to be able to sleep for a while anyway. Not after that dream. But there's no reason for my nightmare to keep us both awake."

Connor watched as Adne donned a robe.

"If you're not going to sleep, where are you going?" His face was drawn.

Adne shrugged. "Maybe to the kitchen. To make some tea."

She could tell that Connor knew she was lying, but he didn't press her for the truth. Maybe he was afraid of what she'd say. She was.

Adne walked back to the bed and brushed a kiss across Connor's cheek. "Get some rest. I'm sorry I kept you up."

"Adne—" Connor grasped her wrist.

"Don't touch me!" Adne jerked her arm free with much more force than she intended.

Connor stared at her, disbelief washing over his features.

"I didn't mean . . . ," Adne began, but she couldn't find any words sufficient to finish.

Hating herself for it but equally desperate to get away, Adne turned and hurried out of Connor's room.

When she was in the hall, she began to run. It wasn't Connor she wanted to flee from. It was the voice that had been whispering ever since she'd woken. Quiet but insistent, it spoke whenever she looked at Connor.

He's not the one you belong to.

Adne reached her room and flung the door open only to find that in her absence someone else had taken up residence. The woman, who was on her hands and knees, picking through the items in a wooden box, shrieked in surprise when Adne burst into the room.

"Sarah?" Adne stared at Sarah Doran in shock. "What are you doing here?"

Sarah paled, her eyes full of panic. She looked at the open box and then at Adne.

"Please, I have to . . ." Sarah closed the box and held it to her chest. "I don't have a choice."

Sarah's eyes cast wildly about the room, reminding Adne of a terrified animal caught in a snare.

Keeping her voice calm, Adne approached Sarah slowly. "Just tell me what's going on. I'd like to help."

Sarah laughed and it was an unnerving sound, tinged with desperation. Adne wouldn't have been at all surprised if Sarah had suddenly attacked her. Then Adne recognized the wooden box Sarah clung to.

"Sarah," Adne said slowly, "when you were looking through that box, did you find what you needed?"

The woman's eyes narrowed as if she suspected Adne was trying to trick her.

Adne walked over to the bedside table and opened its drawer. She withdrew the pendant, holding it up for Sarah to see. "I wear this sometimes," Adne said. "So I don't keep it in the box."

"Please." Sarah scrambled to her feet. "Please give it to me."

"Tell me why you need these things," Adne said.

Shaking her head, Sarah whispered, "I can't say. But you must give it to me."

"You can say, if you truly want this." Adne dropped the pendant into her palm and closed her fist around it, hiding it from view. "I'll make it easier for you. You're taking the box to Logan Bane, aren't you?"

Sarah gave a little gasp.

Adne walked over to Sarah. "Have you made arrangements to meet him somewhere?"

"Yes."

"I'm not going to betray you." Adne took Sarah's hand and laid the necklace in her open palm. "I won't tell anyone about this, but I need you to do something for me."

Sarah's hands were trembling. "What?"

"You're going to take me with you."

"I can't do that," Sarah said.

"Yes, you can." Adne folded her arms across her chest. "And you will. Or you're not leaving the Academy."

"Don't think I won't fight you." Sarah tensed, as if anticipating an attack.

"I'm sure you would," Adne said. "But that's not what I want. I need to talk to Logan. You know where he is, or at least where he's going to be. I'm not going to interfere with whatever your business with Logan is. I have business of my own."

Sarah's gaze searched Adne's expression, seeking some means of escape. Finding none, Sarah nodded in resignation.

"Where are you meeting him?" Adne asked, trying not to show how relieved she was that convincing Sarah to take her along hadn't been harder. It wasn't terribly difficult to see why Sarah had conceded so soon. Beneath her veneer of strength, Adne could glimpse how broken the woman was. Sarah Doran had very little fight left and Adne guessed she was being driven mostly by desperation.

We're not so different.

"A town house in Boston," Sarah told Adne. "I have an address."

"Boston?" Adne frowned. "And how are you planning to get there?"

"I hadn't decided—" Sarah lifted her chin, defiant despite the glaring flaw in her plan. Or the lack of a plan altogether.

Desperate. We're both desperate.

"Well." Adne smiled sadly. "I guess it's a good thing I'm a Weaver."

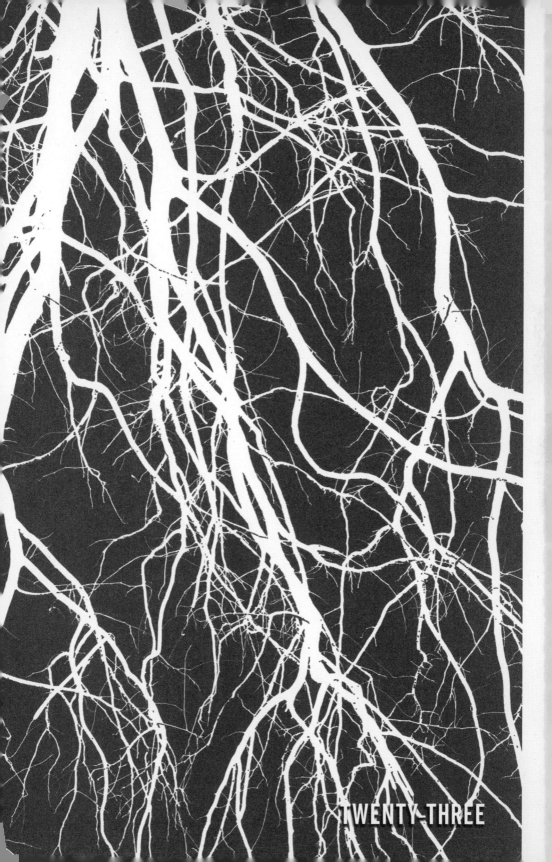

TWENTY-THREE

SABINE FELT AS though she were in the middle of a demented game of hide-and-seek that had gone on for far too long. She couldn't find Adne anywhere and she'd been looking for hours.

When Adne hadn't shown up to guide the tour she'd been assigned, Sabine had simply stepped in and taken over. But given their misadventure the previous day at Haldis, and what Sabine had subsequently learned from Ethan about Adne's bizarre behavior at the training session, Sabine thought it best to find Adne and make sure she was okay.

But Adne seemed to have vanished. Connor grudgingly admitted that Adne had left his bed in the middle of the night and hadn't returned. The Striker was in as sour a mood as Sabine had ever seen. Whether he was smarting from Adne's rejection or the debacle of the mission, which Ethan had also relayed to Sabine, Connor proved less than helpful in Sabine's search.

After hunting through the Academy and asking all of Adne's acquaintances if they'd seen her, Sabine came up with nothing. She even returned to Rowan Estate on the off chance that Adne had somehow ended up at the mansion or in the gardens. But Adne hadn't made an appearance at the Keeper estate since Sabine had left earlier in the day.

Though Sabine wondered if she should just let it be, as a sullen

Connor had suggested in a much less pleasant fashion, she felt somewhat responsible for Adne. Not knowing what else to do, Sabine finally went in search of Anika, despite the fact that the hour crept close to midnight. She'd considered going to Tess, but Sabine had a nagging feeling that Adne's disappearance was a sign of things to come. Very bad things that Anika would need to know about.

When Sabine knocked on the Arrow's door, apology ready to be delivered before her request for help, Anika answered not cross nor groggy-eyed from being woken, but fully dressed and alert.

"It's not a good time, Sabine," Anika said.

"I know," Sabine replied. "But something's happened and I need your help. I think."

"You think?" Anika frowned.

A movement behind the Arrow caught Sabine's eye. Anika wasn't alone.

"I mean, I know I need your help," Sabine said quickly, "but I don't know what the protocol is when it comes to a missing Searcher."

"Missing?" Anika's brow knit together. "You'd better come in."

Sabine entered the Arrow's quarters and Anika closed the door. Without Anika obscuring her view, Sabine was surprised to discover that the second person in the room was Tristan Doran.

"Sabine." Anika was still frowning. "How did you come to know that Sarah Doran is missing?"

"Sarah is missing?" Sabine shook her head in surprise. "I didn't know that. I'm here because I can't find Adne. No one seems to know where she is."

"Adne is missing?" Anika rocked back on her heels. "Are you sure?"

Sabine nodded. "I'm sure."

"Do you think that Sarah and Adne could be missing for the same reason?" Anika asked Tristan.

"I don't know," Tristan said. The man's face was haggard. He looked worse than Connor had.

"Do you have any idea where Sarah went?" Sabine asked him.

"She left a note." Tristan opened his palm to reveal a crumpled piece of paper. "It's not particularly helpful."

Sabine took the note from Tristan and smoothed it open.

I had to try. Please forgive me.

"'I had to try'?" Sabine murmured, mostly to herself, but Tristan sighed.

"I have a few guesses," Tristan said. "None of them are comforting."

Sabine nodded. She could guess too. Sarah Doran hadn't been reluctant to broadcast her hopes for bringing Shay back from his life as a wolf. But how she thought she might accomplish such a thing was difficult to say.

"You don't think she'd go up onto the mountain and try to snare him?" Sabine asked.

"I think that might be a best-case scenario," Anika replied. "I sent a team up to Haldis to see if that's what happened, but Sarah isn't ignorant—she knows how Shay's transformation occurred. If she wanted to undo what's been done, she'll pursue specific channels."

"Magic," Sabine said quietly.

Anika nodded and Tristan's jaw clenched.

"But it's not possible," Sabine continued. "Right? Bringing Shay back is not something Sarah could actually do."

"No," Tristan said. "She can't. But she won't accept it. I've tried to convince her so many times to let it go. I tried."

Anika put her hand on Tristan's shoulder. "We both tried."

"Sorry for being behind the curve," Sabine said. "But if there's no way for Sarah to bring Shay back, then what are you worried she's doing?"

"It's the 'trying' that presents a danger," Anika told Sabine. "Sarah has been spending a lot of time at Rowan Estate."

"I know." Sabine nodded. "I've seen her there."

"We're worried she may have taken some books from the

library," Anika said. "The collections at Rowan Estate skewed heavily toward the occult."

"Sarah can't bring our son back," Tristan said quietly. "But if she uses certain spells to try, even in vain, there could be terrible ramifications."

"But the Rift is closed," Sabine said, more to comfort herself than to argue with Tristan. "Doesn't that kind of mitigate the damage any Keeper spells can do?"

"To the world, yes," Anika answered. "In cases like this, harm doesn't usually extend beyond the caster."

"Oh," Sabine said, feeling foolish. Of course they were trying to protect Sarah from herself. "But maybe that's the connection between Adne and Sarah. What if Adne went along to try to keep Sarah safe?"

"And how would a young Weaver manage that?" There was more spite in Tristan's question than Sabine liked, but she let it go.

"You don't know Adne," Sabine told him. "She's a force to be reckoned with."

"Sabine's telling the truth," Anika agreed. "Adne's an exceptional young woman. But as much as it's comforting to imagine that Sarah's not alone, I'm not certain they're together. Are you aware of any relationship having developed between them?"

"No," Sabine admitted. Adne hadn't talked about Sarah Doran, but then Adne hadn't been inclined to talk much about anything lately.

"For now I think we have to treat the two cases as distinct," Anika told her. "Thank you for bringing Adne's absence to my attention. I'll assign a team to pursue the matter."

Realizing she'd just been dismissed, Sabine nodded and showed herself out of the room. No sooner had she opened the door than Sabine ducked to avoid being struck in the face by a red-faced Striker, who'd been about to knock on the door.

"Watch where you're throwing those fists, friend," Sabine grumbled, pushing past him into the hall.

The Striker ignored her. "I need the Arrow. The Arrow! Is she here?"

Anika was already at the door. "What is it, Mackie?"

"It's Holt, ma'am," Mackie blurted. "He's called an assembly."

"What?" Anika frowned at him. "When?"

"Now!" Mackie told her. "Right now. In the dining hall."

"Damn that man." Anika called over her shoulder, "Tristan! You'd better come with me."

The halls of the Roving Academy were filled with Searchers, flowing as if they were being carried by a current: Strikers, Weavers, Scribes, Elixirs, all streaming toward the dining hall. When Anika, Tristan, Mackie, and Sabine reached the crowded room, they had to push their way through the mass of bodies.

Above the gathered Searchers stood Holt, who had climbed atop a table and was exhorting the crowd.

"See for yourself what they've done," Holt shouted. "The Arrow claims their crimes are all in the past, but I tell you the Keepers have always been and will always be murderers."

A buzz of voices, some agreeing and others disapproving, filled the air.

"They are twisted and evil," Holt continued. "They must be purged from this world. I will not tolerate these horrors, my brothers and sisters." Holt crouched down and gathered something that had been lying at his feet into his arms. He stood again. "Will you?"

"What the—" Sabine stared at Holt in disbelief. He was holding the body of a young woman. That she was dead was obvious. But it was worse than that. Her throat had been cut, sliced so deeply that her neck tipped back, opening like a lid to reveal her spine.

"Who is that?" Sabine whispered to Anika. The Arrow stood beside her, grim faced.

"A Keeper," Anika replied. "We found her at the house where Logan Bane had taken refuge."

"And Holt brought her body back." Sabine shuddered. "But why?"

"For this," Tristan muttered.

Holt scanned the crowd. When his gaze fell on Anika, a smile flitted ever so briefly across his mouth. He turned the corpse toward the Arrow. The girl's lifeless eyes stared out over the amassed Searchers.

"Can you answer for this injustice, Anika?" Holt called to her. "Or will you continue to make apologies for those we've sworn to fight?"

"I don't answer to you, Holt," Anika shouted over the murmurs of uncertainty that swept through the room.

Holt bowed his head and made a show of gently laying the dead girl on the table in a solemn repose. When he rose again, he swept his hand in a broad arc.

"Who do you answer to, Anika?"

Anika remained silent and Holt turned his question to the crowd.

"Who does the Arrow answer to?"

Tristan took Anika by the arm, pulling her closer to him as though he thought he might have to shield her with his body. "You can't stay here. It's not safe. I don't know what Holt's after, but I wouldn't put it past him to send someone after you."

Stricken by Tristan's words, Anika didn't resist as he pushed his way back out of the increasingly riled crowd, taking her with him. Sabine tried to follow, but the mass of Searchers suddenly surged forward. Holt was shouting, but Sabine couldn't make out his words beyond the roar of so many voices. She stumbled and fell to the floor.

A booted foot connected with Sabine's stomach, knocking her breath away.

Someone's knee slammed into the side of her head and dark spots appeared in Sabine's vision. She grabbed at a Searcher's hand, trying to pull herself up, but a sudden kick sent a spear of pain through Sabine's back. Sabine hit the floor and rolled over, curling into a ball as the sea of bodies swallowed her whole.

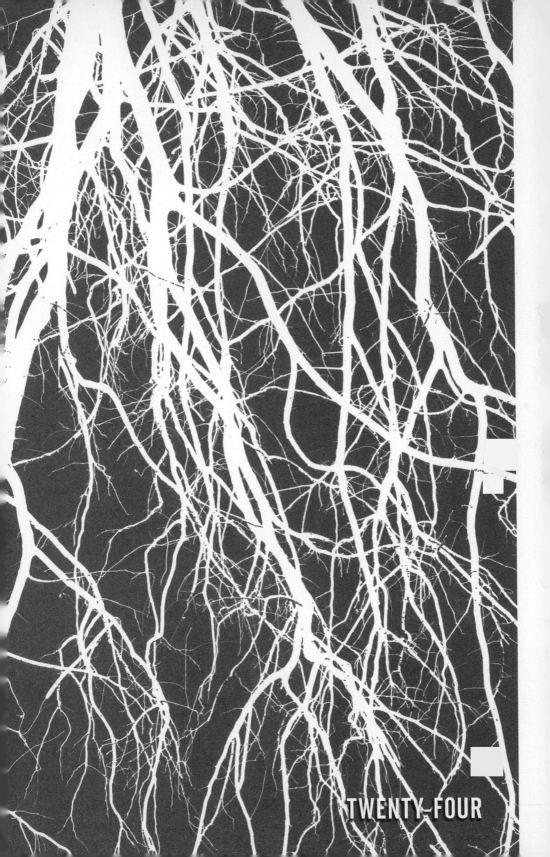

TWENTY-FOUR

REN WASN'T CERTAIN how or when it would be possible, but he knew that he *would* kill Logan. Someday, he would break the arrogant Keeper's neck and the world would be better for it.

"You aren't happy." Logan offered Ren a placid smile.

"Should I be?" Ren snarled.

"It may not be the most ideal situation," Logan replied. "But think of it this way. You could be a restless spirit wandering the earth aimlessly. I'm giving you purpose. You should be grateful."

"I'll keep that in mind," Ren said. "And think of a way to repay you."

Chase, who was sitting beside Logan on the Rococo settee, flinched at Ren's tone, but Logan laughed.

"I know this collar is chafing you, Renier," Logan told him. "But given time, I think you'll find obedience has greater rewards than rebellion. That's a lesson I've had to learn myself. And given the circumstances of your own untimely death, I'd think you'd be inclined to accept the truth of it as well."

Slightly chastened by the sting of Logan's words, Ren fell silent.

"They're late," Chase said, looking at his Rolex for the tenth time in the past five minutes.

"They aren't late," Logan said. "They can't be late when we appointed a day for this meeting and not a specific time."

"I hate waiting," Chase complained. "It makes me anxious."

"That's obvious." Logan glanced irritably at the other Keeper. "If you can't stop fidgeting, then pour yourself a drink. And get me one while you're at it."

Chase jumped up and went to the bar.

When Ren heard the clink of ice cubes, he asked Logan, "Since you have someone to fetch you cocktails and I can't lift a glass or anything else, why the hell am I here?"

"For effect," Logan answered. "The presence of a ghost adds atmosphere. And Sarah knows you. You remind her of Shay. Of why she wants to help us."

"You," Ren said sharply. "Help *you*. There is no *us*."

Logan shrugged.

The doorbell rang and Chase dashed from the room. "I'll get it."

Throwing a longing glance at the abandoned glasses on the bar, Logan sighed. "It really would be a plus if you could fix cocktails, wouldn't it?"

Ren ignored him.

Chase came hurtling back into the sitting room. "She's not alone."

Logan was on his feet, and the alarmed expression on the Keeper's face gave Ren a twinge of satisfaction. "What do you mean she's not alone?"

As if in answer to Logan's question, two women appeared at the room's entrance.

"Sorry to crash the party." Adne stood beside Sarah Doran. "But I think you have room for one more."

Logan's eyes widened briefly, but he quickly recovered and relaxed back onto the settee. "Ariadne. What a pleasant surprise."

"Really?" Adne lifted her eyebrows. "I didn't think we were on the best of terms, Logan."

"Bygones." Logan waved his hand, then gestured to Chase. "My associate, Chase Roth. And of course, this one needs no introduction, does he?" Logan nodded to Ren.

Adne's attention had been focused solely on Logan, but now she was staring at Ren. Her hands became fists.

Ren couldn't speak or move. Though he knew his body had no substance, he felt as if he were made of stone.

"This is a trick." Adne's voice was brittle.

"Strange as it may seem, Ariadne," Logan said, "I'd like to be in your good graces. So no tricks." Logan glanced at Ren. "Aren't you going to greet your sister?"

"Hey, Adne," Ren said, at last finding his voice.

Giving a little cry, Adne rushed forward and flung her arms around her brother, only she grasped nothing.

"Sorry." Ren smiled sadly.

Adne took a step back, staring at him. "Are you a ghost?"

"Spirit," Logan interjected. "But let's not bother with all those details now. You're happy to see your brother, aren't you, Ariadne?"

"Go to hell." Adne glared at Logan.

"I'll take that as a yes," Logan replied smoothly. "His death was such a tragedy, wasn't it? It's a shame the way things turned out. Brother and sister reunited for so brief a time. Wouldn't you like a second chance to know Renier?"

Adne stiffened. Her gaze moved to Sarah Doran, who was still hovering quietly at the edge of the room.

"You're making a lot of promises, Logan," Adne said. "First you say you'll give a mother her son back, and now you're offering me my brother?"

"These aren't *my* offers," Logan replied with a smile. "You know very well I don't have that kind of power. I didn't even have that kind of power *before* the Rift was closed."

Sarah drew a hissing breath. "You said you could bring him back."

Logan shook his head. "Don't fret, dear Searcher. I didn't say anything of the sort. I sent Renier to ask if you wanted to have your son back. That is all."

Suddenly there was a dagger in Sarah's hand. "I will cut your heart out, Keeper."

"Such hysterics!" Logan stood up and went to collect his drink. "Put that blade away. There's no need to jump to conclusions. I'm simply attempting to clarify this situation. Will you do me the kindness of listening? You've come all this way."

Sarah didn't sheath her dagger, but she lowered it.

Logan pursed his lips, but nodded. "I guess that will suffice." Returning to his seat, Logan gestured to the other chairs in the room. "Please make yourselves comfortable."

When neither Sarah nor Adne moved, Logan sighed. "You're making this much more unpleasant than it need be."

"Just talk, Logan," Ren growled at the Keeper. Adne gave her brother a little smile.

"Don't encourage him," Logan said. "Chase, will you get our guests whatever refreshments they'd like?"

"This isn't a social call." Adne's irritation was beginning to show. "Stop grandstanding and tell us what you want."

Ren regarded Adne with admiration. His sister's mettle remained impressive as ever. It was nice to see Logan taken down a peg.

"If you insist." Logan shrugged. "Sarah has something for me, I believe."

Sarah and Adne exchanged a glance, and Adne gave a brief nod. Sarah crossed the room and deposited a satchel on the settee next to Logan.

"Thank you." Logan swirled his drink and took a sip. "That's one thing. And much to my delight, the second thing I wanted arrived today as well. Rather unexpectedly."

"And what's that?" Adne asked.

"Why, Ariadne, I'm surprised at your lack of comprehension." Logan smiled at her. "You really haven't figured it out?"

"I'm sorry to disappoint you," Adne replied blandly. "What's the second thing you wanted?"

Logan set his glass down and folded his arms behind his head, lounging against the back of the settee. "You."

Ren shifted into wolf form, snarling at Logan.

"Ferocious," Logan remarked.

Adne's steely confidence wavered slightly. "What do you mean, me?"

"Someone wants to see you and it was left to me to make the arrangements," Logan said. "You've just made my task that much easier."

"I only came here to find out what you're up to." Adne shook her head. "And to put a stop to it. I'm not a fan of nightmares and I'm pretty sure you're the reason I can't sleep at night."

Logan tilted his head, eyeing her. "What is it that you've been dreaming about? Or should I be asking, who are you dreaming about?"

"As if I would tell you," Adne said, but she blanched.

Ren growled again; he hated where this conversation was headed. He hated even more that he could do nothing to stop it.

"If you don't want to name names, far be it from me to force the issues. But we will need to take a little trip," Logan told her. "Well, *little* perhaps isn't the most precise term."

"Wait," Sarah interjected. Ren saw that she had put her dagger away now, but her expression was a mixture of grief and confusion. "What about Shay?"

Logan nodded. "I haven't forgotten, Sarah. I know that I owe you for recovering these items." He patted the satchel. "But what I said to Ariadne is true. I don't have the kind of power it takes to bring Shay back. No one on this earth does."

"But—"

"I said no one on this earth does," Logan cut her off. "But there is one not of this earth who can give you what you want."

Ren gave up trying to menace Logan and went to Adne's side when he saw that her skin had gone ashen.

Her eyes were closed tight, but Adne said, "He's gone. He's gone and he cannot return."

Logan frowned at Adne. "Are you afraid, Ariadne? You shouldn't be. He needs you."

"Stop," Adne whispered.

Ren shifted forms and glared at Logan. "Leave her alone."

"Don't interfere," Logan said. "In this matter I'm like you, Renier, the intercessor. Your sister has an important role to play. She just has to accept the part."

Adne was shaking her head. A tear slipped from beneath her eyelid.

A subtle change suffused the room. Though it had been a bright day in Boston, the lingering light of the sunset was abruptly snuffed out.

Logan stood up. "He needs to see you, Ariadne."

A column of shadow formed alongside Logan. At first Ren thought it was a wraith, but its shape became more distinct. The silhouette of a tall man stood facing Adne. His features were indistinct, but when he spoke, the voice was unmistakable.

"Ariadne."

The sound of Bosque Mar speaking his sister's name made Ren growl, but no one paid him any attention.

"You don't have to fail," Bosque whispered to Adne.

"Fail?" Adne repeated. She kept her eyes closed, and Ren sensed that she didn't trust herself to stay in control of her mind and body if she looked at Bosque—even in this shadow form.

"What your father asked you to do," Bosque continued. He ignored everyone in the room but Adne.

"No," Adne's voice rasped with uncertainty.

"Yes," Bosque replied. "Tell me. What did your father want? What was the only task he bid you complete so his sacrifice was not an empty gesture?"

Ren flinched. Bosque was talking about Monroe, who wasn't just Adne's father. He was Ren's as well.

"His sacrifice." Adne's hands had begun to shake.

Tendrils of smoke in the shape of large hands stretched toward Adne, enveloping her wrists.

"Tell me, Ariadne."

"I was supposed to save him," Adne whispered. "I was supposed to save Ren. But I didn't."

It's not your fault, Adne. None of this was your fault. Ren was desperate to stop this, to break through Bosque's manipulation, but whatever hold the Harbinger had over Ren prevented him from speaking.

"Will you deny my call, Ariadne?" Bosque Mar's words echoed as if spoken in a vast, empty chamber. "Will you rebuke me when I offer you a chance at redemption?"

Adne didn't reply. Her whole body trembled.

"I can give you a family again," Bosque continued. "Your brother will be restored."

"No!"

It wasn't Adne who shouted at the shadow figure, but Sarah. She looked like a person who'd just woken from a long, exhausting dream and saw the real world again. She stared at Bosque's astral form in utter horror.

At Sarah's cry, Adne's eyes flew open, pulling her out of the trance she'd been captured in since Bosque's arrival.

"Ariadne, don't listen to him. Fight back." Sarah began to move toward Adne. "This is a terrible mistake. We never should have come."

"You disappoint me, Sarah," Bosque said. Beneath the smooth

timbre of his voice, irritation crackled. "I thought you loved your son."

"My son was born to expel you from this world." Sarah's voice shook. "I let myself forget who you are. And I'm glad Shay will never know how close I came to betraying him and everything I've ever fought for."

"You are as foolish as you have always been." Bosque's silhouette crumpled into a dense ball of shadow that hurtled across the room, hitting Sarah full in the chest.

Sarah cried out and dropped to the floor, unmoving.

"Sarah!" Adne rushed to the fallen Searcher's side. She rested the side of her face on Sarah's chest. "She's still breathing."

"Not for long." Logan walked toward the women with purpose.

Adne jumped up, barring his path to Sarah. "I won't let you do this."

Now that Bosque's spirit—or whatever that shadow had been— was gone, Ren was relieved to see that Adne seemed to have recovered her strength. She faced off with Logan, defiant.

Logan smiled at her. "Are you going to kill me, Ariadne? I'm sure you want to, but I don't think you will. You still have too many questions."

"Maybe I do," Adne said. "But as much as I need answers, you need my cooperation."

"I'm listening."

"Let her live," Adne said to Logan, "and I'll go with you. I won't put up a fight. Wherever Bosque has told you to take me, I'll go."

No. The word was burning in Ren's chest, but he couldn't shout it the way he wanted to. He couldn't stop her.

"We're bargaining now, are we?" Logan steepled his fingertips in front of his face. "From where I'm standing, I think I'm the one holding all the cards."

"If you really think that, then you'll have no trouble stopping me when I take Sarah and go," Adne replied.

Logan's hands dropped to his side.

"Somehow you've been talking with Bosque Mar," Adne continued. "And I'm sure you can manage some petty magic, but your real power is gone. You can't summon a wraith to fight for you. Do you really think you can take me on your own?"

Logan stole a glance at Chase, whose eyes bulged as he nearly dropped his glass, and Adne laughed.

"Strength in numbers only works when there's actual strength to back it up."

"Fine." Logan shoved his hands in his trouser pockets. "I'll get an ambulance to take Sarah to the hospital, where she can be cared for."

Adne shook her head. "She was just impaled by a plume of black smoke. There's not a mark on her. How will a hospital help her? She needs to be treated at the Academy."

"So you're just going to run home and then come right back?" Logan snorted. "With an army of Searchers, no doubt."

"No," Adne replied. "I'll open a door to my room and leave Sarah there. And I'll come back alone—with one condition."

"What's that?" Logan asked.

"I have to be sure Sarah gets help," Adne said. "I can't leave her without telling someone where she is."

"How wonderful that I'm beholden to the whims of a lunatic." Logan glared at her. "You are not telling anyone about this."

"You're right," Adne said. "I can't tell anyone. I'd never make it back here." She looked at Ren. "But he can."

"What?" Ren frowned at his sister.

After giving Ren a brief, sad smile, Adne said to Logan, "I'm right, aren't I? You can tell Ren where to go and who to talk to."

Logan nodded.

"Then send him to Tristan," Adne said. "You can wait until I'm here with you and I've closed the door to the Academy."

"At which point you'll hand over the tools of your trade." Logan gestured to the gleaming skeins that hung from Adne's belt.

Adne shrugged. "If it makes you feel better."

Ren remained silent, muzzled as he was, and watched and listened as Adne and Logan reached an agreement. He watched as Adne wove a door made of light and witnessed his sister and Chase carry Sarah's limp form through the passage. When they reappeared, Adne closed the portal and surrendered her skeins to Logan.

Ren saw all of this. And there was nothing he could do.

Nothing.

Except remind himself that one day soon he would find a way to free himself and then he would kill Logan Bane.

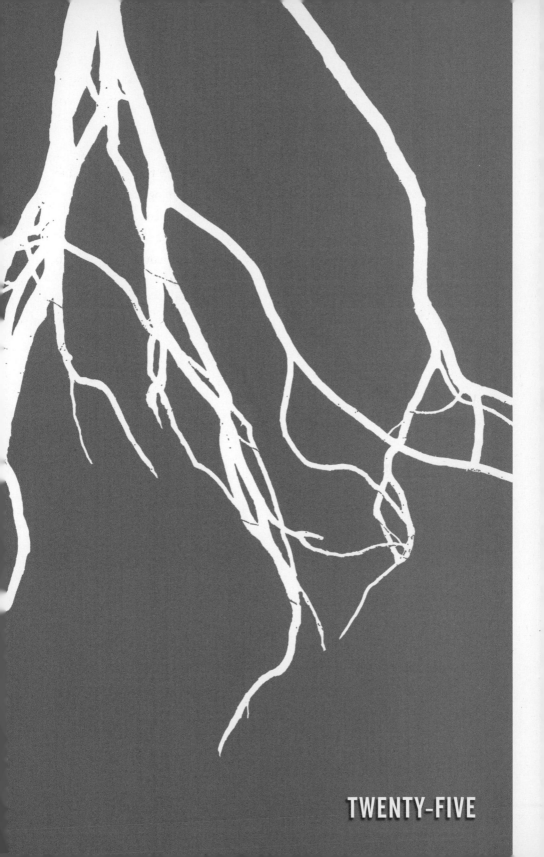

TWENTY-FIVE

THE SCENE IN THE dining hall went from bad to worse as Connor and Ethan watched Tristan grab Anika and shield her with his body. Connor couldn't remember any gathering of Searchers he'd witnessed devolving into nothing more than shouts and accusations, and he didn't even know who was yelling insults at whom, but he was pretty sure that he was hearing curses in at least a dozen languages.

"Good man," Connor muttered to himself when he saw Tristan forcing his way through the press of bodies to get Anika clear of the scene.

He'd made up his mind to follow them. Connor didn't need to hear any more of Holt's grandstanding, but Ethan swore loudly, and when Connor turned, he saw the other Searcher shoving his way further into the room.

Connor surged after his friend. "Where you are going?" he shouted over the din.

For a second Connor thought Ethan had gotten fed up enough to storm to the stage and drag Holt off it. An ill-advised move for sure, but at least it would be fun.

"Sabine went down," Ethan called over his shoulder while pointing at the mob ahead. "These fools will trample her."

Grimly, Connor and Ethan pushed forward, throwing elbows and shoving bodies hard. Like he had been the night before, Connor was filled with shame and disgust in the face of his comrades' behavior.

How could this be happening in the Academy? What the hell has happened to us? We're supposed to be the good guys.

Connor felt as though he was surrounded by strangers, enemies even. Confirming his worst fears, the crowd began to shove back against Ethan and Connor.

What had been annoyed grunts and sour looks became threats. Connor didn't see who threw the first punch. It might have even been Ethan, pushed past the brink of frustration in his effort to reach Sabine. But what had been a surly crowd took no more than a couple of minutes to devolve into a brawl.

For his part, Connor tried not to break any noses or jaws. He still believed that most of the Searchers shared his mindset and had been drawn into this chaos from sheer confusion, lashing out at a threat they couldn't understand.

Connor groaned when someone socked him in the gut. His own fist landed solidly in the middle of another man's chest, sending the attacker reeling back.

"Damn it!" Ethan was trying to knock his assailants aside and keep moving forward, but the fight had turned the crowd into a veritable wall of bodies.

Lowering his shoulder, Connor lunged forward and plowed past Ethan. They rushed through an opening that immediately closed up behind them. Confusion worked to their advantage as the fighting continued at their backs, but no one pursued them. It was obvious that violence was happening for its own sake and no other reason.

"I can't find her," Ethan shouted, wild-eyed. "She should be here. This is where she fell."

A sick feeling seized Connor as he searched for any signs of the girl and saw blood on the floor.

"Sabine!" Ethan turned in a circle, bellowing. "Sabine!"

"Ethan!"

Both men turned toward the sound of Ethan's name. It wasn't Sabine calling to them, but Tess. She was at the edge of the crowd, moving toward the rear of the hall. Shiloh was beside her and he had a body slung over his shoulder.

"Oh God." Ethan threaded through the crowd. When Tess saw them coming, she nodded and then continued with Shiloh to exit the room.

Connor tried not to hit anyone on his way out. Angry as he might be, leaving was more important than throwing a few more punches for good measure. Besides, the only person he really wanted to deck was standing on top of a table like the fool he was.

Holt would get his eventually. Connor was going to make sure of it.

When Ethan and Connor were free of the crowd, which showed no signs of dispersing, and out of the dining hall, they found Tess, Shiloh, and Sabine waiting for them in the corridor. Sabine was on her feet, and though she sported a nasty bruise on her temple, she seemed otherwise unharmed.

Ethan scooped Sabine up, crushing her in his arms.

"Easy there, tiger," Sabine said. "I think I may be concussed."

"We should take you to Eydis." Ethan set her down gently.

Sabine shook her head. "I'll be fine. Just got knocked around a bit. I don't need an Elixir for this. Though I really miss having Guardian blood right about now."

"What the hell was that?" Connor asked Tess, nodding in the direction of the dining hall.

"Who knows?" Tess frowned. "Holt's up to something, but what he hopes to achieve with a stunt like that is beyond me. He'll gain more enemies than friends. You can't just threaten the Arrow, and that's basically what Holt did."

Connor hoped Tess was right, but he had trouble feeling

confident about much of anything, given the general downward spiral of events lately.

"We should find Anika," Tess told them. "Regroup. She needs to know she's not alone in this."

"Do you know where she is?" Ethan asked.

"My best guess: Tactical," Tess answered. "That's where I go when I need a strategy."

"You don't think she'd go to her room?" Shiloh asked. "It was pretty brutal back there. She might be shaken up."

"I'm sure you're right," Tess said. "But Anika won't want to show any weakness. Her authority is being called into question and as much as that's not pleasant, it will also piss her off. She'll fight back." Tess turned to Shiloh. "Would you mind waiting here and keeping an eye on things? I need to know if there are any new developments."

Shiloh nodded and headed back to the dining hall.

"Come on." Tess waved for the others to follow her.

Ethan leaned down and said something to Sabine that Connor couldn't hear, but it earned Ethan a hard shove.

"You are not going to carry me," Sabine said.

"Shiloh was just carrying you," Ethan objected. "You said yourself that you might be concussed."

"If I fall down, you can carry me," Sabine said. "But until I prove infirm, I will walk on my own two feet."

"Besides," Connor added, noting Ethan's sullen expression, "Shiloh's better looking than you. It's the eyes, man, he's got amazing eyes."

With a wicked smile, Sabine said, "He's also taller than both of you."

"Oh, that's low." Connor laughed.

Sabine tossed her hair and abandoned the Strikers in favor of walking alongside Tess.

"Shiloh is not better looking than me," Ethan grumbled, falling into step with Connor.

"Whatever you need to tell yourself, man." Connor chuckled.

Tess's hunch had been right. Anika had gone straight to Haldis Tactical, and Tristan had stayed with the Arrow. But the third member that had joined their party was a surprise to everyone.

Connor wondered how long Anika and Tristan had been standing there, staring at the wolf who sat calmly in the middle of the room, watching them.

Drawing a dagger, Connor moved to Anika's side. "Want to tell me what's going on?"

"He just appeared . . . ," Anika whispered, her eyes locked on the wolf in disbelief. "No more than a minute ago."

"Oh my God." Sabine didn't hesitate or balk as the rest of them had. She went straight to the wolf, crouching in front of him. "Is it really you?"

The wolf stood up and wagged his tail.

Sabine's voice grew hoarse. "But . . . how?"

"Sabine?" Ethan approached her slowly, wary eyes on the wolf. "You know him?"

The wolf glanced at Ethan in annoyance and shifted into the form of a tall young man.

"You Searchers always sucked at remembering us when we changed shape." Ren waved a hand at his new body. "Does this help?"

"Holy shit," Connor murmured. "You're dead."

"Connor!" Sabine shot a deadly look at him. "Don't be rude."

"Rude?" Connor scoffed. "Can it be rude if it's true?"

"Yeah," Ethan told him. "Not saying rude things that are true is called tact."

"Forgive me for not being up to speed on my ghost etiquette," Connor said.

"I forgot how annoying you are," Ren told Connor, but he was smiling, which made the whole situation that much more unsettling. "And I'm not a ghost, I'm a restless spirit. And don't ask what that means. I'm tired of explaining it. Just deal with the fact that I'm here."

"Ren, what *are* you doing here?" Sabine asked.

"I have a message." Ren's gaze shifted to Tristan. "For him."

Tristan frowned. "But I don't know you."

"I just go where I'm told." Ren shrugged. "That's about all I can do now that I'm like this."

He thrust his hand out and it went straight through Sabine's chest.

"Hey!" Sabine jumped back.

"Yeah, 'hey.'" Ethan hooked his arm around her waist. "What the hell?"

"Just demonstrating my non-corporeality." Ren grinned, enjoying their discomfiture. "Trying to get all the ghost stuff out of the way so we can move on."

"I thought you said you were a spirit," Connor noted.

"Like he said," Anika interrupted, "let's move on." Speaking to Ren, the Arrow said, "You're Monroe's son—Ariadne's brother?"

Ren nodded.

"Do you know that she's missing?" Anika asked him.

"That's why I'm here," Ren told her. "Partly."

"You know where Adne is?" Connor felt the blood drain from his face. He couldn't see a ghost knowing about Adne's disappearance as being good in any way.

The flash of anger in Ren's eyes only confirmed Connor's fears.

"What happened to her?" Connor asked.

"I have to deliver my message first," Ren said. "I'm still working out the rules."

Connor frowned. "What?"

"Just give me a second and I'll explain." Ren looked at Tristan. "Sarah is in Adne's room. She needs help from the Elixirs."

Tristan's fists clenched. "What happened to her?"

Ren paused, as if taking the time to choose an answer. "I'm sorry. I can't say anything specific about that."

Tristan stared at Ren a moment longer, then looked to Anika.

"Go," the Arrow told him. "We'll figure this out."

Tristan ran from the room.

"Tess, go to Eydis and send an Elixir to meet Tristan in Adne's room."

Tess nodded, offering Ren an uncertain but kind smile before she left.

Ren glanced around at their worried faces. "I think Sarah will be okay. She hasn't been here very long . . . waiting for help."

"Why are you talking like this, Ren?" Sabine asked. "Everything you say is full of holes. Why are there so many missing pieces?"

"I'm not here by choice," Ren answered. "I have very limited agency in this plane, or so I've discovered. I'm kind of like a puppet and someone else is pulling the strings."

"But is it really you?" Sabine regarded Ren with new suspicion.

"Yes," Ren sighed. "It's me—censored."

"Okay." Ethan nodded. "Can you tell us who's censoring you?"

Ren hesitated, then said, "Logan." He looked surprised when he said the name.

"Logan Bane?" Anika's eyes narrow. "That's troubling."

"Damn it." Connor raked a hand through his hair. "We almost had him at Montauk."

Ethan asked Ren, "Do you know where Logan is now?"

Ren nodded.

"And can you tell us?" Ethan added when Ren didn't offer up the information.

"I already would have if I could."

"Ren." A chill crawled up Connor's spine. "Is Adne with Logan?"

"Yes." The sadness in Ren's voice made Connor feel even colder.

"What does he want with her?" Connor asked.

Ren just shook his head.

"I think an equally important question is, why did Adne go to Logan?" Anika said quietly.

"What are you talking about?" Connor bristled.

"We have to consider the facts at hand, Connor," Anika told him. "The likelihood that Logan could abduct Ariadne or take her anywhere against her will is very, very slim."

Connor shook his head. "Adne wouldn't go to Logan."

"She did." Ren gazed steadily at Connor. Connor could see the wolf's dark eyes were full of unspoken answers.

"Why?" Connor heard his voice was on the verge of breaking. He looked away from Adne's brother, overwhelmed by a sense of loss as he confronted Monroe's dead son and the horror of his missing daughter. It was too much.

"Sarah." Ren said her name and nothing more.

"What?" Ethan gave Ren a quizzical look, but Sabine was nodding.

"He can't tell us," Sabine said. "Because Logan's got him muzzled."

Ren growled at the word, and she offered him an apologetic smile.

"But Sarah was there too," Sabine continued, watching as Ren nodded to confirm her words. "And Sarah knows what happened. She has the answers."

"Okay, fine," Connor said, his head aching with the runaround of this interrogation. "Just tell me one thing: is Adne okay?"

But there was no one to answer. Without warning, Ren had gone.

TWENTY-SIX

SARAH WOKE TO a strange weight, solid, heavy, and emanating warmth, on her breastbone. She glanced down and saw a bloodred stone resting on her bare skin just above a sheet that was folded over to preserve her modesty.

Sarah started to reach for the stone, but someone caught her hand. A woman in a cowled pale blue robe that marked her as an Elixir from Eydis smiled kindly.

"The stone hasn't drawn all of the curse from you yet. Give it more time."

"Sarah?" Tristan appeared beside the Elixir. "How are you feeling?"

Feeling more confused than anything else, Sarah wasn't certain how to answer. She glanced around, puzzled.

"Where am I?"

"I'll give you some privacy," the Elixir said to Tristan, and quietly left the room.

"Ariadne's room," Tristan said quietly. "Do you remember how you got here?"

Sarah shook her head. In her groggy state, she felt the echoes of fear and pain, but she wasn't sure why.

Taking her hand, Tristan asked carefully, "Do you remember what happened before you lost consciousness?"

As sleep cleared away, memories took shape in Sarah's mind. Horrible memories. Sarah closed her eyes, wishing that she'd just woken from an awful dream but knowing she had not.

"Oh, Tristan," Sarah whispered, gripping his fingers tight. "I'm so sorry."

Sarah opened her eyes and looked up at him, finding only love in his gaze. Love she didn't deserve after what she'd done. From the day the wall separating Sarah from this world and from her son was shattered, she'd been blind to anything but the hope of bringing Shay back. But that single-minded focus had taken her down a path so wrong, she could hardly face the choices she'd made. And she hadn't even begun to deal with their consequences.

"Whatever happened, it's over now," Tristan said, brushing Sarah's hair back from her forehead.

It's not over. It's just begun.

The door opened and Sarah recognized Anika's voice.

"I was told she's awake."

Tristan answered, "She is."

Sarah wished she could sit up, but that would send the stone tumbling off her chest. As if reading her thoughts, Tristan put his hand on her shoulder to keep her still.

"You're meant to rest," he said.

Sarah nodded, though she hardly felt relaxed. Weary, yes, but mostly anxious. Things had been set in motion, things she was responsible for. Sarah couldn't hide in a bed while others suffered because of her actions. She had to at least try to undo what had been done.

"The healer tells me you'll be fine." Anika sat on the edge of the bed. "Whatever magic was affecting you had somehow been diluted. It was easy to counteract."

"That's because he's not truly here," Sarah said. "Not yet."

"Who?" Anika's eyes narrowed. "Who did this to you?"

"Bosque Mar." Sarah gave an involuntary shudder.

Anika and Tristan exchanged a look.

"That's not possible, love," Tristan said gently. "The Rift is closed. Bosque was expelled from this world when that happened."

"It was him," Sarah insisted. "Tristan, you know I could never forget his voice. Or the feeling of his presence."

Tristan didn't answer, and Sarah turned her gaze on Anika.

"It was only when Bosque appeared that I realized what a fool I've been. I've acted a coward when I was trained to be a warrior." Sarah lowered her voice. "And now I've opened the gate to the enemy."

"Sarah." Anika sounded wary. "Are you certain you saw the Harbinger?"

"Yes and no," Sarah admitted. "What I saw was a shade, a projection. It didn't have flesh, but it was the Harbinger. He's trying to reach through the veil. He wants to return."

"Where were you that the Harbinger would be present?" Tristan asked through gritted teeth. "What were you thinking, Sarah?"

"He promised to bring Shay back," Sarah answered. "It was what I wanted to hear and so I did what he asked."

"Bosque told you he would bring Shay back?" Tristan sounded both alarmed and brokenhearted.

Sarah shook her head. "Not Bosque. Logan. It was Logan who offered Shay. He proposed an exchange."

"What did Logan want from you?" Anika asked.

"A box," Sarah told her. "A wooden box that had been kept at Rowan Estate but was then taken."

"What box?" Anika frowned. She stood up, pacing beside the bed.

"Carved ebony," Sarah recited, having memorized the instructions Ren gave her for identifying the box. "Containing wedding rings, a pendant, and a bone."

"Does that sound familiar?" Tristan asked the Arrow.

"No," Anika replied. "But that doesn't mean much coming from me. The Tordis Scribes have been cataloging the contents of Rowan Estate."

"The box wasn't cataloged," Sarah interjected. "It was kept apart. I was told where to find it."

The door banged open and Connor stormed into the room.

"I know you asked for time, Anika," he said to the Arrow. "But I can't wait. I have to know what happened to Adne."

Anika grasped Connor's upper arms, trying both to calm him and to keep him away from the bed.

"Soon, Connor. But we need more information."

"Anika, wait!" Sarah sat up, wrapping the sheet around her and not worrying about the stone rolling away to the foot of the bed. She could finish healing later. "Ariadne is a friend of yours?" Sarah asked Connor.

"She's my . . ." Connor hesitated, then said, "She's everything."

Tristan sat behind Sarah so she could lean against him. Folded in Tristan's arms, Sarah was overwhelmed by his acceptance and forgiveness. Despite her mistakes, Tristan loved her; looking at the fear and earnestness in Connor's face, Sarah hoped he would offer the same faithfulness to Ariadne. Sarah had yanked herself back just before darkness descended. Adne had not.

Sarah looked from Connor to Anika. "Ariadne is the one who had the box."

"But why—" Anika began.

"Box?" Connor butted in. "What box? You don't mean that damn thing full of weird Keeper trinkets?"

Anika raised her eyebrows. "Trinkets like wedding rings, a pendant, and a bone."

Connor's indignation faded. "Uh . . . yeah. That sounds right. Adne found the box right after the robbery."

"And she kept it?" Anika pressed him.

"She did." Connor scratched the back of his neck, uneasy. "She seemed attached to it, though I never could figure out why." With a frown, he asked, "What does the box have to do with what happened to Adne?"

"Logan wanted it back," Sarah told him. "And I was the one who accepted that task."

Drawing a long breath, Sarah continued, "But Adne caught me searching her room for the pendant. I found the box right away, but the pendant wasn't inside. I would never have found it . . . Adne kept it separate from the other things. She had it in a drawer. She told me she'd taken to wearing it sometimes."

"She wears the pendant?" Connor sounded surprised. "Eira's pendant?"

Silence gripped the room, choking off their conversation.

Finally, Tristan said, "Ariadne feels compelled to wear a pendant that belonged to my grandmother?"

"Your grandmother?" Connor looked at Tristan in surprise.

"The line of the Keepers began with Eira," Tristan answered. "I'm her direct descendant."

"It's just a necklace, though," Connor said. "How could Adne wearing a necklace matter? I admit, it's a little creepy that this particular piece of jewelry belonged to the first Keeper, but . . ." Connor's voice trailed off.

"I wish I could agree," Sarah told Connor. "But from what I saw, Adne wears the pendant because she feels some affinity to Eira."

"Why would you say that?" Connor whispered. "That's insane."

"Logan wanted the box," Sarah said. "But when Adne found me, she insisted on coming along. She had questions for Logan, or so she said. I thought Logan would be furious that I hadn't come alone, but he was just the opposite. Logan wanted Adne there."

"What does he want with her?" Connor's skin had taken on a gray pallor.

"It's not Logan who wants her," Tristan said slowly. "Is it, Sarah?"

"Logan is simply doing his master's bidding," Sarah answered. "It's Bosque who seeks Ariadne."

"Why?" Connor demanded. "Why the hell would Bosque go after Adne?"

Anika said to Connor, "If the Harbinger is trying to find a way back into this world, he must think that Ariadne can help him."

"But she wouldn't." Connor's fists clenched. "She wouldn't."

"I don't think she's acting completely of her own free will." Sarah struggled for comforting words. "When the Harbinger spoke to her, she was obviously trying to fight him, but—" Sarah stopped. She didn't want to finish the thought, knowing it would only cause Connor more pain.

"But what?" Connor asked, unable to keep the panic from his voice.

"I don't know if she'll be strong enough to resist," Sarah said reluctantly. "His power is corrupting and absolute. If she's already under his sway, it might be too late."

Connor went very still. Then, in a quiet voice, he said, "Never say that to me again."

Sarah started to apologize, but Connor turned his back on them and left the room, slamming the door behind him.

Guilt gnawed at Sarah. She cast a pleading look at Anika. "I'm so sorry."

"It's time to stop apologizing," Anika replied in a stern voice. "Regret helps no one."

Sarah nodded and Tristan kissed the crown of her head. "You've brought us vital information, Sarah."

With a flat smile, Anika said, "He's right. If the Harbinger is seeking a way to return, we must prevent it at all costs. The power plays and bickering that have overtaken the Academy mean nothing compared to this."

Anika went to Adne's desk and picked up a pen and notepad. She handed them to Sarah and said, "Write down everything you remember about your encounter with Logan and the Harbinger. Every detail, no matter how insignificant it seems. We need to determine what Logan's next move is. He's already set a plan in motion. We're going to have to catch up if we want to stop him."

"Thank you," Sarah said.

"For what?" Anika asked.

"For letting me help," Sarah replied. "I want to help however I can."

"I'm not letting you do anything," Anika told her. "You're one of us, Sarah. A Searcher and a Striker. I haven't forgotten that. Neither should you."

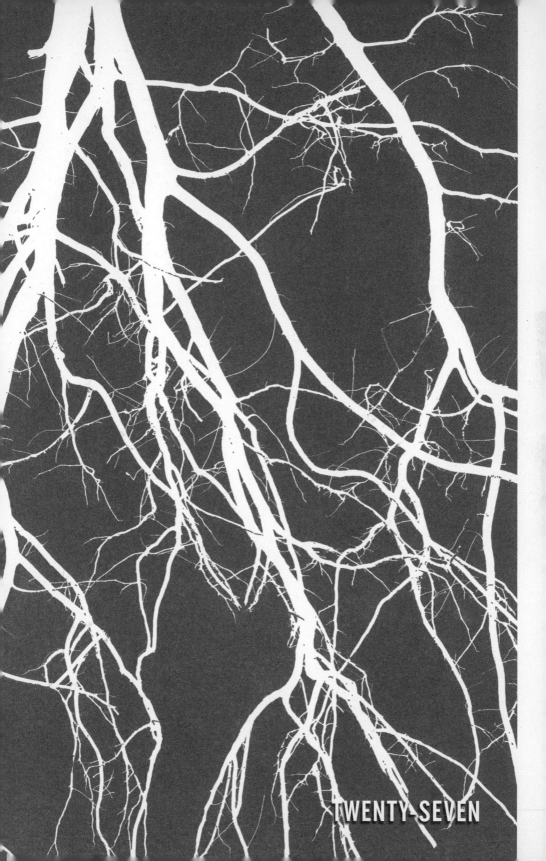

TWENTY-SEVEN

THOUGH THE FIRST-CLASS cabin of the aircraft was spacious, Logan couldn't imagine why anyone thought the gaudy colors were a good decorating choice. It made Logan feel like he'd been dropped into a gumball machine.

"I can't believe we're taking a commercial flight." Chase signaled the flight attendant to bring him another cocktail.

"We're in first class," Logan said. "It's not that bad."

"Please." Chase gave him a hard look. "It's a *commercial* flight."

Across the aisle, Adne murmured, "I've never been on a plane."

"No?" Logan's gaze slid over to her. "I suppose planes wouldn't be much use to a Weaver."

Adne gave Logan a startled glance, making it clear that she hadn't intended to be overheard. "Don't talk to me," she said, turning her face away from the pair of Keepers.

"This is going to be the best vacation ever." Chase finished his vodka and donned a sleep mask. "Wake me up when we're across the Atlantic."

"What a wonderful traveling companion you are," Logan said.

Chase gave him the finger. A few minutes later he was snoring elegantly. Logan hadn't realized that snores could have elegance, but Chase somehow managed it as only a Montauk Keeper could.

Logan glanced at Adne. She was in the window seat, and the aisle seat beside her was empty. Logan got up and moved to the vacant seat.

Adne shot him a poisoned look. "I told you to leave me alone."

"And I'm not comfortable with you thinking I take your orders," Logan answered. "So this is your first time on a plane? Are you frightened?"

"That question is so lame, I'm not bothering with it," Adne said, keeping her face turned toward the window.

Logan smiled. Prickly as Adne might be, Logan sensed how restless the girl was. She wanted to talk, needed to. And Logan was feeling the same way. So he waited.

After what he supposed Adne considered a sufficient snub, she asked, "Do you think he's in pain?"

"Chase?" Logan laughed. "No. He just gets whiny when he's tired."

"I meant Ren," Adne said. "Do you think Ren is in pain?"

"Why would he be in pain?"

Adne turned to face Logan. "Because he's trapped, isn't he? He died, which means he isn't supposed to be here, but he is."

"I don't know if a spirit feels pain," Logan said. "But to be honest, I'm sure he isn't happy. He hates taking orders from me."

"Why is it that he has to obey you?" Adne frowned.

"I couldn't get into specifics," Logan said with a shrug, "but it has something to do with Bosque. Ren serves as a conduit, letting Bosque exert a fraction of his power on this plane."

At the mention of Bosque's name, Adne shrank into her seat.

"Are you afraid of him?" Logan asked. From what he'd witnessed of Ariadne, she was steely and cowed by little. But in Bosque's presence, the Weaver had quailed as if her will was being sapped and she could do nothing other than submit.

Logan thought it had been rather glorious.

Adne said quietly, "Aren't you?"

"Not really," Logan replied.

Adne's mouth quirked in a mocking smile. "I find that hard to believe. Bosque can't have forgotten that you summoned him and forced him to reveal his true form. You're the reason Shay was able to close the Rift."

Logan maintained his nonchalant tone. "We all make mistakes."

"Is that what you told Bosque?" Adne asked, incredulous. "That you just made a mistake?"

"I didn't understand who Bosque was," Logan said stiffly. "I do now. And he knows that I've changed."

"You mean you know he's your grandfather," Adne supplied.

Logan sucked in a sharp breath. Trying not to show his alarm, he asked, "How do you know that?"

"I found a family tree," Adne said. "Eira and Bosque had children. You're a part of that line. So is Shay."

Logan nodded. "That's why he could close the Rift."

"And why you can open it." Adne finished the thought.

Logan searched Adne's face for signs of deception. Is that what she thought? That he was the one who could open the Rift? She had no idea of the part she had to play in all of this. She'd been cast in the leading role and she thought she'd just be in the audience.

"Yes," Logan answered simply. Better to let this scene play out than give away the plot twist now.

"Does Bosque really trust you to pull off something this big?" Adne didn't bother to hide her smirk.

"I've demonstrated my skill." Slightly ruffled, both by the new knowledge of Adne's misconceptions and her insult, Logan shot back, "And I've proven my loyalty."

"How?"

"I got you here, didn't I?" Logan smirked.

"That was a fluke and you know it," Adne replied. "I came here on my own. Not because of you."

"Why are you here?" Logan countered.

The direct question took Adne by surprise. "I—I don't know."

"You must, though," Logan said. "Throwing yourself into the belly of the beast. If you've gone mad, you hide it well."

"I'm not crazy," Adne said, though her voice was quiet.

"I don't think you are," Logan said. "But that means there's reason behind your choices."

"Never mind." Adne fidgeted in her seat. "Let's just say I am crazy."

"I know why I decided to summon Bosque." Logan ignored her attempt to dodge the issue. "After the war, I learned very quickly that wealth means little without power, and we Keepers had Bosque to thank for the power we wielded. I didn't understand that until he was gone."

"Good for you," Adne muttered.

"Is that what you're after?" Logan continued. "True power?" He leaned close to Adne and murmured, "I remember what he said to you in the library. About your power. He wouldn't be seeking you now if you weren't extraordinary. That's the key, isn't it? Bosque knows who you really are, but you don't, and you want to."

"I think you should go back to your side of the plane now." Adne returned her gaze to the window.

Satisfied, Logan went back to his original seat. Though Adne's unexpected arrival had been something of a boon, Logan had been worried he'd have to constantly contend with her for control of the situation. But now he saw things differently. For reasons she didn't want to or wasn't ready to admit, Adne was no longer Logan's enemy. And Logan was beginning to think she might turn into a surprising ally.

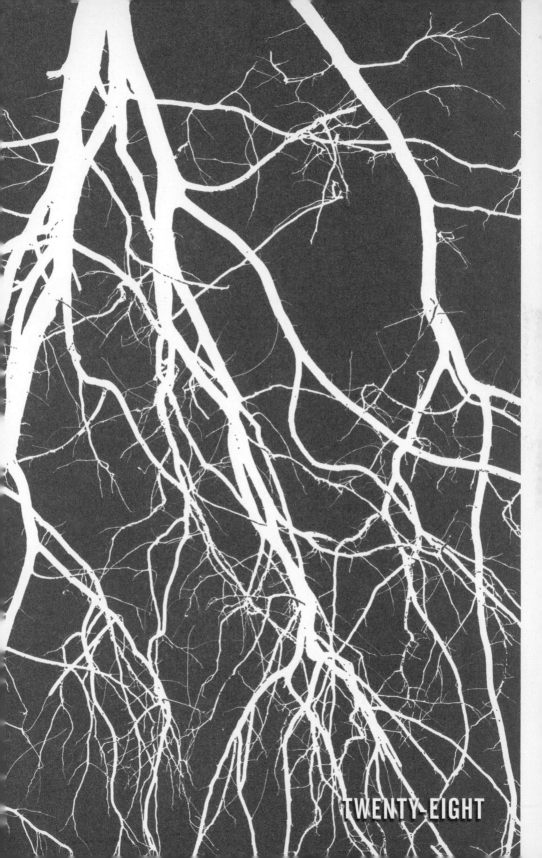

TWENTY-EIGHT

AFTER CONSIDERABLE discussion, it was decided that four of their number would go to meet Holt: Anika, Tristan, Ethan, and Sabine.

Anika, as the Arrow, was an obvious choice, and Tristan was deemed a good counterpart to Anika because he would be able to emphasize the threat that the Harbinger posed. Ethan was to play the "common man," a warrior of the Searchers. And Sabine, as Anika put it, represented their future.

"The future?" Sabine frowned at the Arrow. "How does that work?"

"You're a Guardian who became an ally," Anika replied. "You represent the potential for peace."

"I represent peace?" Sabine laughed, glancing at Ethan. "She doesn't know me very well, does she?"

"You expect me to walk into that trap?" Ethan lifted his eyebrows. Sabine jabbed an elbow into his ribs.

"As painful as it will be," Anika told them, ignoring Ethan and Sabine's exchange, "we need to keep Holt happy, within reason. The goal here is a united front. If we don't get to Logan in time, we may be looking at the beginning of a new war."

"We get it, Anika," Ethan said. "We can suck up to Holt for the greater good."

"All right then." Anika smiled at him. "Let's go."

They waited outside the door to Holt's offices in Pyralis for at least five minutes before someone finally came to greet them.

"I appreciate your taking the time to speak with us," Anika said.

"I assume you'd like to reach a détente." Holt didn't bother to stand when they filed into the room.

Two Strikers flanked Holt, standing tall and silent, with their weapons displayed prominently. They were even wearing sunglasses. And while the crystals running through the walls of Pyralis boasted the bright, flickering tones of burning flames, the shades were just unnecessary. Sabine wished she could tell them how lame they looked, but that wouldn't make Anika very happy.

Holt gazed at them from his seat, wearing a smug smile, as if he were a king sitting upon a throne and about to receive petitioners.

Watching him, Sabine thought, *A man who feels it necessary to flaunt his power has no real power at all.*

If he hadn't been making such a mess of things at the Academy, Sabine might have felt a little sorry for Holt. He was a petty man grasping at power, his ambition no doubt fueled by self-doubt and fear.

"I'd still like to think we have the same goals," Anika said to Holt. "Goals that compel us to work together rather than against one another."

"And what is your goal, Anika?" Holt asked.

"The same as it has ever been," Anika replied. "To protect the earth from the corruption of the Nether."

"You say that." Holt leaned back in his chair. "And yet you seek to hinder my efforts to rid our world of the lingering threat posed by the Keepers who survived the war."

"You're right." Anika clasped her hands behind her back. "We don't see eye to eye on that issue. But new information has come to my attention that I wanted to share with you before I brought it to the other guides. Something that requires immediate action."

Holt straightened up. "Really? I'm intrigued."

Of course you are, Sabine thought. The offer of exclusive access to information. She was surprised he wasn't drooling all over his desk.

"You heard about the incident in the garden," Anika said, waiting until Holt nodded. "It turns out that the robbery at Rowan Estate and the other event were connected. The girl who was found on the grounds of Rowan Estate, Ariadne, has recently gone missing. And until early this morning, Tristan's wife—Sarah—was missing as well. We've learned from Sarah that they were together and it was at the behest of Logan Bane."

"The Keeper? Whose house we just raided?"

"It wasn't Logan's house," Ethan corrected. "He was just staying there."

Holt gave Ethan a sour look.

"Sorry," Ethan mumbled.

"Logan has been attempting to make contact with the Harbinger," Anika continued, hurrying past the awkward moment. "He's using magic to reach through the veil and apparently he's been successful. The Harbinger wants to return to our world, and Logan Bane is serving him in this quest."

"Can you run that by me again?" Holt asked.

He listened as Anika repeated the information they'd gathered from Sarah Doran. When she finished, he nodded.

"So it all comes down to the Harbinger," Holt said. "The great Nether lord who was expelled from the earth when the Scion closed the Rift."

"Yes," Anika said, wearing a smile but clearly losing patience.

"And according to Sarah Doran, the Harbinger is planning his great comeback."

Uh-oh. Sabine threw a worried glance at Ethan. He gave a slight nod, confirming her fears.

"Do you have any other evidence?" Holt asked the Arrow.

"Other evidence?" Anika repeated with a frown.

"Forgive me," Holt continued, "but the story you've presented is a bit far-fetched and, as far as I can tell, supported by rather unreliable sources."

"Ariadne and Sarah are hardly unreliable," Anika countered.

"I'm afraid there are other reasons I'm not particularly inclined to believe you." Holt glanced at Sabine. "For example, the company you keep."

"I guess I'm not the future after all," Sabine murmured.

"Seriously?" Ethan scoffed at Holt. "Did you sleep through the end of the war? We would have lost without the help of Guardians."

"I'm not entirely convinced that's true," Holt replied, straightening his jacket. "From what I've observed, the end of the war saw far too many compromises of what Searchers always stood for. We tainted ourselves by making deals with the devil. I'm trying to undo that damage and restore our cause to its former glory."

"Former glory?" Sabine laughed. "You mean all those years that you were losing? Someone needs a history lesson."

"I'd rather not learn my history from a Guardian." Holt regarded Sabine with disdain. "I maintain a healthy doubt about where your loyalties lie."

"Take that back." Ethan's hand was on his dagger hilt.

Sabine shot Anika a warning look.

"We're here to talk." Anika put her hand on Ethan's arm. "Not fight."

"I don't mean to give offense." Holt raised his hands in apology. "I only speak the truth as I see it."

"The truth as you see it?" Ethan spat. "What kind of crap is that?"

"Ethan." Anika's tone silenced Ethan, but he pushed his duster back to keep the hilt of his dagger in Holt's view.

"A few items stolen from a library and some cockamamie tales don't add up to a conspiracy to restore the Harbinger's power," Holt said.

"These aren't just cockamamie tales," Tristan objected. "Logan Bane is a direct descendant of Bosque Mar. Logan's existence grants Bosque the ability to keep a tenuous connection to this world. And I'm certain he's planning to use Logan to try to reopen the Rift."

"What are you talking about?" Holt glared at Tristan for interrupting his catalog of objections.

"The truth of it was closely guarded by the Keepers," Tristan told him. "But Eira wasn't just the first Keeper, she was the mother of Bosque's children, and her bloodline was what sustained Bosque's ties to this world. That's why my son, Shay, could banish him. And that's why Logan Bane can summon him now."

Holt gave Tristan a long look. "If what you say is true, then you, Tristan, also share Eira's bloodline."

"I do," Tristan said.

"It follows then that you pose an equal threat to our cause, since you also have the power to open the Rift." Holt gave Tristan an ugly smile. "It's in your blood, after all."

"Lock me up if you want to," Tristan snapped at Holt. "But don't pretend what I've said isn't true."

"I don't believe throwing you in a cell is necessary, Tristan. Not unless you continue to incite dissention in the Searcher ranks by causing a panic." Holt stood up. "Let me tell you what I think. A clearly troubled girl has run off, no doubt in a desperate ploy for attention. And a woman deranged by grief concocts stories about the reemergence of the Harbinger, and you believe her?"

The veins in Tristan's neck bulged, but he remained silent.

Ethan leaned over to Sabine. "It's really good that we didn't bring Connor."

"No kidding."

Holt shook his head. "I've been debating whether or not to go forward with a particular matter, and you've just made it clear that I must. I'm bringing up a vote of no confidence at the next Council meeting. You've had a tenuous grasp on power and now you're making desperate ploys to maintain your authority. You aren't fit to be the Arrow, Anika."

Sabine waited for Anika to jump onto the desk and kick Holt in the face, because Sabine thought that would be a perfectly appropriate reaction, but the Arrow just nodded.

"Do what you have to do, Holt. We'll leave you to your business."

Anika pivoted on her heel and walked out of the room. The others began to follow, but Sabine lagged behind.

"Tell me, Holt," she said. "Did you hear the story of how I killed my former master? You know, Efron Bane?"

Holt's eyes widened only slightly, but it was enough to make Sabine smile.

"Good." Sabine nodded. "I just wanted to be sure."

She caught up to the others in the hall. Anika was walking at a fast clip out of Pyralis, slowing only when they were well away from Holt's office.

"I guess we can't count on a united front," Tristan said.

Anika nodded. "I wish I could say I'm surprised."

"What now?" Ethan asked.

"We deal with this ourselves," Anika said. "Sabine and Ethan, go get Connor. I'll find Tess, Shiloh, and Mikaela. Meet us in Tactical with gear for a mission."

"A mission?" Ethan frowned at her. "Do we know where Logan is?"

"No," Anika admitted. "But I'm hoping that by putting our heads together we'll be able to figure it out."

Sabine grabbed Ethan's hand. "Come on."

The knowledge that she'd be going into the field, that she'd be in the fight again, thrilled Sabine in a way that took her by surprise.

She'd have to learn to rely on weapons instead of her teeth, but that also struck Sabine as exciting. A new adventure.

"You okay?" Ethan glanced at Sabine and then down at their hands, and she realized she'd been crushing his fingers in her grip.

"Yeah." Sabine smiled at him. She knew she was no longer a wolf, but inside, she was howling.

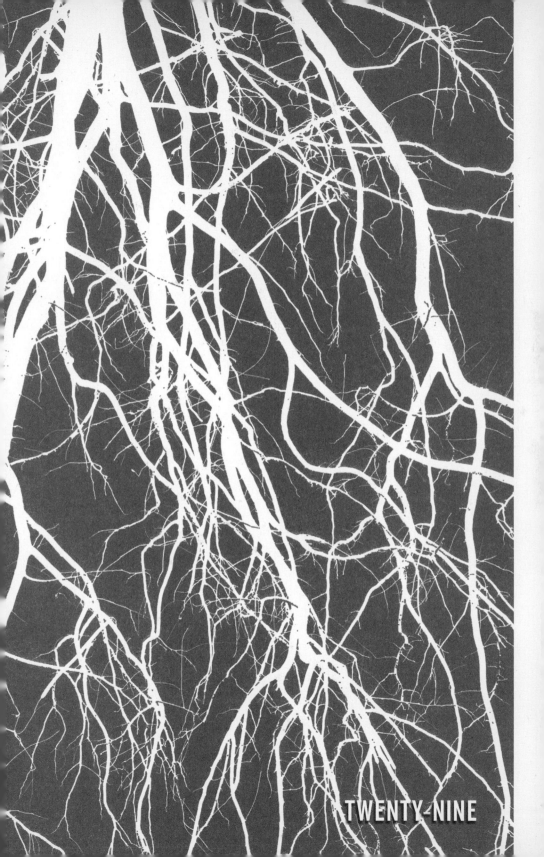

TWENTY-NINE

THE SMALL PARTY of Searchers bearing the news that the Harbinger posed an immediate threat to the world had spent a good part of the afternoon arguing about what to do with that information. There had been an even split between those who believed Holt could be reasoned with and those who expected him to continue acting like the ass he was. They had all agreed, however, that Connor should not be part of the group that reached out to Holt.

Except Connor.

Connor absolutely thought he should be part of that team.

"What happens when you need someone to punch him?" Connor had asked. "Because there will obviously be a point in the conversation where hitting him becomes necessary."

And with that question, Anika had ordered Connor to the barracks, where he could punch inanimate objects for as long as he liked, but he was much less likely to muck up an important meeting.

So while his friends tried to save the world via diplomatic negotiations with a dick, Connor set about the important task of hitting things. Because that's what the others thought he was good for. Hitting.

Despite his resentment, Connor threw himself into the work of jabbing, kicking, and elbowing the heavy bag that hung in one corner of the training room. It wasn't long before he'd broken a sweat. Connor stripped off his shirt and kept going.

He didn't hear anyone enter the room, but the voice that spoke was suddenly right behind him.

"You wouldn't believe how jealous I am right now."

Connor whirled around and discovered Renier Laroche standing no more than a foot away. Ren nodded at the punching bag.

"To be able to hit things," Ren added. "I really miss it. Particularly when I have to spend so much time listening to Logan."

"Is that why you're here?" Connor asked. "Logan sent you back with a message for me? If he didn't send flowers too, tell him he needs to class up his act."

"I'm not here for Logan," Ren answered. "I'm here for Adne."

Connor turned back to the bag, this time working on uppercuts. "So even as a ghost, you want to play big brother. Are you going to tell me that I messed up? That I should have seen this coming?"

"Did you see it coming?" Ren asked.

Connor kept hitting the bag. "Maybe."

"Could you elaborate a little more?"

"Why?" Connor replied. "You've been around, haven't you? I mean, you've seen her. You've seen what Adne's been like. You're no Casper, but if you're a ghost, I assume you can keep tabs on whoever you like. Except for when you're running an errand for that bratty warlock."

"That's a pretty good description of my life, actually," Ren said with a dry laugh. "And you're right. I have been watching Adne, and I don't like what I've seen."

"That makes two of us," Connor growled, bringing his knee up hard into the bag.

"Really?" Ren gave a low whistle. "Knee to the crotch. You fight dirty."

"Whatever it takes," Connor said.

"See, that's what I always thought about you," Ren commented as Connor threw more jabs at the bag. "You go for the throat. No hesitation. No regrets. You're a fighter through and through."

"I'm a Striker." Connor sent the bag spinning with an uppercut. "It's in the job description."

"You say that," Ren replied. "But we both know it's always been more."

Connor grabbed the bag, breathing hard, and looked at Ren. "What's your point?"

"That you've been acting out of character," Ren said. "Or rather, not acting. You've been benchwarming, when you're a starter. What's the deal?"

"Too many metaphors, man." Connor picked up a towel and mopped sweat from his face. "Try again."

"Why didn't you stop my sister?" Ren's question came with a snarl that made Connor's skin crawl. "You saw what was happening to her, but you did nothing. You let her go to him."

"I didn't let her do anything. No one can tell Adne what to do, and no one can stop her when she makes her mind up about anything." Connor turned on the wolf and shouted, "Who the hell do you think you're talking to? You might be her blood, but you barely knew Adne. I've loved her for years."

Ren said quietly, "Then why haven't you been fighting for her?"

"Go screw yourself."

"That would be a neat trick, but I prefer company." Ren glanced around the room, surveying the weapons that hung on racks along the walls. "Answer my question. You're a fighter, so why didn't you fight for Adne?"

"Maybe I don't know how," Connor snapped.

"Wrong answer," Ren said. "We've already established that you know how. You helped win the war. I know. I was there."

"So?"

"So at the eleventh hour, when all the odds were against us, you crashed into Bosque Mar's mansion like you had nothing to lose," Ren replied. "When you fight, you're fearless."

"Are you trying to tell me I'm afraid now?" Connor frowned at Ren. "Are you calling me a coward?"

"Something like that," Ren answered. "Though *coward* wouldn't be my word of choice. I'd rather use a phrase. My description of you would be 'paralyzed by fear.'"

"Really?" Connor smirked. "You just claimed that the last time you saw me in a fight I was fearless. So how is it that I'm so afraid now?"

"Because now it's not the war that you're fighting for, it's Adne," Ren said. "It would be easier for you to have the world end than it would be to lose her."

Connor didn't respond. Ren might not have been corporeal, but his words hit like a sucker punch.

"You know, as her brother, I put that in the plus column for you," Ren added.

"Thanks." Connor picked up a water bottle and took several gulps. "So why did you come to find me?"

"Because I'm starting to see how this is going to play out," Ren said. "Benefit of the not-quite-afterlife or something. It's going to be ugly. For everyone, but especially for Adne."

Connor grimaced. "So you're the motivational speaker, I see."

Ren laughed. "That's going to help you. Humor. As annoying as it is, it will help."

"We all have our gifts." Connor frowned at Ren. "Is that all?"

"She needs a champion," Ren said, all mirth gone from his face. "And it has to be you."

"What are you talking about?" Connor asked. "A champion? Are you going to tell me to go find the One Ring now?"

"I've already told you," Ren answered. "I've seen the shape of things to come. This is how it's going down. I'm just giving you some advance notice."

Connor grunted to hide his confusion. "Don't you want to be champion?"

"It's hard to be champion when you can't pick up a sword."

"Right." Connor looked at Ren. Tall, strong, ready to fight. It had to suck. "You know, kid, I'm sorry about how things ended for you. You deserved better."

Ren shrugged. "How often do people get what they deserve? Good or bad."

"Very Zen." Connor took another swig of water.

"I suppose," Ren said with a slight smile. "I may be dead, but apparently I still have choices. So I could brood and mope and try my best to learn how to rattle chains. Or I can try to save my sister."

A shiver traveled through Connor's limbs. "Point taken."

Connor regarded Ren for a minute, then said, "I can't believe Logan would put his stamp of approval on this conversation. So forgive the turn of phrase, but how did you get off your leash?"

"I'm getting the hang of this ghost thing," Ren told him. "Learning via trial and error. At first I could only go where Logan sent me, but sometimes where he sends me lets me cross paths with people other than those he intended me to see. I figured out that, once someone has seen me, I can go back to visit them at will. You saw me earlier. So now you're on the list."

"Lucky me." Connor went to the wall and took down a long sword. Brandishing the weapon, he asked, "So you want me to save your sister. Can you tell me where she is?"

"No." Ren watched Connor cut the air with sweeping strokes of his blade. "But she already has."

Connor stopped swinging the sword. "You've got some misinformation there. Adne didn't leave a note. She just left." He could hear the resentment in his voice.

Ren managed to give Connor a sympathetic look. "We're dealing in subtleties, man. I'm talking about clues, not a sign in neon lights. Think about what Adne's been going through. What she's done recently. The choices she's made. Follow Adne's lead and you'll find her."

"Do all ghosts talk in riddles?" Connor asked. "Or do you just like pissing me off?"

"I like pissing you off," Ren answered. "But the riddles aren't my choice. I'm toeing the line here, but I can't cross it. If I could tell you everything I know, I would. But I'm not free."

"Sorry," Connor muttered, passing the sword hilt from hand to hand.

"Don't be," Ren said. "You should get angry. It will help you find Adne."

"Has Logan hurt her?" Connor asked. He didn't want to voice the question, but suddenly it was there and he couldn't hold it back.

"Logan isn't the real threat to Adne," Ren replied. "She's a danger to herself in ways she doesn't realize. We're losing her."

Connor wheeled around and ran the punching bag through with the long sword.

"Oh, good," Ren said as Connor jerked the blade free. "I was worried that bag was going to take you."

"I am not losing Ariadne," Connor said in a voice sharper than the sword edge.

Ren nodded, then flinched as if something had hurt him. "I have to go."

"Go where?" Connor looked at the space around Ren, hoping that he might see or sense whatever force was affecting the spirit. But Connor found nothing.

With a brief nod of understanding, Ren said, "See you around." And he was gone.

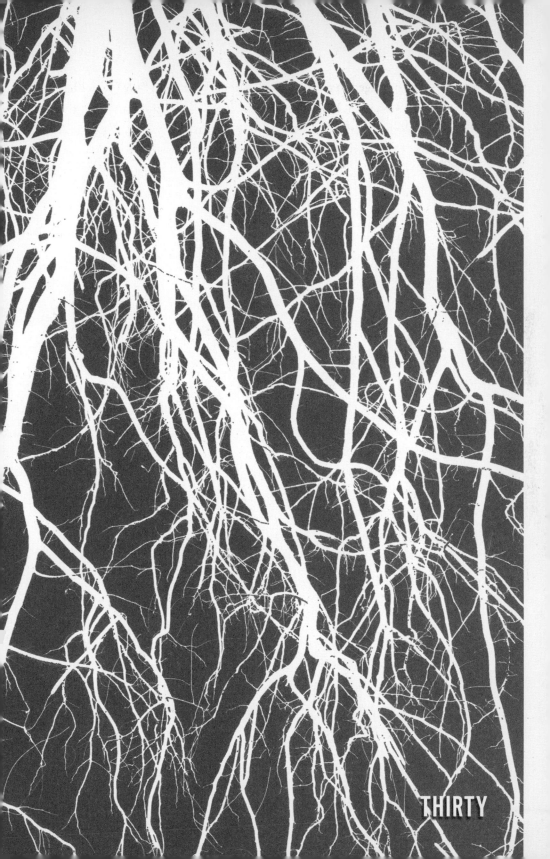

THIRTY

THOUGH GENERALLY disheartened by all that had transpired in the past hours, days, even months, Sarah tried to focus on the small and very recent improvements in her circumstance. She had graduated from bed rest to a rocking chair and she'd been moved from Adne's room to her own. Taking the stone off too soon, it turned out, had been a bad idea. Disrupting the draw of the curse from her body had allowed it to take hold again. Now Sarah's blood felt like sludge and the Elixirs had her drinking a tea that tasted like dirt. Sarah half suspected that they could have just used a stone again but that the dirt-tea was retribution for failing to follow their original instructions.

When the door to her room opened, Sarah expected it to be Tristan returning. Instead, a group of heavily armed men stomped into the room and took up sentinel-like stances on either side of Sarah's rocking chair. Another man entered a moment later, and while he wasn't boasting the same amount of steel as the others, this last man had a more imperious bearing.

"Sarah Doran?" the man asked Sarah.

Sarah set down her cup of tea. She didn't like the way her hand had begun to shake. "Do I know you?"

"My name is Holt," he said. "The Pyralis Guide."

"It's an honor to meet a Guide," Sarah said, out of sheer politeness. "And yes, I'm Sarah Doran."

"I'm afraid you'll have to come with us," Holt told Sarah. "You need to answer the charge that has been brought against you."

"The charge?" Sarah couldn't believe that she'd heard him right.

"Treason."

Sarah didn't know what was worse, the word itself or the way that saying it had made Holt smile.

THIRTY-ONE

ETHAN WAS EYEING Connor with suspicion. "Something's different about you. You seem . . . like you."

Connor barked a laugh. He hadn't realized how far from himself he'd been until Ren forced him to face it head-on.

"I had a close encounter," Connor told Ethan.

They were taking inventory of armor and weapons while they waited in Haldis Tactical for Anika to arrive.

"You had what?" Ethan asked.

"A close encounter," Connor said. "With a ghost."

"Close enounters are with aliens," Shiloh interjected as he stowed a pair of short-handled sickles boasting wickedly curved blades in his pack. "Not ghosts. You're mixing up your paranormal beings. That's sloppy."

Ethan grinned at Connor. "I like this one."

"Just don't forget that he's taller and better-looking than you," Connor reminded him.

"Excuse me?" Shiloh said.

"And he's really cute when he blushes," Connor added. "Just look at that. Can you blush like that?"

"Leave him alone," Sabine chided Connor. "Or you'll be one Striker short on this mission."

"He can take it," Connor told her. "Can't you, Shiloh?"

"I couldn't say," Shiloh said. "I'm too busy being cute while blushing."

"Yeah." Connor looked at Ethan and nodded. "I like him too."

"Shut the door!"

Connor looked up and saw that Anika, Tristan, Tess, and Mikaela had run into the room. Tess slammed Tactical's door and brought down its heavy wooden bolt, sealing them in.

Tristan glared at Anika, spewing curses. "I have to go back!"

"And do what?" Anika shouted at him. "Tell me how you can help your wife by storming the stockade alone."

Tristan seethed but held his tongue.

"Huh," Connor said to Ethan. "That can't be good. I didn't even know the door had a bolt."

"Neither did I," Ethan said.

"We don't have much time." Anika waved the Strikers and Sabine over.

"What's wrong?" Sabine asked.

"Holt's making his move," Anika told them. "And it's much worse than I expected. He didn't wait for the next meeting of the Council. He and his lackeys are making arrests. It's only a matter of time before they come here looking for us."

"Arrests?" Ethan's brow knit together. "For what?"

"For nothing," Tristan snarled. "He's taking down potential threats to his political ascendancy. That's all."

"He's bringing charges of conspiracy, insurrection," Anika replied. "And treason. They took Sarah Doran first and they were trying to arrest Tristan when we intervened. I don't know how many of you he'll come after, but there's no doubt that I'm one of his targets."

"We're just going to let him do this? Stand by while he tries to usurp you? While he throws people in prison?" Connor demanded of Anika.

"Thank you. That's what I've been saying since Holt made his move," Tristan said to Connor, but Tess shook her head at them.

"It's already done," Tess said. "Holt's calling the shots and there's nothing we can do about it for the time being. As far as the Academy is concerned, we're at damage control. Let us handle it. You need to focus on the mission."

"I don't understand why anyone would follow that blowhard." Connor slammed his fist into the wall and winced. The punching bag had a lot more give.

"Because blood wants blood," Sabine replied. "Holt's shown us that he can turn the Searchers into a mob. They got a taste of destruction and they want more. Mindless but purposeful violence is the easiest to promote."

"So we're just going to fall in line?" Ethan frowned. "We're not going to fight back?"

"This fight isn't yours, not right now," Anika said. "I truly believe that the elder Searchers will prevail in this matter and that reason will trump Holt's power grab. But you can't afford to waste time on Holt. Your battle is elsewhere."

"Really, Anika?" Tristan asked. "Don't you think getting your house in order takes precedent over what's happening with Logan?"

"You're not seeing past Sarah's involvement," Anika chided gently. "And that's understandable, but you know better than anyone, Tristan, what Bosque is capable of."

Tristan started to object, but then his shoulders slumped. "Yes. I do know."

"Speaking of Bosque and Logan," Ethan said, "any progress on where this battle of ours will be happening?"

"Connor." Anika turned to the Striker.

"What?" Connor said, surprised that the Arrow was looking to him for an answer.

"You're the closest to Adne," Anika continued. "Do you have any idea of where she might be going? Where Logan would be taking her?"

Connor ruffled his hair, nervous but resolved. "I'm not sure. Hang on. There might be one thing . . ."

"I'll take anything," Anika said.

The sound of voices came through the door, followed by a commotion as whoever was outside discovered that the way in had been blocked.

"I think we're out of time," Tess said. "Connor?"

"The necklace," Connor told them. "Eira's necklace. Sarah said that it meant Adne must have some sort of connection to Eira."

Sabine began to nod. "What did Adne say when we first found the box? Something about Logan going back."

"Back to the beginning," Ethan said.

"The beginning," Sabine repeated. "Back to Eira, the first Keeper."

"Okay, that's a who." Tess glanced nervously at the door, from which shouts and pounding fists emanated. "Do we have a where to go with it? Because I don't think the pitchforks and torches outside are going to wait much longer."

"Tearmunn," Anika said.

"What's Tearmunn?" Sabine asked with a frown.

"It was a Conatus fortress in the Middle Ages," Anika said.

"A fortress?" Shiloh piped up. When they all looked at him, he smiled sheepishly. "Sorry. It just sounds cool."

"It's a ruin now. I can't say for sure what you'll find there," Anika told them, and Shiloh managed to look sincerely disappointed. "Most of the structure was destroyed in the early years of the war. But Tearmunn is the site where the first Rift was opened."

"Okay, I'm in," Connor said. "That's as good a guess as any."

"Sure." Ethan was nodding. "So this ruin. Where is it?"

"Scotland," Anika said. "In the Highlands."

The pounding at the door had transformed into a ramming sound, shoulders being thrown heavily against the wood.

"Do they not realize that they could just get a Weaver to open a door and come in that way?" Sabine asked.

"The Weavers don't like Holt," Mikaela said in a tiny voice.

"What?" Anika asked the girl.

Ducking her head at the sudden attention, Mikaela said, "We don't like Holt. He's a bully and he only cares about fighting. Weaving is an art. It requires thoughtfulness and grace. Holt doesn't understand that."

Tess and Anika exchanged a look. "Well, that's something."

Encouraged by her elders' approval, Mikaela added, "The Scribes aren't his biggest fans either."

"Thank you, Mikaela." Anika smiled at the girl. "That gives me something real to work with."

"It could prove vital. If Holt has been strong-arming with only a handful of Strikers at his back, he really is only playing at power," Tess said to Anika, then turned to the diminutive Weaver. "Now, Mikaela, make us a door. Take us near Kyle of Lochalsh. I think we should regroup and find a place to use as a base of operations before we end up in the middle of the wilderness."

Mikaela nodded and began to weave a portal.

"What are Highland winters like?" Connor asked ruefully. "Balmy?"

"Don't worry, Connor." Sabine patted him on the shoulder. "We'll just find you a sheep to cuddle up with. I hear they have lots of them in Scotland."

Connor made a sour face. "When we find Adne, I'm going to tell her you said that."

"Good for you." Sabine laughed.

As a snow-covered landscape came into focus amid the shimmering threads of Mikaela's weaving, Connor leaned over to Ethan.

"I don't know about you, but I'm gonna get a kilt," Connor said. "I mean, hey, it's Scotland."

Ethan just smiled and shook his head, but Shiloh asked, "A kilt?"

"I've got great legs," Connor said solemnly.

Shiloh looked to Ethan for a reprieve. "Is he always like this?"

"Yep," Ethan said.

"Of course I am." Connor grinned. "I'm a goddamn champion."

"You're a what?" Sabine asked.

"Close encounter," Connor replied. "You wouldn't understand."

The portal now offered a clear view of a hillside with the glittering lights of a village at the base of the slope.

Tess hugged Anika. "Good luck."

"You too," Anika said. "Don't contact us unless you have to. I don't want Holt to come after you. I'll try to keep him too focused on the problems here to even think about interfering with your mission."

"So we're on our own," Sabine said, glancing at Ethan.

"No," Anika answered. "You'll have an original descendant of the Harbinger to help you find your way."

"What?" Tristan stared at Anika. "I'm not leaving. Not with Sarah imprisoned and Holt running the show."

"Sarah is my best friend. You know I'll do everything I can to help her," Anika told him. "It's my task to face Holt and take him down. You're the only one who actually knows Bosque. You'll see things, put pieces together that the others can't. You need to go with them."

"She's right, Tristan. I may be the Guide, but we need you to show us the way," Tess said. "Anika will deal with Holt. We'll stop Logan."

Tristan's face was drawn, but he nodded.

"She makes it sound so simple," Connor said wistfully.

"Get going." Ethan shoved Connor toward the portal. "Your kilt awaits you."

Connor's skin prickled as he stepped through the light-filled doorway, leaving Haldis Tactical behind. Though he'd been a Striker for years, Connor felt as though he were heading into the field for the first time. A mission without the backing of the Academy and its Searchers made this a new beginning for all of them.

She needs a champion.

That label still made Connor uneasy. It wasn't a word he'd use to describe himself except in jest. But if that was who he needed to become for Adne's sake, then that was who he would be. The thought gave him a bit of comfort. He might only be at the beginning, but a champion could see the battle through to the end.

ACKNOWLEDGMENTS

I'm thrilled to continue writing in the world of Nightshade. *Snakeroot* wouldn't have been possible without the aid of so many colleagues, friends, and family. My team at InkWell Management, Richard Pine, Charlie Olsen, and Lyndsey Blessing, do more for my books and my life than I could ever truly express. Every time I name Penguin Young Readers Group as my publisher, I feel overwhelming gratitude and pride. There could be no better home for this writer. Thank you to Don Weisberg and Jen Loja for your constant encouragement. I love popping in at 345 Hudson to catch up with the sales, marketing, publicity, and school and library teams, who do so much to bring my novels to life. Thanks especially to Shanta, Emily R., Erin, Elyse, Lisa, Elizabeth, Marisa, Jessica, Kristina, Molly, Courtney, Anna, Scottie, Laura, and Felicia. The beautiful paperback editions of the Nightshade series are thanks to the lovely Puffin team, particularly Eileen and Dana. Thanks to Tara for being so, so excited.

Nightshade thrives under the guidance and support of Michael Green, who is taking me to a baseball game soon . . .

I am so glad Jill Santopolo is my editor and I'm beyond lucky that she's also my friend and neighbor in New York. UWS FTW. Thanks to Kiffin and Brian, too, for all their work.

Writers need other writers with whom to be silly and neurotic: David Levithan, Eliot Schrefer, and Sandy London take exceptional care of me. Beth Revis, Marie Lu, and Jessica Spotswood keep me sane and honest. Elizabeth Eulberg and Michelle Hodkin take care of important shenanigans.

My family remains at the heart of my writing endeavors. Thanks to my mom and dad for weathering transitions and keeping joy in focus. This book is dedicated to my brother, Garth, and his wife, Sharon, who made me believe in love again and remind me every day that nothing is more precious than family.

Turn the page for sneak peek at

EMBER BROUGHT HER sword down without warning and her aim was true. Her blade whistled through the air, hitting its mark and smoothly halving her adversary.

Her enemy might only have been a kirtle she'd outgrown and put to use by stuffing it with straw. Even so, the kirtle now lay in pieces, and bits of golden debris floated in the air around Ember as if celebrating her victory. With a yelp of joy she twirled around, brandishing her sword.

She held up the blade, letting its surface catch the sunlight. She was pleased, not only because she'd destroyed her poppet but also because her success meant she'd given her weapon the care it needed. Her sword was bright and sharp. The blade showed no signs of rust though she had to keep it hidden in the small niche she'd dug in this hollow, where it couldn't be fully protected from the elements.

Ember brought the sword up once more and swung it down in a broad arc as her body turned, following the path of the blade. The effortless stroke ended abruptly when her sword met resistance. The sound of steel on steel rang in her ears a moment before the shock of impact jolted up her arm.

"I thought I'd find you here." The familiar voice made Ember's shriek of horror transform to one of delight. Though his clothing had changed, Alistair Hart had not. His ebony curls still shone in the sun and his eyes still rivaled the spring sky.

She began to lower her sword, but Alistair stepped forward. His blade rasped, pressing into hers and forcing her to push back.

He smiled at her. "Tsk. Don't lower your defenses, Em. Is that how you'd respond to an ambush?"

"But—" Ember's brow knit together. She couldn't believe he was here.

"We'll have a proper reunion after you've shown me that you've been practicing," Alistair said, glancing at the remnants of the poppet. "It's a bit more of a challenge when your adversary can fight back."

His blue eyes shone with mirth that made Ember want to laugh, but she gritted her teeth. With a twist of her wrist she knocked Alistair's sword away and struck. He dodged, deftly wielding his blade to parry her swing. Ember met his blow and pushed their swords up so she could aim a kick at Alistair's stomach. Catching her sudden movement, Alistair tried to jump back but not quickly enough. He grunted as her heel dug into his gut.

Doubling over, he stumbled away. Ember cried out, dropping her sword.

"Oh, Alistair, I'm sorry." She ran to him. "I got carried away."

His shoulders were shaking and she gripped them, leaning down in hopes of peering at his face. "I didn't mean to hurt you."

When he looked up, grinning, she stomped her foot. His body shook not with pain, but with laughter.

"You're horrid." Ember's cheeks were hot with embarrassment. "I thought I'd hurt you."

"Only my ego, sweet Ember," Alistair said, still laughing. "Fortunately my stomach can withstand a gentle kick."

Ember winced at the word *gentle*. She certainly hadn't meant to be gentle.

"I'm impressed," Alistair continued. "You have been practicing."

Though she wanted to stay cross with him, Ember couldn't help but smile. "I have . . . If I don't sneak out to this hollow, I'll be forced to spin. I hate spinning."

Her fingers twitched at the thought. She didn't mind the calluses that made her hands rough from gripping her sword's hilt, but she resented the blisters that covered her fingers after the tedium of carding wool and pulling thread from a wheel. With a sigh, Ember turned to rescue her blade from the dirt where she'd dropped it, but Alistair took her arm and pulled her back.

"Have you forgotten already?" he asked with an impish smile. "Now that you've proven yourself, it's time to welcome me home."

Ember laughed and threw herself into his open arms. He crushed her into his chest, so she couldn't draw a breath, but Ember didn't care. She had missed Alistair every day since he'd left the marches. He was the only person who would know to look for Ember in the hidden glen. The only person she trusted with her secrets. The one who'd secreted a sword into her possession and helped her learn how to use it. In this last year, his absence had meant she had no sparring partner and no one to reassure her that wishing of a life of adventure wasn't a silly dream for a girl.

He laughed and spun her around so quickly that her feet swished through the air. "Ah, I've missed you, Em."

Ember wriggled against him until she was able to gulp in air. The question pounding in her veins rushed out. "Have you come to take me away?"

Alistair buried his face in the crown of her hair. "Did you have doubts? I keep my promises."

"But my father—" Ember tried to pull free, but Alistair's arms were tight around her body, holding her close.

"There are some powers in this world that even your father must answer to," Alistair told her. "And I'm here representing one of them."

Though he seemed reluctant to let her go, Ember managed to

wrestle herself out of Alistair's embrace. "It's wonderful that they sent you."

"It was decided that things would be easier if I were to come," he said. "For all of us." He reached out, letting his fingers rest on her cheek. "After today things will be better. Forever."

Ember nodded, though the lingering touch of his hand felt strange. Her mind was working too quickly to give the gesture much thought. Even with Alistair returned, she wouldn't believe that her father would let her leave his home, be free of his rule, until she was well away from the family estate.

When Alistair had left his own father's manor—only an hour on foot from Ember's home—to join Conatus, Ember had been delighted to receive word that he'd been chosen to serve in their elite Guard. He'd always bested his brothers in combat. He'd made his preference known, and not many would give up the comforts of domesticity for a life of war, even the sacred war of the Church. But Alistair was the third son of a noble, which meant his father's fortunes would pass to his elder brothers. Though he could have sought the hand of an heiress, Alistair claimed he'd prefer living by his sword than winning his fortune through a marriage.

Ember's situation was the reverse. She was the ideal fiancée for someone in Alistair's position. He'd even jested that they could marry to please their families. But two things kept Ember from ever considering that course. First, she knew marrying Alistair wouldn't please her father. He had an eye on husbands who would extend his holdings in France or Scotland. Alistair might be noble in name, but he brought nothing to the table that would gain her father's favor: no inheritance, no land of his own.

Second, and much more pressing, was the protest of her spirit. She was certain she'd suffocate trapped in a manor as some lord's wife. Even as a girl she'd longed to escape the monotony of spinning, weaving, and needlework. She'd been plagued by jealousy as Alistair and his brothers learned swordplay and horsemanship while she and Agnes were cooped up in the manor. Alistair had become her closest friend and confidant because of his willingness to thwart convention, stealing away to meet her in the hollow so she could at least have a taste of martial training.

Ember ached for a life where she could live by her sword and her courage. A life unavailable to the daughter of a nobleman. Except for this single possibility. Her father's debt to Conatus meant that she might be called to serve at Tearmunn. In what capacity she couldn't know. Even with her obligations to Conatus she might still be destined for a politically expedient union.

Her hopes were futile. Ember knew as much. But over the past year she'd too often allowed herself to imagine otherwise. Alistair's letters had encouraged her dreaming, hinting that joining the order would forever alter her life's path.

No work could be greater than the sacred duties of Conatus, he'd written. But what was that work? Despite his reassurances she still found herself doubting that she'd have a place within this strange order. Perhaps she'd been a girl who played with swords and slaughtered straw dolls, but now she was a woman. And women warriors were aberrations, creatures of legend but not the world she inhabited. Though it might be at the ends of the earth, Tearmunn was still of this world, and that meant she had to live as women did. As a wife. As a mother.

But now Alistair had returned, as he'd promised. Her pulse jumped at the thought that her daydreams of another life might be realized. With opposing currents of hope and fear sloshing against each other in her mind, Ember clambered up the grassy bank after Alistair.

Alistair's horse, a glossy bay mare, was gorging itself on the spring-green shoots that appeared in thick tufts throughout the pasture. The horse blew out in annoyance at having such a lovely meal interrupted when Alistair took up the reins. They started across the green fields toward the tall manor that loomed over the glen. The mare snorted, craning her neck in an attempt to snatch another mouthful of the grass.

"She's beautiful," Ember said, looking over the long lines of the mare's form.

"Her name is Alkippe. The horses at Tearmunn are exceptional," he told her. "Everything there is exceptional."

"And they haven't made a monk of you?" she asked, easily falling into their old pattern of teasing each other about romance. Alistair had always boasted that one day no woman would resist his knightly charm. Ember had countered that no man could ever have charm enough to make her want to marry.

Expecting Alistair's laughter, the suddenly harsh cut of his mouth startled her. "Of course not," he said. "Conatus may be an arm of the church, but we're not a monastery."

"I was only making fun," Ember said. "Your letters spoke of taking vows."

"The vows are of loyalty." Alistair's pace quickened. "Not chastity."

"But you said as a knight of Conatus you can't marry," she argued. "And that you continue the work of the Templars—who were chaste, were they not?"

The words left her mouth and Ember's heart became tight as a fist when she remembered that the Templars had been disbanded and many tortured and burned because of charges they'd broken their vows.

Alarmed, she murmured, "I shouldn't have jested about something so serious."

He grimaced. "You don't understand the function of the vows. They exist only because of the danger . . . Never mind. You'll learn the truth of this soon enough yourself. Now our task is to deal with your father."

Ember fell silent, lost in her own thoughts about the strange world that Alistair had called home for the past year. The world that was intended to be her home too.

"Are you so worried about my prospects for marriage?" Alistair smiled and tried to take her hand.

Ember shied away. She'd missed him, but twining their fingers wasn't something they had ever been in the habit of doing. He frowned when Ember pulled her hand back, causing a twinge in her chest that made her regret her choice. She quickly took his hand, squeezing, and was pleased when he smiled.

"You know I don't bother with such things," she said. "My father and mother have their plans. I have others. We shall see who wins the day."

Her words carried courage that Ember didn't feel. In truth she'd fled her house that morning in a desperate attempt to keep her mind occupied, just as she had every morning since her sixteenth birthday passed. Fear that an emissary from Conatus would never arrive, that her hopes wouldn't be fulfilled, had rendered her sleepless night after night.

"We shall." Alistair's tone grew serious. He halted, covering her hand with both of his. "Your arrival at Conatus is considered a harbinger of the order's future. One way or the other."

He dropped her hand, but only after briefly raising her fingers to his lips. An unpleasant shiver coursed through Ember. The flood of happiness filling her at Alistair's return was seeping away, leaving a cold foreboding in its wake. Why was he acting so strange? Touching her too often and in ways that were unbefitting of their friendship.

"How can that be?" Ember asked, hoping to avoid more awkward interactions. If she kept Alistair talking about his life at Tearmunn, perhaps it would make things more comfortable between them.

"You're the daughter of a noble," he said.

"You're of noble birth," she countered. "Wasn't your arrival equally auspicious?"

He shook his head. "I went to Tearmunn voluntarily. You are being called because your life is owed to Conatus."

Ember went quiet. Though she had no memory of it, the story never failed to unsettle her. When her mother's labor pains began, the birth hadn't progressed as it should. Death hovered over mother and unborn child. The sudden arrival of an extraordinary healer—a woman trained by Conatus—had offered salvation. But miracles came with a price. And the price named was the infant girl when she reached her sixteenth year.

Growing up with this memory following her like a shadow had been strange. That she was pledged to Conatus hadn't been hidden from her, but whenever it was mentioned, her mother fretted and her father roared. Even lacking her own memory of the event, Ember felt as though the circumstances of her birth had left her only loosely tethered to this world. That her survival had been a mistake, leaving her with a half-formed and chaotic soul. And that was why she wanted things she wasn't meant to have and dreamed impossible dreams. Because her very existence was ephemeral. Unintended.

As the manor rose before them, its hulking shape looming over the fields owned by her father and worked by his peasants, Ember's heart dropped like a stone in a well. Alistair had fallen silent, as lost in his thoughts as she'd been in her own. Ember wondered if her friend's outward confidence belied his own doubts.

A groomsman intercepted them in the courtyard, taking Alistair's horse and leading the animal to the stables.

"Your father is in the great hall," Alistair told her as they passed through the manor's tall oak doors. "With quite a feast prepared."

"He was hoping to impress Conatus," Ember said. "And he's likely disappointed that he's spent a fortune only to have young Alistair Hart appear to collect me."

"Not only me," he said with a quirk of his lips that might have been a smile or a grimace.

"Someone else is here?" Ember could hear her father's booming voice as they approached the great hall. He was using the expansive tone Ember knew meant he wanted to convey his importance.

Alistair leaned close, whispering, "Someone more intimidating than young Master Hart. Though I'm loath to admit such a man lives. But in truth, it is someone your father would be less likely to dismiss."

Curiosity brimming, Ember walked as quickly as she could without running. The hall was bursting with color, scent, and sound. Lord Edmund Morrow sat in a carved wooden chair, taller than its counterparts. A long table was overspread by silver platters laden with roasted pheasant, venison, and suckling pig. Wooden bowls were close to toppling under the weight of sweetbreads, piping hot fish stew, and savory pottage. Servants scurried about the hall, refilling empty glasses with crimson wine and amber cider.

Despite her pattering heart, Ember's stomach rumbled. This feast was far greater than even the Christmas celebration her father had thrown. Was he so concerned about his reputation with Conatus? After all, hadn't he spoken of them as a strange, isolated sect that had little to do with the world of court and kings?

Ember's mother, Lady Ossia Morrow, sat to the left of her husband. She was dressed in one of her finest gowns of ebony silk. Her hair was pulled into an intricate knot and adorned with gems. Ember's sister, Agnes, sat to her mother's left. She was also dressed in a favorite gown of rose and cream silks. Her eyes were downcast as she picked through the meats on her plate.

The other guests at the meal were warriors—the men-at-arms who served Lord Morrow. Burly and riled up by an excess of food and drink, they toasted and jostled each other, making the most of this unexpected bounty.

The only person in the room Ember didn't recognize was the man sitting at her father's right hand. Unlike the other revelers, the stranger's demeanor was stiff. Both uneasy and wary. Even though he was seated, Ember could tell he was a great deal taller than her father.

Catching sight of the new arrivals, Ember's mother extended her hands. "Alistair! You found her."

Edmund jabbed the tip of his knife at them. "Good lad, Alistair. As for you, errant girl, you might have taken a moment to don appropriate attire for this feast honoring our guests."

Ember glanced down at her plain and rumpled gown, its hem covered with dirt. "I was walking in the pasture," she said, cheeks warming with blood.

"Agnes, take your sister and help her make herself presentable," her father said. He glanced at the tall man on his right.

Agnes began to rise, but the stranger frowned. "There's no need for your daughter to adorn herself."

He waved for Agnes to return to her seat, but she hovered, uncertain what to do. When her father's eyes narrowed, she stood and scurried to Ember's side.

"You might hail from the wild north, good knight," Edmund answered him. "But I expect my daughter to act as befits her station, not as some peasant girl who runs around with straw in her hair."

Ember reached up, gingerly running her hands over her tangled locks. Blushing more deeply, she picked several pieces of straw from her hair. The stranger watched her closely, and Ember thought he might be on the verge of smiling. Her embarrassment melted into irritation. Was seeing her scolded like a child so entertaining to this man?

Still holding her gaze, the knight stood up. He was at least a head taller than her father and even a bit taller than Alistair. Ember glanced at the younger man beside her. Both knights of Conatus had dark hair, but where Alistair had curls as glossy as a raven's wing, the stranger's smooth hair was shorn so it fell just below his ears and had a rich color, like a tree's bark after rain.

She looked away from him only when Agnes took her hand. "Come, sister. I think the green silk gown would be a fine choice."

"Hold!" The knight's booming call stopped Ember from following her sister. Before her father could speak again, the stranger said to Ember, "My lady Morrow, I am Barrow Hess. Lord Hart and I have come to escort you to the Conatus keep of Tearmunn in Glen Shiel."

Ember freed her hand from Agnes's tight grip and dropped into a curtsy. "I understand, my lord."

"Are you prepared to leave now?" Barrow asked her. "We've already enjoyed too much of your father's generous hospitality. If you are amenable, we would take food for the journey and leave within the hour."

Beside Barrow, Ember's father began to sputter. Her mother gasped in horror. Agnes grasped Ember's arm, as if that gesture alone would keep her in their father's house.

Ember looked from her father to the tall knight. "I—"

"What sort of insult is this?" Edmund jumped up, squaring his shoulders. "I prepare a feast for you and you can't be bothered to share in it."

Barrow gave him a measured look. "I've eaten my fill, Lord Morrow. This gesture was a rich gift, but unnecessary. Lord Hart and I are here only to collect what you owe Conatus. Now that your daughter is here, we should be on our way."

A chill crept over Ember's skin. *What you owe.* Was that all she meant to Conatus? A debt to be paid?

She felt even colder when Alistair stepped forward, gaining her father's attention.

"The Circle bade me remind you, Lord Morrow," Alistair said slowly. "One life for another. These are the terms."

Agnes's fingers dug into Ember's skin, but Ember didn't flinch nor did she speak, even when her sister began to cry softly.

Their father paled. "Mercenaries you are. Cruel and demanding."

"One life for another," Alistair said again. His gaze fell upon Ember's mother. Ossia's lip quivered, but she laid her hand atop her husband's.

"You cannot forswear your oath, my lord," she murmured.

Edmund snatched his hand from hers and stood. "No. I shall not forswear myself. But I shall journey north with you. We all shall."

Agnes threw a pleading look at her mother and sniffled. "But my wedding . . ."

Ossia nodded, turning to her husband. "My lord, our daughter is but a month from her sea journey."

"Her trunks can be packed by servants." Edmund snorted. "She needn't be here. Our house travels to Tearmunn on the morrow."

Barrow coughed. "Lord Morrow. My orders are to bring the younger lady Morrow to Conatus today."

"Tomorrow is as good as today." Edmund glowered at the knight. "You shall not further offend me by refusing to share this feast and spend the night as guests in my home. We will leave at dawn."

"If you insist on making this journey north," Barrow said, with a slight shake of his head, "we will depart within the hour."

Edmund's face purpled. "You dare to command me in my own house."

His warriors ruffled at the exchange. Ember felt as though someone had grabbed her by the throat when she saw several of her father's men reach for their weapons. She could feel Agnes trembling.

"Father, please." Ember started forward, but Alistair put up his hand, signaling for her to keep still.

"Just wait," he murmured.

"I do not command you," Barrow told her father quietly. "But I will not fail in my own duties. I take your daughter to Tearmunn today. If you travel with us, you will already slow our progress. Three riders would make the trip quickly. The entourage you seem to be suggesting will make our journey longer by days. Delay is simply untenable."

Ember was holding her breath, her gaze locked on Barrow. He towered over her father with shoulders set, face calm but unyielding. She couldn't look away from him. No man had ever spoken thus to her father. Without fear. Without apology. Her pulse rippled with anticipation. It was marvelous.

Ember's father puffed up his chest. "I will not suffer this humiliation. Nor will I send my daughter off on a horse with two men like some common woman. She shall arrive at Tearmunn with her maids and her belongings."

Barrow glanced at Ember. "The lady alone will return with us today. You may send her things to the north as you wish. There is no place for her maids at Tearmunn."

"Enough!" Edmund brought his fist down on the table, the force of the blow toppling several platters and overturning cups. "I will hear no more of this."

"Perhaps we can resolve our differences another way," Barrow said quietly.

Red-faced and huffing with fury, Edmund scowled. "And what way would that be?"

"Pick your best men." Barrow waved at the cluster of warriors in the hall. "If they can defeat me in combat, we'll depart tomorrow."

Edmund squinted at Barrow. "Did you say *men*?"

The warriors guffawed, trading grins. Edmund raised his hands and the hall fell silent.

All traces of Ember's father's rage had been wiped away. With a hearty laugh, he said, "I'm tempted to hold you to your words, knight. And guarantee myself victory."

"I didn't misspeak, my lord," Barrow answered without hesitation. "Your best men. Name them."

The chortling of Lord Morrow's men quieted and soon became angry rumbles.

"A bold challenge," Edmund said, his smile hard. His gaze swept over his men. "Hugh! Gordon! Felix!"

Ember drew closer to her sister as the three warriors eased their bulk from their chairs. Her father had picked well. Not only were these his most seasoned knights, but they were among Ember's least favorite. Hugh wasn't horrible, but when she was a girl, his scarred face and missing teeth had frightened her. Gordon and Felix had a habit of leering at Ember and her sister when they passed in the hall. Even worse, Felix had a reputation for cruelty to both the manor's servants and his hunting dogs. These men would fight hard and, if given the chance, wouldn't hesitate to seriously injure Barrow out of spite.

Barrow nodded at the three men. "My lords, choose your weapons." He turned to Ember's mother. "My lady, I would not sully your home with combat. Might we move into the courtyard?"

Ossia nodded, taking her husband's arm. Edmund led his wife from the room, beckoning his chosen champions to follow.

The buzz of anticipation in the hall broke into a low roar. The men-at-arms surged after their lord, leaving the hall and barreling to the courtyard. Alistair hung back, offering his body as a barrier between the rabble of men and Ember and Agnes.

Watching the tide of warriors ebb from the room, Ember jumped in surprise when a low voice, very close, said, "I apologize for this spectacle, Lady Morrow. I hope I haven't given offense."

Barrow had appeared suddenly out of the mob, standing at her shoulder. She looked up and found him searching her face intently. What he was looking for she couldn't say, but her own gaze was caught in the dark blue-gray of his eyes, their shade like that of a storm-ridden sea. Unable to find her voice, Ember simply shook her head.

"Are you sure this is necessary?" Alistair asked Barrow.

"Lord Morrow is in need of a lesson," Barrow answered.

Alistair frowned. "Perhaps. But Ember's father will like us even less afterward, which will hardly please the Circle. Also, I know those men. You're in for a dirty fight."

"Don't worry about me." A smile flickered over Barrow's mouth. He shrugged off his cloak and handed it to Alistair.

Alistair sighed, muttering, "I wonder if Kael could have avoided a fight."

"Your mentor in the Guard?" Ember asked, remembering the name from one of Alistair's letters.

"Yes," he said. "He has a lighter touch than Barrow—but our commander didn't think a cheerful countenance would persuade Lord Morrow."

"Your commander is probably right," Ember said, and Alistair's only answer was a rough laugh.

As Ember and her sister hurried to match the long strides of the two Conatus knights, Agnes whispered, "How horrible! Can't you stop this?"

Ember glanced at her. "How could I stop this?"

"They're fighting over you," Agnes said. "Alistair has been our friend since we were children. Plead your cause to him. Surely he'll convince Lord Hess to release you from Father's promise. You were but a babe and our father was desperate. This burden shouldn't fall to you."

Gritting her teeth, Ember said, "You know how dear you are to me, Agnes. But I have no desire to be released. I want to go with them."

Agnes sighed. "You say that now, but what do you know of Conatus?"

Ember pulled her gaze away from her sister's worried face, frustrated by the truth in her words. Conatus was shrouded in mystery—an order of knights sanctioned by the Church, but one whose tasks were known only to its members.

"You told me that Alistair's letters spoke of vows." Agnes stared at Alistair's back as she spoke. "Vows wherein you would forsake a life of your own."

"My life now is not my own," Ember hissed through her teeth. "If I stay here, I am but Father's to give to whatsoever noble he chooses."

A mewling sound of sorrow emerged from Agnes's throat and Ember put her arm around her sister.

"Forgive me, Agnes," Ember said, cringing at her own thought-lessness. "I should not say such things."

"I know you look upon marriage with scorn." Agnes kept her eyes on the floor as they walked. "But it is only because you haven't been struck by love's arrow."

Ember would have snorted, but she'd already hurt Agnes enough. "I hope you find the love you seek in France."

Agnes glanced up, but at Alistair rather than Ember. "So do I."

Bright sunlight made Ember squint as they emerged into the courtyard. Her father's warriors had already formed a ring in the open space. Within the circle Hugh, Gordon, and Felix brandished their weapons. Hugh bore a short sword and had a shield strapped to his left arm. Gordon carried a halberd and Felix a spiked mace.

Lord Morrow's men stepped aside to let Barrow enter the ring. Alistair led Ember and Agnes to a nearby slope where their parents stood, overlooking the ring. Barrow had drawn his sword. Unlike Hugh's thick, squat blade, Barrow's sword was sleek and curving. The men about to fight bore as much resemblance to one another as their weapons did. Like Ember's father, the three warriors he had chosen to face Barrow were thickly muscled with an impressive girth of chest and shoulders. Their hulking bodies were built like piles of large stones. By contrast Barrow was tall and lean, his form drawn in long, taut lines.

Barrow searched the courtyard until he found Edmund. "My lord?"

"Whoever does not fall or does not yield," Edmund shouted. "My men or this knight of Conatus shall be declared the victor!"

Brutish hollering rose from the ring of warriors. Agnes shuddered, pleading with her sister once more: "How can you bear this, Ember?"

Ember barely heard her sister's question. Her blood was roaring in her ears, her heart drumming heavy against her ribs. Her hands moved restlessly, fists clenching and unclenching. She wished she could hold her sword, even if only to mimic the exhilarating match that was playing out before her.

Barrow raised his sword in salute to his trio of adversaries. They grunted and shrugged in reply. Hugh and Felix exchanged grins, signaling their anticipation of an easy win.

As the warriors around them roared for blood, the men within the ring began to move. Barrow kept his sword low, watching his opponents. Gordon bellowed, rushing at Barrow, his halberd aimed to impale. Barrow sidestepped, letting Gordon's spring carry him past the point of attack. As Gordon blew by him, Barrow twisted and brought the flat of his sword down on Gordon's skull. The crack of steel on bone made Agnes shriek.

"I can't watch!" She buried her face in Ember's shoulder. Ember didn't blink. It was as if she could feel Barrow's muscles tensing and exploding into action as he fought. Her body hummed with his strength and grace. She'd never felt more alive.

Gordon crumpled and lay unmoving. With Barrow's back turned, Felix and Hugh were already on the attack. Felix leapt at the knight, swinging his mace in a broad arc, while Hugh darted around their adversary, keeping his shield up but his sword low.

Barrow dove, rolling in the dirt as Felix's mace whistled past his ear. Hugh struck as Barrow lay on his back, but the knight managed to kick Hugh in the stomach with both feet. As Barrow sprang to his feet, Felix brought his mace around. A cry of warning rose in Ember's throat, but Conatus's champion spun around, his blade sweeping up to meet Felix's mace mid-blow. Metal clanged as they struck over and over.

Recovering from having the breath kicked out of his lungs, Hugh scrambled from the dirt to rejoin the fight. He tossed aside his shield and threw himself at Barrow's unguarded back. As Felix swung his mace, Barrow dropped to the ground flat as a board. Hugh tripped over Barrow and fell forward. Bone crunched, and a groan rose from the circled warriors when Felix's spiked mace buried itself in Hugh's shoulder.

Hugh screamed as Felix swore and wrenched his weapon free. Blood poured from Hugh's wound and his left arm hung limply at his side. Barrow had already rolled away from them and was on his feet again. Without pause he darted toward Felix, his curved blade flicking through the air. Gashes began to appear on Felix's arms and shoulders. Felix winced, stumbling back. With a strangled cry he wheeled around, flailing as Barrow continued his relentless strikes. Felix's shirt was in tatters, his chest covered with cuts that looked like whiplashes. Breathing hard, he dropped to one knee. Only then did Barrow's blade pause.

"I yield," Felix rasped, his head bowed.

Barrow nodded. He turned to face Hugh, who though bleeding and groaning in pain was still standing in the ring.

"Do you yield?" Barrow asked him.

Hugh spat on the ground just short of Barrow's feet, but he nodded. As Barrow sheathed his sword and turned to leave the ring, Hugh began to laugh. Felix had risen from the dirt, his eyes bulging with outrage. Without a battle cry, Felix lunged at Barrow, bringing his mace around in a high arc so it would smash into Barrow's skull.

In a movement eerily similar to Felix's submission, Barrow pivoted and dropped to one knee, but his hand was moving, sliding his blade from its sheath and slashing the air. He easily met Felix's swing, but Barrow hadn't aimed his blow to block Felix's attack. A shriek pierced the air as Felix's mace and his forearm dropped to the ground, hewn from his body by Barrow's sword.

Felix fell to the ground, still screaming and holding the bloody stump of his arm. Without looking back at the fallen warrior, Barrow left the ring. He didn't break stride until he stood before Ember. The slight incline upon which she stood put them face-to-face, and she found she couldn't breathe.

Ember stared at the tall knight. Every muscle in her body was taut as if she'd been in the ring herself. Her gaze lingered on his arms, his chest, the muscles of his thighs. Ember had seen dozens of men fight in her sixteen years at her father's estate. She'd never seen anyone move the way Barrow had.

Though she couldn't fathom why she would merit such a gesture, Barrow bowed to her.

"My lady."

She was still shaking when he turned to her father and said, "We leave for Tearmunn in an hour."

Edmund Morrow, pale with rage, answered. "An hour."

Turn the page for sneak peek at

The
Inventor's
Secret

1.

EVERY HEARTBEAT BROUGHT the boy closer. Charlotte heard the shallow pulls of his breath, the uneven, heavy pounding of his footfalls. She stayed curled within the hollows of the massive tree's roots, body perfectly still other than the sweat that beaded on her forehead in the close air. A single drop of moisture trailed along her temple, dripped from her jaw, and disappeared into her bodice.

The boy threw another glance over his shoulder. Five more steps, and he'd hit the tripwire. Four. Three. Two. One.

He cried out in alarm as his ankle hooked on the taut line stretched between two trees. His yelp cut off when his body slammed into the forest floor, forcing the air from his lungs.

Charlotte lunged from her hiding place, muscles shrieking in relief as they snapped out of the tight crouch. Her practiced feet barely touched the ground and she ran with as much silence as the low rustle of her skirts would allow.

The boy moaned and started to push himself up on one elbow. He grunted when Charlotte kicked him over onto his back and pinned him against the ground with one foot.

His wide eyes fixed on the revolver she had aimed at his chest.

"Please," he whispered.

She adjusted her aim—right between his eyes—and shook her head. "I'm not in the habit of granting the requests of strangers."

Charlotte put more weight onto her foot, and he squirmed.

"Who are you?" she asked, and wished her voice were gritty instead of gentle.

He didn't blink; his eyes mirrored the rust-tinged gleam of the breaking dawn.

"I don't know."

"Say again?" She frowned.

Fear bloomed in his tawny irises. "I . . . I don't know."

"You don't know," she repeated.

He shook his head.

She glanced at the tangle of brush from which he'd emerged. "What are you running from?"

He frowned, and again said, "I don't know."

"If you don't know, then why were you running?" she snapped.

"The sounds." He shuddered.

"Sounds?" Charlotte felt as though frost had formed on the bare skin of her arms. She scanned the forest, dread building in her chest.

The whistle shrieked as though her fear had summoned it. The iron beast, tall as the trees around it, emerged from the thick woods on the same deer trail the boy had followed. Imperial Labor Gatherers were built like giants. The square, blunt head of the machine pushed through the higher branches of the trees, snapping them like twigs. Two multijointed brass arms sprouted on each side of its wide torso and its long fingers were spread wide, ready to clutch and capture. Charlotte's eyes immediately found the thick bars of its hollow rib cage.

Empty.

"Who sent a Gatherer after you?"

His voice shook. "Is that what it is?"

"Are you an idiot?" She spat on the ground beside him. "You must know a Rotpot when you see one! Everyone out here knows how the Empire hunts."

The screech of metal in need of oiling cooled Charlotte's boiling temper. A horn sounded. Another answered in the distance. But not nearly distant enough.

She didn't have time to mull over options. She lifted her foot from the boy's chest and offered him her hand. The only advantage they had over the Rotpots was that the lumbering iron men maneuvered slowly in the forest.

"We need to leave this place. Now."

The boy gripped her fingers without hesitation, but he shot a terrified glance at the approaching Gatherer. They were partially concealed from view by a huge oak, but the machine was close enough that Charlotte could see its operator shifting gears from within the giant's iron skull. She watched as the man reached up, pulled down a helmet with telescoping goggles, and began to swivel the Rotpot's head around.

Charlotte hesitated a moment too long. And he saw her.

Cranking hard on a wheel, which made steam spout from the machine's shoulders, the operator turned the iron man to pursue them.

"Go!" Charlotte shoved the boy away from her. "Run east! I'll catch up."

"What are you—" he started to ask, but began to run when she pushed him so hard that he almost fell over.

When she was certain he wasn't looking back, Charlotte reached into her skirt pocket. Her hand found cool metal, and she pulled a small object from within the folds of muslin. It only took a few winds of the key before sputters and sparks leapt from her palm. She sighed and regretfully set the magnet mouse on the ground, pointing it at the encroaching machine. The little creature whirred and skittered away, its spring-anchored wheels accommodating the rough path she'd set it upon.

"Come on."

When Charlotte caught up with the boy, she ignored the puzzled look on his face and grasped his hand, forcing him to run with her into the dark western wood, away from the now bloodred haze of early sun that stretched through the forest canopy.

Between gasps of breath, his fingers tightened on hers. She glanced at him.

His tawny eyes had sharpened, and he peered at her like a hawk. "What's your name?" he asked.

Charlotte dropped his hand and gathered her skirts to accommodate her leap over a moss-covered log.

"Charlotte."

"Thank you for not leaving me back there, Charlotte."

She looked away from him, nodded, and ran a bit faster. Behind them she heard the explosion she'd been waiting for. Though they were hardly out of danger, Charlotte smiled, feeling a surge of triumph. But a moment later, a single thought chased her giddiness away.

Ash is going to kill me.

HE LAST BEAMS of sunlight were cutting through the forest by the time they reached the tree.

"Bloody hell!" Charlotte groped through the tangle of roots in search of subtle tactile differentiation. Her companion gasped at her outburst, and she spared him a glance. Not that he could tell. She'd tied a kerchief around his eyes when the sounds of the Gatherers seemed far off enough to risk slowing down.

The boy's face scrunched up, as if he was thinking hard. After a moment, he said, "Girls shouldn't use that kind of language. Someone told me that . . . I think . . ."

Though he appeared to be running from the Brits, she couldn't risk letting a stranger learn the way to the Catacombs. The Empire's attempts at finding their hideaway had been limited to Gatherer sweeps and a few crowscopes, none of which had been successful. It wasn't out of the realm of possibility that they'd stoop to sending a real person out to hunt for them. And someone like this boy, who seemed so vulnerable, would be the perfect spy. If he was and this was a trap she'd sprung, Charlotte would never forgive herself.

"Well, you may not know who you are, but apparently you were brought up in polite society," Charlotte said sourly, her mood darkened by new suspicions about who he might be. "If you're planning on sticking around, you'll find girls here do a lot of things they aren't meant to do."

He simply turned his head in her direction, puzzled and waiting for an explanation. Charlotte's answer was an unkind laugh. Perhaps she should have been more compassionate, but the consequences of revealing their hideout were too dangerous. And Birch was almost too clever with his inventions. She'd never been able to locate the false branch without effort, and delays could be very costly. The Rotpots might have been stopped by her mouse, but nothing was certain. A slowed Gatherer was still a threat.

"I . . . I . . ." Beside her the boy was stammering as if unsure whether to apologize.

"Hush," she said, keeping her voice gentle, and he felt silent.

Her fingers brushed over a root with bark harder and colder than the others.

"Here it is."

"Here's what?" He waggled his head around pointlessly.

"I said hush." Charlotte stifled laughter at the boy's bobbing head, knowing it was cruel given his helpless state.

She found the latch on the underside of the thick root, and a compartment in the artificial wood popped open. Quickly turning the crank hidden within the compartment, Charlotte held her breath until the voice came crackling through.

"Verification?"

"Iphigenia," Charlotte said with a little smile. *Birch and his myths.*

The boy drew a sharp breath. "Who is that? Who's there?" He sounded genuinely afraid.

"It's all right," she whispered and leaned closer to the voicebox. "And there are two of us, so you'll need to open both channels."

There was a long pause in which Charlotte's heart began to beat heavily, once again making her question the decision to bring the strange boy with her.

"The basket will be waiting," the voice confirmed, and a little relief seeped through her veins.

The pale boy was still twisting his neck, as if somehow doing so would enlighten him as to the origin of the voice despite his blindfold.

"What's happening?" he asked, facing away from Charlotte. Rather than attempt an explanation, Charlotte grabbed his wrist and tugged him toward the roaring falls.

As the pounding of water on rocks grew louder, the boy resisted Charlotte's guidance for the first time.

"Stop! Please!" He jerked back, throwing her off balance.

"Don't do that!" Charlotte whirled around and grabbed his arms. "We're about to cross a narrow and quite slippery path. If you make me lose my footing, we'll both be in the drink, and I don't fancy a swim, no matter how hot the summer air may be."

"Is it a river?" he asked. "Where are we?"

Charlotte couldn't blame the boy for his questions, but she was close to losing her patience. Hadn't she already done enough to help him? All she wanted was to get inside the Catacombs, where they would be hidden from any Gatherers that might still be combing the forest. What did Meg always say when she was fighting with Ash?

Meg's warm voice slipped into Charlotte's mind. *Try to see it from his point of view. It's a horrible burden, Lottie. The weight of leadership.*

Charlotte looked at the pale boy, frowning. His burden wasn't that of her brother's—a responsibility for a ramshackle group aged five to seventeen—but this boy bore the weight of fear and, at the moment, blindness. Both of which must be awful to contend with. With that in mind, Charlotte said, "I'm taking you to a hiding place beneath the falls. I promise it's safe. The machines won't find us there. I can't tell you more."

The boy tilted his head toward the sound of her voice. He groped the air until he found her hands.

"Okay."

She smiled, though he couldn't see it, and drew him over the moss-covered rocks that paved the way to the falls. As they came closer, the spray from the falls dampened their clothing and their hair. Charlotte was grateful the boy had decided to trust her and ask no further questions because at this point she would have had to shout to be heard.

When they passed beneath the torrent of water, the air shimmered as the native moss gave way to the bioluminescent variety Birch had cultivated to light the pathway into the Catacombs.

Charlotte wished she could remove the boy's blindfold. Entering the passageway that led into the Catacombs delighted her each time she returned. Not only because it meant she was almost home, but also because the glowing jade moss gave light that was welcoming. Seeing it might ease the boy's mind, reassuring him that she led him to a place of safety rather than danger.

She turned left, taking them into a narrow side passage that at first glance would have appeared to be nothing more than a shadow cast by the tumbling cascade. Within the twisting cavern, the shimmering green moss forfeited its place to mounds of fungus. Their long stems and umbrella-like tops glowed blue instead of green, throwing the cavern into a perpetual twilight.

The boy remained silent, but from the way he gripped her fingers, Charlotte knew his fear hadn't abated.

"We're almost there," she whispered and squeezed his hand, garnering a weak smile from him.

The passage abruptly opened up to a massive cavern—the place where the falls hid its priceless treasure: a refuge, one of the only sites hidden from the far-seeing eyes of the Empire. While from the outside the falls appeared to cover a solid rock base, several meters beneath the cascade, the earth opened into a maze of caves. Some were narrow tunnels like the one from which they'd just emerged. Others were enormous open spaces, large enough to house a dirigible. Far below them, the surface of an underground lake rippled with the current that tugged it into an underground river. A dark twin that snaked beneath earth and stone to meet its aboveground counterpart some two leagues past the falls.

They were standing on a platform. Smooth stone reinforced by iron bracings and a brass railing that featured a hinged gate. On the other side of the gate, as had been promised, the basket was waiting, dangling from a long iron chain that stretched up until it disappeared into a rock shelf high above them. The lift resembled a birdcage more than a basket. Charlotte opened the gate and the basket door, pushing the boy inside and following him after she'd secured the gate once more. The basket swung under their weight, and the boy gripped the brass weave that held them.

"You put me in a cage?" Panic crept into his question.

"Shhh." She took his hand again as much to stop him from ripping the blindfold off as to reassure him. "I'm here too. It's not a cage—it's an elevator."

With her free hand, she reached up and pulled the wooden handle attached to a brass chain that hung from the ceiling of the basket. Far above them, a bell sounded, its chiming bounced off the cavern walls. A flurry of tinkling notes melded with the roar of the falls for a few moments.

Charlotte shushed the boy before he could ask what the bell meant. Now that she was out of the forest, away from the Gatherers and a short ride from home, she was tired and more than a little anxious about what awaited her on the upper platform. Not so much what as who, she had to admit.

As the clicking of gears and the steady winding of the chain filled the basket, they began to move up. The swiftness of the lift's ascent never failed to surprise Charlotte slightly, but it caught the boy completely off guard. He lurched to the side, and the basket swung out over the lake.

"Stop that!" Charlotte grabbed him, holding him still at the center of the swaying basket. "If you don't move, the lift won't swing out."

"S-sorry." The boy's teeth chattered with nerves.

Peering at him, Charlotte felt a creeping fear tickle her spine. She'd assumed his awful colorless skin had been a result of his fear, but looking at him closely, she thought it might be the natural state of his flesh. And it struck Charlotte as quite odd. Flesh so pale it had an ashen cast. She forced herself to hang on to him so he wouldn't unbalance the lift again, but she now worried his wan quality was a harbinger of illness. And that it might be catching.

Her nagging thoughts were interrupted when they passed the lip of the upper platform and the gears slowly ground to a halt.

The first sight that greeted her was three pairs of boots. The first was black, thick-soled, and scarred with burn marks. The second pair was also black, but polished and trimmer of cut and heel, showing only their shiny tips rather than stretching to the knee like the first pair. The third pair made her groan. Faded brown and featuring an array of loops and buckles that held knives in place, this pair was soon joined by a grinning face as their owner crouched to peer into the basket.

Jack, clad in his regular garb of leather breeches and two low-slung, gun-heavy belts, threaded his fingers through the brass weaving of the basket, rising with it until he was standing. "Well, well. What a fine catch we have today, mateys."

"Cap it, Jack," Charlotte said.

He pushed stray locks of his bronze hair beneath his tweed cap and continued to smile as he opened the platform gate. "A mermaid and a . . . what?"

Jack's mirthful expression vanished as he stared at the blindfolded boy.

Charlotte swallowed the hardness that had formed in her throat. Jack turned to look at the wearer of the polished boots. Charlotte was looking that way too.

The boots were mostly covered by black military pants, close fitting with brass buttons from knee to ankle and looser to the waist where they met with a band-collared white shirt and burgundy vest with matching cravat. The owner of the boots carried an ebony cane tipped with a brass globe.

Ashley wasn't wearing his usual black overcoat, but its absence did nothing to impede his air of authority.

"Pip called in that two were arriving instead of just one," he told Charlotte.

She glanced over to the wheelhouse where a slight girl wearing goggles was mostly hidden by pulls, levers, and cranks. Pip gave Charlotte a quick, apologetic wave and then ducked out of sight.

Throwing her shoulders back, Charlotte exited the basket, dragging the boy with her.

"The Rotpots were after him," she said, meeting her brother's stern gaze. "I had to help him."

"Of course *you* had to." Ash tapped a shiny boot on the stone platform.

She didn't offer further explanation but refused to look away. Charlotte didn't want to quail before her brother because rumors of her unexpected guest seemed to have spread throughout the Catacombs. From the mouth of the caverns that led to their living quarters, half a dozen little faces with wide eyes peeked out, watching Charlotte and Ashley's exchange. The children should have been at their lessons or chores, but Charlotte knew well enough that when something this unusual took place in their mostly cloistered lives, it was irresistible. When she'd been younger, Charlotte had snuck away from her responsibilities many a time for events much less exciting than the arrival of a stranger. Ash had always chided her for her impetuous behavior. Her brother had been born a leader, all sobriety and steadfastness. He was never tempted away from duty the way Charlotte so often had been.

Ash frowned and walked up to the blindfolded boy.

"And what do you have to say for yourself?" Ash asked him. "Who has my sister brought us?"

"I . . . I can't . . ." The boy strained toward the sound of Ash's voice.

Ash put the brass tip of his cane beneath the boy's chin. "I know you can't see, boy. If you'll tell me how you came to be in the forest, perhaps we can show you a bit more hospitality."

Charlotte stepped forward, hitting the length of the cane so it thwacked away from the stranger. She jerked the kerchief down so the boy blinked into the sudden light.

"Leave him be. You weren't the one being chased by an iron beast with a cage for a belly."

Ash stared at her, his dark brown eyes full of incredulity and budding fury. He didn't speak to Charlotte, though, instead turning his hard gaze on the faces peering out from the cavern opening. Ashley didn't have to say anything. The children bolted away, the pitter-patter of their speedy steps echoing in the cavern like sudden rainfall.

"Do you know if he's hurt, Charlotte?" The boy wearing the burn-scarred black boots scampered forward, peering at the new arrival.

Jack, who'd taken a few steps back as if to survey the unfolding scene from a safe distance, answered as he threaded his thumbs into his wide belt loops. "He looks fine to me. Are you sure he was really running from them?"

Charlotte ignored Jack, instead smiling at Birch, who trotted over to the boy's side.

"Let's have a look." The boots weren't the only pockmarked part of Birch's wardrobe. From his thick apron to his elbow-length gloves, the tinker's brown leather clothing boasted enough black marks to rival a leopard's spots.

The boy was shivering, but he nodded and didn't object when Birch inspected him.

"No injuries I can see. He's not feverish. If anything, I'd say he's a little clammy." Birch scratched his thatch of wheat-colored hair.

A tiny head capped by large round ears peeked around one side of Birch's neck. Its wide black eyes stared at the strange boy. The boy stared back as the bat climbed from Birch's neck onto his shoulder. Its minuscule claws fastened to one of the straps of the tinker's leather apron, never losing its grip as Birch moved.

"There's, there's something on you," the boy said, his tone wary, but also curious.

"What?" Birch glanced at the shoulder the boy pointed to. "Oh. That's just Moses. He's usually crawling somewhere on my apron. Doesn't like to roost anymore, understandably. Fell when he was just a baby and broke both wings. I found him floating in the river one day when I was collecting guano to make gunpowder. Had to rebuild his wings myself."

Birch coaxed Moses onto his hand and then gently stretched out one of the bat's wings, which produced a soft clicking sound as the appendage unfurled. The underside of Moses's wing glinted with silver.

"The key was creating a new bone structure using hollow tubes," Birch explained. "Light enough so he could fly."

"What proof do you have that he was trying to escape?" Ash was still watching Charlotte instead of looking at the boy.

Charlotte's charge seemed content conversing with Birch, so she gave Ash her full attention.

"Only that he was alone in the forest and running from Rotpots." Charlotte thrust her chin out. "That was good enough for me."

"How reassuring," Ash said. "And you failed to notice that he's dressed in clothes from the Hive?"

Charlotte's eyes went wide. She turned to look at her companion, feeling blood leach from her face. Her brother was right. While the trio waiting to meet them wore a mishmash of clothes cobbled together into outfits favored by each, the boy wore gray tweed pants and a matching fitted jacket with button and chain closures. His wardrobe marked him as belonging to the Hive: the artisan caste of the New York metropolis.

Ash released her from his glare, but before he said anything more, the strange boy jerked hard to the right. The sudden movement pulled his hand free of Charlotte's grasp.

Until that moment, the boy had been leaning close to Birch's shoulder, examining Moses's mechanical wing. Now he stood straight as an iron rod, gazing at Birch.

"Maker. Maker. Maker," the boy said. His limbs began to shake violently.

"What the—" Jack leapt forward, drawing a knife from his boot and holding it low, putting himself between Charlotte and the now flailing boy.

"Maker! Maker! Maker!" the boy cried. His shouts bounced off the cavern ceiling and walls, filling the air with a haunting chorus of echoes: *Maker! Maker! Maker!*

"Rustbuckets. He's having a fit." Ash raised his cane. "Easy, Jack."

"Grab him, or he'll go right over the edge," Birch warned, but Ash was already moving. While the boy's arms lashed, Ash slipped his cane through the stranger's belt and hauled him away from the precipice. With another deft movement, Ash freed his cane just before the boy flopped to the ground, lolling about with no control of his body's violent movements..

With a horrible shudder, he gave a slow, whining cry and went still.

"Oh, Athene, he's not dead, is he?" Charlotte's hands went to her mouth.

Birch knelt beside the boy and laid his head on the prostrate figure's chest. With a sigh, he said, "I don't hear a heartbeat, but . . ."

The boy moaned. Birch frowned and sat up quickly.

Charlotte gulped air in relief. "What happened? Did Moses do something to scare him?"

"Why would anyone be frightened by Moses?" Birch asked. Hearing his name, the bat peered toward Charlotte, as if daring her to answer.

Charlotte ignored the question, knowing that pointing out to Birch that most people considered bats frightening little creatures would only provoke an endless debate with the tinker about fear and rationality.

Jack returned the knife to his boot.

"You've brought home a strange pet. I definitely prefer the bat," he said to Charlotte, earning an elbow in the ribs. "Ouch!" Jack rubbed at his side. "Now you have to kiss me so my feelings aren't hurt."

"I meant to hurt your feelings," Charlotte said.

"I guess that means I'll have to kiss you myself so I feel better."

Charlotte jumped out of his reach. "Don't you dare."

"Jack, get over here," Ash said. He was leaning over the boy, who despite making a sound, still appeared to be unconscious. "Help Birch take him inside. Then get Meg. Between the two of them, maybe we can sort this one out."

Birch grabbed the boy around his shoulders, while Jack grabbed his legs. His body swung limply between them as they carried him off the platform. Charlotte began to inch away from the basket.

"And you're going where?" Ash blocked her path with his cane.

"With them," she declared, hoping her confident tone would get her out of any punishment Ash had in mind.

"Not until we've had a chance to discuss your heroic exploits of the afternoon," Ash said. "Come with me."

Charlotte stood up tall until her brother turned away. Then her shoulders slumped and she reluctantly followed him into the Catacombs.